fo fum flarey

Fo Fum Flarey

The people in this story are my creation. Any resemblance they bear to actual people, living or dead, is purely coincidental.

ISBN: 978-1-7356523-7-5

www.KirstenMortensen.com
www.ConcealedBeauties.com

To the stealers of hearts and the lovers who love them.

1

So okay, Tibbs, New York isn't the fanciest place in the world, and all we'd planned to do was stop at Dingo's for a beer, then walk across the street for a slice of pizza. But a date is a date and really???

Fletcher Beal canceled—AGAIN?

What kind of prince keeps canceling dates?

Okay, okay. Maybe "canceled" is the wrong choice of words. It wasn't his fault. He was in the Philadelphia airport and about to board his plane, and one of his partners called "literally just as I got to my gate," and something-something Houston something-something need you here something-something has to be in person.

And he was sorry. So sorry. "I'm so sorry, Marion," he said.

Ugh.

And also, why did nobody warn me that my road down Happily Ever After would be the route with all the speed bumps?

I told myself that now was not the time to cry. It wasn't like we were crashing into an actual wall. No actual wall had sprung up between me and the prince I'd once lost and then finally re-found.

This was a speed bump. And speed bumps aren't pleasant. But they are speed bumps, and that's all. They slow you down. They don't stop you.

I struggled bravely to regain my composure. "Are you sure you need to be there?" I said in a little voice. "Can't you do a conference call or something?"

"Geez, Marion. I'm sorry."

His voice sounded pained.

So I felt a flash of alarm. Because Fletcher Beal is the guy I wanted. With all my heart. And guess what, Marion Flarey, this is now real life. And even if he wasn't an actual prince, Fletcher Beal was smart and well-off, and the perfect blend of elegant sophistication and muscular athleticism, and wow, the way he made me feel when he gathered me into his arms and studied my face with those gorgeous light brown eyes, and wow that calm confidence he wore the way other people wear their favorite pair of blue jeans...

But Fletcher was not only my personal private prince. He was also a successful businessperson. A man of the world. And as a successful businessperson and man of the world, he happened to be juggling multiple ventures in various cities. And yes, one of them was Booch4U, the kombucha brewery in Tibbs where I'd gotten a job as tasting room manager, which is how we ended up finding each other again. But he also owned kombucha breweries in other cities, too. Like Houston, for example.

And what was I doing? Did I not realize that getting ouchie might make him feel guilty? And couldn't that potentially initiate the sort of downward spiral of resentment and recrimination that causes relationships to crash and burn?

Be brave, Marion Flarey. Be brave enough to leave fairy tales behind and accept Fletcher Beal as he is, instead of wanting just some bits of Fletcher Beal and not the others.

"No, it's me who's sorry. I understand. It's fine," I said, bravely.

"I'll be in Tibbs day after tomorrow."

The day after tomorrow. You can wait two days. Right, Marion Flarey?

"And Marion, I've been thinking. We were going to take that trip to New York. Let's do it. How about the week after next?" he said.

"Oooh!" I said.

"I'm driving to our Vermont location that weekend, but I can be in Manhattan on Monday."

"Oooh!" I repeated.

I was standing in the tiny bathroom of our camper-trailer during this conversation, by the way, because I'd just gotten out of the shower when Fletcher's call came. And now I met my own eyes in the mirror. My hair was wrapped in my towel and my eyes and cheeks stood out, and I looked so bright and expectant and girlfriend-y. And I felt a million times better because, A. he was obviously trying to spend time with me despite being a businessperson with many ventures in many different cities, so stop being so insecure, Marion, and, B. I'd obviously been overreacting when I'd felt disappointed about him canceling our silly Tibbs date, and, C. who wouldn't take an upgrade from slice of pizza in silly Tibbs to a real meal cooked by an actual chef in New York City?

Reality wasn't so bad, after all.

"You'll get to see my place, finally," he said. "And meet my friends."

He meant his Manhattan place and his Manhattan friends.

Meaning that he was bringing me into his other life. A necessary step when the prince prepares to marry the commoner he fell in love with when he was visiting one of his lands. He needs to introduce her to the courtiers. Preparatory to ascending to the throne and elevating his princess into his queen.

"That sounds wonderful, Fletcher," I breathed, although he may not have heard me because a lady announcer's voice was suddenly jangling through the phone, warning everyone that it was final call for flight something-something to somewhere-somewhere and if you don't get to your gate in one nanosecond you'll be left behind and I guess you'll have to walk, instead, so good luck with that.

Airports.

"Hang on," Fletcher said over the lady announcer voice, and then when it was quiet again, he added, "So if that works for you, I'll go ahead and make dinner reservations when I get to Texas. Hey, what was it you were going to ask me?"

"Never mind. It can wait." And I met my eyes in the mirror again, but this time I quickly looked away.

Because yes, I'd been planning to broach a certain topic to Fletcher, that night. And it was a delicate subject. I'd planned to ask him if it was okay if I could store some of my stuff—books, mostly—in his house. Which would arguably be a practical arrangement, seeing as there wasn't a lot of room at my parents' and my family was starting to get cranky about all those boxes stacked in their living room. And Fletcher's house in Tibbs had plenty of room. That big stone house of his. The one I once thought of as a castle.

But I had a problem. Because I didn't want to give the impression I was in a huge hurry to move in with Fletcher. I mean, eventually we'd co-habitate. Obviously. We were meant to be together. Because fairy tales aren't real, exactly, but they have left traces in, I guess, our collective unconscious. And, in my case, the fairy tale traces around me were crystal clear.

On the other hand, we'd only gotten back together again a few weeks ago and his divorce wasn't even final yet. I didn't want to seem overly eager. And fairy tales plots can include twists and setbacks. It pays to be careful.

Storing a bunch of my stuff in Fletcher's castle was not a subject to discuss over the phone.

It had to be face-to-face. And nuanced.

"What time is your flight?" I asked, deftly changing the subject.

He didn't hear me. He was walking as he talked, apparently, because instead of answering he grunted and then muttered, "Watch where you're going," and then in a louder voice, "I'd better let you go, Marion. It's a bit of a trek to my new gate and I don't want to miss my flight."

"Okay," I said. "Fly safe."

I set my phone down on the edge of the tiny sink.

I made a face at myself in the mirror and picked up a tube of moisturizer and squeezed some into my palm.

I told myself to get over it.

Fletcher Beal was my prince. And in the 21st Century that's what princes are like, right? Off conquering new kingdoms. Only not by horseback. Plus we have our modern technology. We'd be able to call and text.

And sooner or later things would calm down and we'd settle into our new life. And sure, things weren't perfect at the moment. I was living with my parents, for example. At age twenty-nine. In Tibbs, New York. Which was not something I'd exactly planned for my life.

But Tibbs was also where Fletcher Beal owned a brewery and his family had a house, which meant that Tibbs was not just my hometown, anymore.

It was our hometown.

And we were together. Fletcher Beal and Marion Flarey.

That's what mattered.

2

So I love fairy tales and there is no doubt in my mind that one can draw deep and important life lessons from them.

But I admit, fairy tales also have a few inadequacies. One being that once the princess and the prince get together and, you know, consummate their love, pledge their troth, graduate from princess and prince to queen and king, etc., etc., the stories tend to go dark. We have no idea if the two royal lovers discover they have less in common than they realized (other than their mutual passion of course) or need to work on their communication skills, let alone whether any mundane issues begin to intrude and how they partner to solve them. You know, the kingdom's tax revenues are inadequate to cover the royal budget and now the prince-turned-king must sally forth to war and conquest to refill the dwindling coffers, while the princess-turned-queen sits in the tiny camper parked on her parents' property feeling vaguely jealous that the young king is off on adventures while she is stuck at home.

I started thinking about all that as I picked out a tee shirt and combed my hair, and then I realized I was dawdling a bit and really needed to get over to the dome and pack a lunch for work.

That's a geodesic dome, by the way. Winchell built it back in the day and then my mom moved us in when they got together, so that's where I grew up. Only when I was fourteen, I announced that I was claiming the camper as my own, because it was ridiculous that I was still sharing a room with Candace, plus I needed a place to store my books. My fairy tale books, of which I already owned stacks and stacks by then. And the camper was the perfect solution. Winchell had lived in it while he was building the dome, but it had sat empty ever since, used for storage and as a guest house when out-of-town relatives visited, which wasn't often. So it was available.

And it became my space.

Until earlier this year and unbeknownst to me, Candace tried to take it over. I found out when I returned to Tibbs and discovered that my stepsister had left her husband, and instead of moving into the dome, like she should have, she'd taken the camper. And at least she let me have the camper bedroom, but it still meant there were three of us crammed into a very tiny space.

Me, Candace, and her boy, Quill.

Complicated. Families are complicated.

Speaking of Quill, after I finished getting dressed that morning and stepped outside, there he was, sitting on the bottom row of the stacked cinderblocks that serve as the camper's front steps.

"Watcha got?" I said as I stepped around him. He was holding something cupped in his hands.

"I caught a moth. Surprise eats them."

Surprise is our three-legged cat. The cat that disappeared and then reappeared but before you get any ideas, the reappearance had nothing to do with magic. Or my so-called fairy godmother. It was a coincidence. That's all.

"You shouldn't feed moths to Surprise," I said. "You should feed her cat food."

"But she likes moths," he said. "Hey, Aunt Marion, can we go visit Effie?"

Yikes.

I glanced toward the dome. The windows were open, because it was summer and the Weekes-Flareys don't have AC, so they always leave the windows open in the summer.

Would Candace be able to overhear this conversation?

"I don't think Effie is, uh, home right now," I said. "Plus your mom doesn't really want you visiting her."

Quill's eyes got wide. "Did Effie's house disappear again?" And he must have forgotten about the moth because his hands uncupped and it fluttered, a little brown thing, into the air and then up and over the roof of the camper.

"Her house doesn't disappear." I glanced back at the dome. "Who told you her house disappears?" Thinking to myself, oh crap, if he starts talking to Candace about Effie's house disappearing or whatever other stories he's heard, I'd be the one who'd get the blame.

But he didn't answer my question. He just shrugged. An exaggerated shrug. His thin little shoulders squeezed up and in and nearly touched his ears.

"Well," I said in my best adult voice and intending to nip this in the bud that instant if at all possible, "whoever told you that was wrong. Her house doesn't disappear."

"But if you were in it when it disappeared, would you disappear, too?"

"Geez, Quill," I said, my voice no longer very adult but more pleading. "Knock it off. You gotta stop asking questions about Effie or you'll get me in deep doodoo with your mom. So let's drop it please, and why don't you come into the house and have your breakfast?"

But he jumped up, shook his head, and ran around to the back of the camper, his little body a carbon copy of RB's body at that age. So that watching him run off I had one of those sudden flashbacks I get, sometimes, of RB, running away from me on the playground when we were kids. Like he'd just kissed me, the way kids sometimes kiss other kids on the playground. Kissed me and ran away, embarrassed.

And dang, enough reminiscing about grade school. I needed to focus here. Because Fletcher and I didn't have a date, but as I mentioned, it was his tasting room I was managing and if I really thought about it, the best way to demonstrate my stoutheartedness and faithfulness and trueness was to go to work and do a great job and sell lots of kombucha and make my boyfriend proud. Because something suddenly occurred to me. In the real world, seeing that Fletcher Beal was a businessperson, what better way to forge our golden future together than by becoming a businessperson myself, worthy of his admiration and respect?

Arguably, becoming a businessperson looked a great deal less frivolous than being a fairy tale person. I mean, come on. And in fact, hadn't I just stumbled on the bit that is missing from the fairy tales? The bit where the young queen—far from being some passive little creature who'd lucked into her role and was now moping around the castle while her king dashed forth busily ruling and conquering—actually has will and vision and agency? Seizes her destiny, forges herself into a vibrant, capable leader, a problem-solver, a respected pillar of her community, loved and admired by all? Especially her king?

And so right then and there, as I stood in front of the camper that fine morning, I resolved to change everything. To forge a new destiny.

Starting immediately.

Only I wasn't quite sure how, yet. Other than, vaguely, I'd need to do a major personal and professional overhaul, which would involve a great deal of planning and re-training and re-education.

But I'd figure it out. I'd become an entirely new Marion Flarey. I'd leave the world of fairy tales behind forever and fully embrace reality.

And Fletcher Beal wouldn't be able to believe his luck.

I practically floated through the air as I made my way to the dome and my new future.

• • • • •

The dome, of course, bore no resemblance to my new future.

It looked like it usually did on workdays.

Candace was in the kitchen already, and dressed for the office, because during the summer she has to be in around nine. She likes what they call bold colors, and given her personality she could pull them off. Unlike yours truly, who sticks to earth tones and jeans. And wow, was her top bright that morning. Canary yellow. Made me blink to see it, like walking out of a cave where you've been held by an underground gnome and seeing the sun for the first time in weeks. Blink, blink.

She was pouring herself a mug of coffee when I came in.

I went to the fridge, but then got the immediate sensation that I was in her way. Mostly because she stood directly behind me as I pawed around in the drawers looking at the cold cut selection.

"If you're looking for turkey," she said, "it's all gone."

Typical Candace. Did she have to talk to me like that? "Whaddya mean, all gone?"

She reached past me to grab her beloved caramel-flavored non-dairy creamer, her arm brushing me as she reached. "I finished it last night."

"There's plenty of ham left, honey." Mom speaking, now. She was sitting at a tiny student desk shoved up against the far wall of the dome, trying to get something done on their ancient PC. Probably working on her Etsy shop. Surprise was on her lap but instead of settling down to nap was arching her back and pressing her head against Mom's chin and generally getting in the way of the screen.

And ham? Great. This day was going great. First, no date tonight with Fletcher and now, instead of a turkey sandwich, I'd be stuck with pink, salty, fatty ham.

Be stout-hearted and resolute, Marion Flarey.

I bit my lip and laid my sandwich fixings on the counter.

And how was I supposed to keep my focus on my plans for a major personal and professional overhaul when I had to contend, constantly, with my annoying family?

The bread seemed a little dry.

In fairy tales, meals are never boring. You have your feasts at the end of the tale or the provisions you pack at the beginning when you set off on a journey. And, of course, there are those magical meals that appear when you open the magical tablecloth or reach into the magical bull's ear. But back here in reality, meals are prosaic. Ham and yellow mustard and bread that is supposed to be rye but tastes like regular old wheat bread, and is a little dried out to boot.

No wonder Quill wanted to go to Effie's.

"So," Candace stuck the carton of her flavored non-dairy creamer back in the fridge and the door clunked shut. "Did you hear Quill, last night?"

I startled. Not from the sound of the fridge door but hearing Quill's name. It was too much like Candace had read my thoughts. Also, that edge in her voice I'd detected when she made the comment about eating all the sliced turkey? It was still there. Only sharper. Like I was in trouble for something.

"Quill?" I asked innocently.

"He woke up screaming. Nightmare. About giants."

Uh oh. "Aw, poor kid," I said cautiously.

"I think you need to stop reading him those fairy tales."

"Uh, well. I haven't read him any fairy tales about giants," I said, then remembered that maybe we had done Jack in the Beanstalk last week. Oops. "At least, not recently," I added. "We mostly read out of my Grimm collections, and for the most part you find giants in the English fairy tales, not the German ones."

It's funny, actually, how you start to see differences like that when you study fairy tales. How the French and Italian fairy tales are the ones where you're most likely to find actual, exotic fairies dropping in to help us mortals solve our problems. And the mortals are almost always royalty or at least very wealthy. Whereas a lot of the German fairy tales have characters who are working class. Millers and tailors. Sure, they have kings and queens and princes and princesses, too, but a lot of the German stories are about regular people.

The English fairy tales are like that, too. So even a story like Jack and the Beanstalk. It's not about a prince, going off to distant lands and eventually winning a kingdom. Jack's the son of a poor widow. He's a nobody, basically. Also a bit of a simpleton who starts the story off by being stupid and gullible. But when the beans he takes from the merchant in trade for the precious milk cow turn out to be magical for real, ol' Jack climbs up in the world, literally as well as metaphorically. The lesson here, I suppose, being that when you are young, you make stupid mistakes in your career, but things have a way of turning out in the long run, so don't let it bother you too much. Good advice for yours truly, don't you think?

Of course the other thing about Jack is that, if you want to be a stickler about it, he gains his fortune by stealing. The hen that lays golden eggs, the golden harp? They belonged to the giant, technically. And sure, the giant was an evil ogre who ate people and probably got his hands on his treasures by stealing them himself. But thievery is thievery, and maybe the story had disturbed Quill on some level?

"Last night," I said, because this train of thought was making me uneasy, "we read the Princess on the Glass Hill. No giants. Just a farmer's son who, because he is very brave, wins three horses and uses them to climb up a glass hill, and then marries a princess." I began to warm to the subject as I thought it over. "And since the story is about being brave, it's probably good for him, if he's been having nightmares."

"Oh, come on, Marion. Seriously?" Candace said.

I glanced over at her in time to catch her look of mixed annoyance and disdain. Like I cared what she thought. Because nothing mattered less, to me, than Candace's opinion about fairy tales. Even though by some measures she was a more successful human being than I was, since she had a child and a salaried job in an office. "Calm down, Candace," I said in a reasonable tone of voice. "Quill knows they're just stories."

A bit of a bluff, of course. Because I was pretty sure he knew the stories I read to him were "just stories," but when it came to the odd old lady living up the road...

"Can't you read him a different kind of story? For once?"

"I don't own any different kinds of stories," I said.

"You know your problem, Marion?" Candace picked up her mug and phone. "You're stubborn. Stubborn as a jackass."

"Like you're not?" I snipped in self-righteous retort.

"Girls," Mom said.

I began layering slices of ham on my bread, and was wondering if there was any fruit left or if Candace had eaten all of that, too, when there was a thud somewhere behind me.

Followed immediately by Candace shrieking. "MAYFLY!"

My nickname. Used by people who knew me growing up. But usually not when they are mad.

"You need to get your crap out of here!" she shrieked.

I looked up from my sandwich. Candace was standing by my stacks of boxes, which as I've mentioned are piled behind the living room couch. Because I couldn't fit them anywhere else and, as you know, I hadn't had the chance, yet, to ask Fletcher if I could store them at his house. Oh, and I say "living room," but imagine more of an open area with an arc of furniture—couch, coupla chairs, Winchell's sagging recliner—facing a television. Because being a dome, the back half is two floors of bedrooms, bathrooms, closets, and Winchell's "spa," which used to be Candace's bedroom, but at some point he'd taken it over and installed his beloved jacuzzi. But the front half is all open. Kitchen on one side. Faux living room on the other.

And my boxed-up stuff was stacked in that gray zone that marks where the kitchen ends and the living room begins. And now Candace was standing next to the boxes, holding her mug out and away from her body, and her astonishingly bright yellow top had big coffee-brown splashes splurshed down the front, some large enough and wet enough to make her top cling to her bra. And since the top was pretty sheer, the bra was more visible than usual, which is saying a lot because Candace requires, er, a lot of support in that department. Her bra cups could probably do as shelters for a pair of small dogs in the event of a nuclear emergency. Whereas I am on the scrawny side. You've seen a real mayfly, right? Very thin, small, easy to squish?

There's a reason I earned that nickname.

"That's the third time I've tripped on your crap THIS WEEK!" she yelled, glaring at me. Expecting a response, obviously.

"Try watching where you're going?" I suggested. Because if she'd been watching where she was going, none of this would have happened. Hahahahaha.

She didn't find my remark amusing. "Are you kidding me?" she snarled. Only insert a couple eff bombs midway through. "I've had it, Marion. That's the last straw. If you don't find someplace else to put all your crap, I will. And you're not going to like it!"

"Girls," I heard Mom say.

But now it was my turn to get pissy. "Don't you DARE touch any of my boxes, Candace!" I yipped, although to be honest there was a touch of fear in my yip, because I wouldn't put it past her. I wouldn't put it past Candace to haul my boxes to work one day while I was sleeping in and toss them in the dumpster. She could be like that when she was in a mood. She could be mean.

And she was in a mood that morning. "I'm not joking, Marion." She marched back to the kitchen and began blotting her top with paper towels. "You need to—"

"Girls." Mom, again, from where she was sitting by her PC. That weary tone of voice mothers get. Like they are soooo tired of the bickering. And the language. Although to be honest I still wasn't really paying attention to her, because that touch of fear about what Candace might do with my books was deepening into something approaching panic, and also was that my phone buzzing? And it must be, but I couldn't remember where I'd left it? And it could be Fletcher. Or my best friend Teagan who I hadn't talked to in days.

"Don't you dare touch my books, Candy," I snapped as I paced the kitchen looking for my phone.

"Don't you 'Candy' me," she snapped back. "You can't just store your crap indefinitely in Mom and Dad's living room. Right, Dad?"

Ah, Winchell. My plus-sized stepfather. He'd materialized from the master bedroom. An accident on his part. No way would he have walked into this if he'd been forewarned. So now he stood on the narrow upstairs balcony, looking down at us and frozen in horror.

Candace, meanwhile, was still going at it, proving that she hardly needed reinforcements to make her point. "I mean it, Marion. We're all sick to death of your crappy old books."

Well. If there is anything my family needs to understand, it's that my books are the most important thing in my life. Other than Fletcher, of course. "If you lay a single finger on one of my books, I will MURDER you, Candace Weekes!"

And for some reason, that did it.

Mom snapped.

"GIRLS!" she shouted, jumping up from her seat by the PC so that Surprise hit the floor with a thud and darted under the couch.

Now it was our turn to freeze.

My mother never yells.

She never gets upset about anything.

Ever.

"Lana," Winchell said to her in a peculiar voice.

He sounded almost scared.

Not scared of my mother. It was something else.

Scared for her.

And I got it. I felt it, too. Maybe it was the look on her face. Her mouth. It was moving even though no sounds were coming out. And the rims of her eyes were suddenly bright red, the way eyes look when someone has been crying.

"Mom?" I whispered. "What's wrong?"

But she didn't answer. She clamped her lips together and crossed the room and disappeared through the front door.

"Holy shit," Candace said under her breath.

"Good one, girls," Winchell growled from the balcony. "Now look what you've done."

Okay. Tell you what. I felt pretty horrid in that moment. Because, you know. Mom. She never yells. She never gets upset.

Candace and I have bickered like that our entire lives.

I had no idea it might upset Mom that much.

I glanced over at my stepsister. Her cheeks were drained of color. And she met my eyes, and I could tell she felt it, too.

She felt as crappy as I did.

Winchell, meanwhile, came down the steps, growling indecipherably, and went out the door. Following after Mom. So it was just Candace and me, alone in the dome, which now had that deadly quiet feel that houses do when there's been an out-of-control blow-up that probably never should have happened in the first place.

"Geez," I whispered.

My phone buzzed again and this time I was able to locate it. I'd left it on the counter on the other side of the fridge. And it was Fletcher, texting me. And the last text in the string:

sry, u must be busy. plane taking off, gotta shut down

So damn it, I'd missed him.

The screen door rattled.

Winchell was back. And he looked odd. He stood inside the front door, and the expression on his face reminded me of the way Surprise looks when she's caught outside in the rain.

"What happened?" Candace said.

"She locked herself in her shop," he said. "Broken is as broken does. She won't come out. A downturning spiral of uncontrollable events."

He looked stricken. So much so, that for once, his silly made-up aphorisms seemed almost poignant.

We all three stood there a moment, considering what to do. If anything.

Then Candace spoke. "Marion?" Her voice cracked a little. "It's up to you. You need to go talk to her."

I gave a quick little shake of my head, because my first reaction was "no." I didn't want this, I didn't want to take responsibility for this. And up until that summer I'd been away for a long time. Seven years. Whereas Candace had lived in Tibbs all along.

Maybe she should be the one to try to patch things up?

But something else kicked in before I could speak. Call it a family dynamics override switch, I guess. Because back when Candace and

I were little kids—newly-made sisters, the exact same age, in a newly-blended family—we'd made a couple of pacts, and one of them was that, logically, Dad should be her responsibility and Mom should be mine. Our respective biological parents.

And be brave, Marion Flarey. Because isn't this exactly the sort of problem a young queen would solve, if some sort of interpersonal conflict erupted unexpectedly in her household?

I shoved my phone in the pocket of my jeans, and headed to the door, and past Winchell, and down the front steps.

Thinking to myself: Mom never gets ruffled. Not really. She's probably already calmed down. I'll have this all patched up in a jiff.

And then I'd text Fletcher back, he'd have Wi-Fi on the plane by then, and everything would be smoothed over and back on track, and I could turn my attention to my boyfriend and my future.

Right?

3

Mom's workshop is a shed behind the dome. One of those prefab metal sheds, only Winchell had added insulation so she could work out there year-round.

And it was getting to that time of morning when the sun was high enough that its beams were piercing the tops of the trees beyond the dome. No breeze, but I could see some of the tree leaves moving here and there, like the air was waking up. And the birds were going crazy, the way they do when the sun first starts to warm things, darting and flashing through the treetops, hunting for bugs, I suppose, and all the while making their little chirpy noises so their friends knew exactly where they were. And above them, above the trees, the sky was completely clear except for a couple white contrails that made an enormous X drifting against the blue.

I banged on the door to the shed. "Mom?"

Nothing. Nada. Silence.

"Mom. What's going on? Are you okay?"

Still nothing.

Hmmm.

And okay. I'm not the sort to panic over nothing, but my mom wasn't the sort of person who would—I dunno—shut herself into her workshop and off herself.

Was she?

She couldn't be that upset, could she?

I took a step back.

There were no windows on the front of the shed. But I circled around to the side, and yes, I'd remembered right, there was a window there. A smallish window, about four feet off the ground. Although unfortunately, it was guarded by a large and bristling clump of weeds, and naturally the weeds were pricker bushes and burdocks. And the burdocks were in bloom and were being visited, already that morning, by a half dozen enormous bumblebees.

I returned to the front of the shed and knocked on the door again. "Mom? We're sorry, Mom. Me and Candace, both. We stopped fighting. We won't do it again. And I'll move my books. If that's what it takes to make her happy. I'll get my books out of the dome."

Silence.

Okay, then.

I went back around to the side of the shed and side-stepped the bee-covered burdock plant and pushed the pricker bush canes aside, only of course one of them sproinged back at me, and I felt it snatch my tee shirt with its little prickery hooks, and of course it was one of my favorite tops, and now a line of threads was yanked into little loops across the front.

Argh.

Ruined.

Karma for the coffee on Candace's top, I suppose.

I sighed and leaned forward and put my face up to the window. The glass was dusty on the inside and gray with water spots on the outside, so I cupped my hands around my eyes to cut back on the glare.

And Mom must have realized what I was doing, because there she was. Not more than about arm's length from the window. Looking straight at me. And her mouth was pursed and her brows were beetled, and I saw her body lift up and down in one of those sniffy-sounding snorts you make through your nose when you have just about had it with someone.

She stepped up to the window and lifted the sash.

"Marion. What exactly are you trying to accomplish?"

"Um. Get you to talk to me?"

"Am I not entitled to a little alone time once in a while?"

Ah. Well. I considered how to answer. Because I'm not sure storming off and locking yourself into a shed really qualifies as me-time. At least, not high-quality me-time.

But pointing that out might not have been a fruitful course of action. And I was a bit relieved, frankly, that she was standing there, annoyed at me for bothering her, instead of curled up on the floor, resolving to never have anything to do with either of her daughters ever again.

"I just wanted to check on you. Is everything okay?"

She sighed, and her expression shifted from purse-lips to that smile-not-smile where you lift one corner of your mouth and your eyes stay somber. "It's complicated, Marion," she said. "Please just go finish making your sandwich. I'll see you after work."

"I'm sorry about fighting with Candace and all that, Mom. We didn't mean to upset you."

And she let out a noise that was a half-snort, half-laugh. And then she shook her head, and shut the window, and turned her back on me, and between how dim the shed was inside and the film on the glass it was like she started to fade as she walked away.

And I felt a stabbing sensation in my chest, because this was my mom, and was she really going to just walk away like that? Fade away into the dark, like that?

But fortunately, at that very moment, I heard the camper door slam. And I had an amazing inspiration, if I do say so myself. Because the camper door slamming reminded me that Quill still hadn't had his breakfast, and if anything could get Mom back to the dome, it was her grandson.

"Well," I called out in a loud voice, tapping on the glass as I spoke to make extra sure I had Mom's attention. "Quill's probably pretty hungry by now. So if you're busy, I guess I'll go fix him some breakfast, okay?"

Smart, right? Because you see, although my mother had never cooked for any of us growing up—the Weekes-Flarey clan has never sat down together to eat home-cooked meals, we've always been a TV dinner or make-your-own-sandwich sort of family—to my utter astonishment, when I moved back to Tibbs, I learned that Mom was fixing her grandson a from-scratch hot breakfast. Every morning. Well, from-scratch meaning she added milk and eggs to the pancake mix. Or waffle mix. But still.

And it made for a heart-warming scene. And yeah, I was astonished when I first noticed it. But you know, becoming a grandma apparently does peculiar things to people.

So my instantaneous plan was a simple one.

No way would she surrender breakfast-cooking duties to her daughter.

And guess what happened next? Synchronicity, that's what. A sign.

Quill, in the flesh, running full speed around the corner of the workshop.

He stopped short when he saw me.

"What're you doing in the pricker bush, Aunt Marion?" he said. "Where's Grandma?"

"She's in her shop. Grandma!" I tapped on the glass again. "Quill's asking for you." And then, in a jovial-type voice loud enough so Mom would hear. "Quill, you want pancakes this morning? Or French toast?"

Hah.

It worked.

I could see her dim form moving toward the front of the shed.

I backed carefully out of the pricker bush and around the bees.

The bolt on the door of the shed rattled. It was one of those old flimsy faux brass bolts, and tended to stick because the shed had settled since it was put up.

I got back around to the front just as the door opened, and Quill was throwing his arms around Mom's hips in a little-boy hug. "Hi, Grandma!"

"Hi, sweetheart."

She dropped her hands around his shoulders and held him tight, then looked up and looked over at me. And there was something in her expression that I don't think I'd ever seen before. Or maybe I'd seen it but hadn't paid enough attention. And I can't describe it. Like sadness, in a way, but more resigned than sadness.

Had Candace and my bickering upset her that much? "Mom," I whispered. "Something's wrong. Tell me what's wrong."

But she shook her head at me and spoke only to Quill. "Come on, honey, let's go get some breakfast."

I followed the two of them back to the dome, walking slowly, feeling a little knot of worry growing in the pit of my stomach. Thinking to myself how you go along in life, playing out your story in your head, and then all at once you realize that someone you thought you knew is playing out a different story, and how is it possible that could be happening, and how could I have no idea what Mom's story was?

Winchell was outside, standing next to his truck, and Mom passed him without saying anything or making eye contact.

And I realized something else. Something else about Mom's secret story.

There was something in the air between her and my stepdad. Something that hadn't been there in the olden days, before I started college—before I went out into the world and basically cut off all contact with them for seven years. And I realized that I'd been picking up on it ever since I'd moved back to Tibbs, even though I hadn't really let it register. And now Winchell's eyes didn't leave her, even when he gave me a little wave and said something about how he'd be ready to leave at 10:30.

He was watching her.

I followed Mom and Quill inside.

Candace had changed into a different top. Gaudy floral print which would doubtless do a better job hiding food or beverage stains.

I finished making my sandwich.

Winchell came back indoors, only now I was secretly watching him and Mom.

"Need anything from the store, Lana?" he asked her. And although his voice sounded completely normal, it wasn't. It wasn't normal.

And Mom didn't answer. She picked up a slip of paper and pencil from the counter and went to the freezer and opened it. Doing a little inventory of our stash of TV dinners.

Was she angry at him about something? Was that it?

"We need more deli turkey," Candace spoke up. Her voice sounded funny, too, though, and I could feel her trying to catch my eye with meaningful looks that I interpreted as some variation of told-ya-so with a smattering of so-what-happened.

"And, uh, how are we on blackberry sorbet?" I said. Because this was all so upsetting in a can't-put-my-finger-on-why way that I wanted ever more to be super nice to Candace, and although I can't stand blackberry sorbet personally, Candace was apparently fond of it, and heaven forbid we run out.

Mom jotted sorbet on the list.

And then Dad went upstairs, and Candace left for work, and I pretended I was reading stuff on my phone while in reality I was watching Mom as she made pancakes for Quill. And then I poured myself another mug of coffee, wondering if I dared ask her, again, whether something was really wrong.

Because sometimes, my mother seemed like the mothers in fairy tales. They hang around in the background, most of the time. Good-hearted, and quiet, and never making waves, never a part of the plot other than nodding quietly once in a while from where they sit in the corner embroidering or mending their daughters' stockings or shelling peas.

But of course she wasn't a mother in a fairy tale.

She finished filling out the grocery list and sat back down at the PC.

I shuffled over to the living room and snuck a look at the computer screen.

And then I did a little double take. Because Mom's an artist and sells stuff on Etsy, so naturally I assumed that's why she was online. I assumed she was busy posting pictures in her Etsy shop of those clay wind chimes she said were selling so well, or reviewing her orders, printing packing slips or whatever.

But instead, she was on a site with a big headline about the stock market.

I sidled a bit closer. "Whatcha doing?"

But it was almost like she didn't want me to see. She clicked the little dash in the corner of her browser window to minimize it and said, "Financial news." Then she stood and pushed the chair back under the desk. "I like to keep up."

Okay, that was odd. Why would Mom be reading the financial news?

And for the second time that day, I got a very strange sense that I didn't know my mother as well as I thought I did. Although maybe she read the financial news because, as an Etsy shop owner, she needed to stay abreast of consumer spending trends or something?

And then something else occurred to me.

Here I was, planning to re-invent myself as a businessperson.

And here was my mother. And although a few minutes ago I'd never have thought of my mother as the person capable of teaching me businessy things, I'd be foolish to rule it out.

She ran an Etsy shop. And it wasn't making them rich, obviously, but still, wasn't this a new way our stories might be overlapping? And could I use this as a way to re-connect? And hey, wait a minute, maybe I could open an Etsy shop and sell Booch4U merchandise and generate a second income stream for the brewery? And wouldn't Fletcher think that was amazing?

"So, Mom," I said. She'd crossed the dome to the kitchen and now I followed her. "How's the store going?"

"Store?" she said. She closed the box of pancake mix and stuck it back into the cupboard.

"Your Etsy store. The wind chimes, right? They sell pretty well?"

Mom put the batter bowl in the sink and began to rinse it out. "Yes. I do okay."

"That one on your desk, what's it go for?" She'd brought one of her bell-style chimes into the dome, probably getting ready to pack it up and mail it to a customer. The bell part was nearly the size of a football and was glazed in mostly sapphire, with brown and yellow streaks running down the sides.

"That one was listed for six-fifty," she said.

"Wow." So that was how she and Dad had managed to hang onto the dome despite the fact that neither had anything like regular jobs. And if she could sell 650-dollar wind chimes online, surely I could sell ten-dollar Booch4U swag. "Mom, could you give me some pointers, some time, on setting up an Etsy shop? I'm thinking of doing one for the brewery. We could sell our tee shirts and glassware and stuff."

"Sure, honey," she said.

And then Winchell came back downstairs and asked me if I was ready to leave, and to my relief the two of them pecked lips when he said good-bye. So maybe I'd been imagining things. Maybe there wasn't anything off between them. Maybe they were behaving the way people do when they've been married for twenty-whatever years.

I was still thinking about it a few minutes later, as I sat in Winchell's truck watching the greenery zip by.

A lot could have happened in the seven years that I was off on my own. People have their lives, they have their marriages. And there's a reason for the expression about the consequences of making your bed in a certain way. And it's not like Mom had asked my advice before she married Winchell and moved us into his dome which now that I thought about it was shaped like a bubble. Well, half a bubble.

Symbolic, eh? Living in a bubble and we all know what happens to bubbles.

But if I couldn't do anything to help my Mom, I could maybe learn from all this. In fact, maybe cultivating shared interests, becoming partners on multiple fronts instead of just in bed, was more important than I'd even considered. Maybe it was key to ensuring that with

Fletcher and me, our lives and our time and our very selves would be intertwined, symbiotic. We'd become a single organism, forever comfortable and relaxed, no odd, strained notes creeping into our voices, no running out and shutting ourselves in sheds.

I texted Fletcher.

how was your flight. am soooo excited about nyc trip!!!!

Followed by a string of hearts.

We reached the brewery—a little later than I'd expected, because we had to stop for gas, and Winchell refuses to patronize the gas station that we pass, conveniently, on the way to the brewery. He insists on detouring to another, out-of-the-way place six miles west of Tibbs where gas is three cents a gallon cheaper.

But at long last, Winchell pulled into the parking lot and stopped the truck, and I opened the door and gathered my purse and my insulated lunch bag. "Thanks for the ride," I said.

He didn't answer.

And ugh. He didn't even seem to notice that I'd spoken.

Was he still brooding about what had happened at the dome this morning?

And I thought about letting it drop, but I didn't. "Hey, Dad?" I heard myself say. "Is Mom okay?"

And he answered really fast, like he had already considered the question.

"Of course. Nothing is going on with Mom."

4

"Something's going on with Mom," Candace said.

Ugh.

It was closing on nine pm. And I'd expected Winchell to pick me up after work, because normally he was the one who ferried me around. So imagine my surprise when, fifteen minutes before closing time, Candace walked in the front door and said, "Surprise, it's me tonight."

"What happened to Dad?" I asked suspiciously.

"He was watching a game, so I'm being nice. But didn't you have a date tonight?"

"Change of plans," I said, picking up a couple dirty glasses and slushing them in the sink.

"Well, I'm glad he cancelled, because we need to talk."

"He didn't cancel," I said, rinsing the glasses and setting them on the drying rack. "He got called out of town for an urgent meeting. Talk about what?"

"You know. Us. And Mom."

Oh, great.

"What about Mom?" I said warily.

Which is when she said that "something is going on with Mom" thing. Which struck me spooky weird, since Winchell had said the exact opposite using almost the exact same words.

"Dad says there's nothing going on with Mom," I said.

"Dad's in denial, obviously. She's been acting very, very strange."

"Mom's always acted strange," I countered, partly in the spirit of devil's advocate and partly because I really, really didn't want to believe anything was going on with Mom. So I guess that made two of us in denial. I dipped a bar rag in the wash water. "She's an artist, remember?" I walked to the far end of the bar to give it the final wipe-down of the night. "And think about it, Candace. After how many years of no kids in the house, in we walk. It's got to be hard on her. She had her life, and now she's got one daughter with a marriage in shambles—"

"Oh, come on, Marion—"

"Chill, Candace! I'm not blaming you! My life is as effed up as yours in its own way." Which it was, although I didn't list all the flaws out loud. I was in debt, I'd been chronically underemployed for years, and I'd started a master's program—one reason for the debt—but then dropped out, or in fairness chickened out, because I realized a master's degree in fairy tales is an exercise in career futility.

I picked up the last dirty glass from the far end of the bar. "Mom is a total introvert. And suddenly her peaceful, empty nest is full of fledglings who were supposed to leave, but then came back, and now we're jostling and pecking and squawking at each other like a couple of hormone-crazy teenagers." I passed Candace as I spoke, carefully wiping the bar as I walked. "Before, she had this quiet, artist-y world where all she has to worry about is what designs she's gonna paint on her wind chimes. Now she's stressed." I cleared my throat. "So, I guess maybe one thing we should work on is to hold things together on our end." I cleared my throat again. "So that, uh, Mom has a solid foundation, psychologically speaking, under her feet. You know. While she works through whatever is bothering her. To keep her grounded and everything."

"Sure, Marion, sure," Candace said. "Or we could just try to stop fighting in front of her."

I suppressed a smile. "Yeah. That's what I meant."

"How much longer will you be?"

"I can lock up now," I said. "Wait for me out front."

• • • • •

I climbed into Candace's car. Feeling on the one hand relieved that she and I were negotiating some sort of truce, but on the other hand also a bit wary because she was, after all, Candace.

And sure enough, instead of starting the engine after I got in, she just sat there.

"Okay," I said. "What?"

Despite the orangish light pooling down from the brewery parking lot's single light pole, it was too dark in the car for me to read the expression on my stepsister's face. "What?" I said again.

"Here's the thing, Marion." Her shoulders lifted and fell as she drew a silent breath. "I think Mom is—I think she may be cheating on Dad."

OMG.

I admit. When I first heard the words, I felt that sudden stab of fear. Like when you rub your hand over your arm and think you feel a weird lump and think oh crap, it's cancer I'm gonna die. But then on second thought you check again, and the lump is actually a wrinkle in your shirt and calm down, honey, it's not actually a tumor that's going to kill you in six weeks.

It's a wrinkle.

In your shirt.

Don't be an idiot.

I burst out laughing. "You must be kidding! Mom? Cheating? On Winchell?"

"I don't think it's funny, Marion."

"Oh, come on!" I gasped. "How on earth could Mom possibly have an affair? Even if she wanted to? Sneak off after the rest of us have gone to bed? Hide a lover in her shop? Oh my God, is that why she ran out to her shop this morning? To have a tryst with her lover?"

My laughter reached a nearly full guffaw at the thought.

Which didn't please Candace. "Marion! Come on!" she sputtered. "You need to take this seriously!"

So then I felt a little guilty for laughing. I mean, Candace was genuinely concerned and for sure something was going on with Mom. Not an affair. But something. So I controlled myself. Wiped my eyes, then reached over and touched my stepsister on the arm. "Okay, Candace, I'm sorry I reacted that way. But let's look at this rationally, okay? What makes you think she's having an affair?"

"I am being rational," she said to me. "Mom's been acting very strange, lately, for starters. Like she forgets to pay attention to things. And the only time she seems really happy is when she's packing up to go to a show."

Hmmm. I thought this over. "So you think she's rendezvousing with her lover at her shows?"

"It's possible, isn't it?"

Ugh. I hadn't thought of that.

But really? Mom? An affair? "I dunno, Candace," I said slowly, because—I admit—I really didn't like the idea of Mom having an affair. So I was prepared to talk Candace out of the idea, as if talking her out of the idea had the magic-wand-power needed to turn a cheating mother back into a faithful wife. "She's happy other times. She loves hanging out with Quill."

But Candace shook her head vigorously, so that in the dim orangish light I saw the wavy bit of bangs that she usually keeps swept up off her forehead fall down like a horse's forelock. "You missed a lot, Mayfly, being away for so long." She pushed her bangs back into place, and her bangles—she wears a lot of bangles—jangled softly. "Her and Dad? Even before I moved back. They're never lovey-dovey like they used to be. I've been noticing it for a while, now. Years."

Hmmm again.

Maybe Candace had a point.

But still. My mother? An affair? I wasn't ready to accept it. "They've been married a long time. Maybe they're just not in love anymore. That doesn't mean she's—" I broke off. Aware that I didn't want to say "having an affair" out loud. Like saying it out loud would have the magic-wand-power to make it suddenly real. So I tried again. "It doesn't mean she's found someone else. Maybe after raising three kids and putting up with Winchell for twenty-plus years, it's fun to go to shows and get away from things for a few days."

Candace was fiddling with her bracelets. "I suppose."

"Have you ever seen any actual evidence of it? Of another man?"

I tried to think what kind of affair evidence a woman Mom's age would leave lying around. Expensive jewelry? Unexplainable credit card charges? The scent of strange cologne on the sleeve of her tee shirts? Startling changes in her preferred style of lingerie?

Candace, meanwhile, shook her head. "Nothing specific. No."

Okay. I felt a little better. "And anyway, Candace, even if she is having an affair, I don't see much we can do about it. I mean, it's her life, I guess."

Her story.

I looked out the window, past the pool of light to the dark road and the darker trees beyond.

Each of us has our own story. To work out as we must.

"But she and Dad are made for each other," Candace interrupted my thoughts, her voice glum. And I wondered for a second if maybe, for Candace, this had more to do with her than our parents. I mean, talk about peoples' stories. Had she thought she and her husband, Garth, were made for each other? Until she realized she was wrong and walked out on him, and now she was thinking the person made for her was RB? Who had fathered her child and, given the way he was hanging around a lot lately, was apparently poised to queue himself up as husband #2?

And wasn't I the lucky one? Because I had Fletcher, now, and unlike the other women in my family, I really was with the man who was made for me, and was therefore safe from these kinds of silly doubts?

"Look," I said. "If Mom's having an affair, our job is to support her. No matter what decision she makes."

"Gawd," Candace groaned. "I know what you're saying. But I can't stand the idea of them breaking up. Mom and Dad."

"Of course you can't. You and I both went through that once before. Even though we can't really remember it very well, it's still—"

"What do you mean?" she interrupted. "I remember it."

"What?" My head tilted sideways in disbelief. "You remember Winchell divorcing your mom?"

"Well, yeah."

"Candace. You were three."

"I remember it."

Argh. She can be so aggravating. How can she possibly remember something that happened when she was that little? I mean, I last saw my bio dad when I was five or six, and I barely remember the guy.

"I remember it, Marion," she repeated for the third time. Stubbornly. "Also, what about your promise?"

Ugh, again. "What promise would that be, Candace?" I said but I was bluffing, now, wishing that I didn't know the answer. "I'll get my stuff out of the dome. I said I would, and I will."

But that wasn't the promise she meant. "Oh, come on, Mayfly. I mean, thanks for finally dealing with that mess. It's about time. But that's not what I'm talking about and you know it."

Okay. She sounded different, now.

She sounded small.

I felt my head tip to the side, the way a dog's does when it hears a peculiar sound. Because I was used to Candace being pushy and abrupt and bullying and loud. But now she sounded fragile and tentative. She sounded like a little kid. Like she used to sound back when my mom and I first moved into the dome.

"No. I don't know what you mean," I said. Only my voice had changed, too, it sounded small, too, and it was catching in my throat a little bit.

Like I knew what was coming, even before my mind caught up.

"Your oath," she said.

That word, again.

Oath.

It thunked against me, thunked against my chest, over my heart. And I looked down at my hands, where they were folded in my lap, illuminated softly by the light from the Booch4U sign. And something about them, about them being a woman's hands. Not a little girl's hands...

"You remember." She was watching me, she was almost whispering, now. "You have to remember."

And I didn't answer. But not answering was the same as saying yes. Because of course, I remembered. And no wonder her tone of voice had changed so much, because what she was talking about was something that she and I had agreed when we were little, seven or eight years old, when we first became sisters, and we felt close, when we were secret allies, paired off against things adults had done that we didn't understand, trying to make sense of this new blended family that our parents had negotiated behind our backs, thrusting us into a new arrangement without our having a voice in their decision.

Trying to make sense of how I had a mother, and Candace had a father, but now we were also suddenly sharing these parents with each other. Trying to turn what had happened to us into a shared story.

And that word. Oath. It was the word I'd picked, of course. Candace hadn't even known what it meant, until I explained it to her. It was a word from the world of fairy tales that I loved so much. And so I'd explained that an oath was like a promise, but more serious. That it was a promise but if you broke it, awful things would happen. That it was almost like a spell, a magical spell.

Our oath had been that we would make sure our parents—Lana Flarey and Winchell Weekes—stayed together. Always.

"Remember?" she repeated.

"It was a long time ago," I said.

"Does that matter?"

"You don't even believe in that shit," I muttered, because to be honest, she was freaking me out a little.

"But you do. And you're the one who said it was a big fucking deal, to swear an oath."

"We were little kids," I muttered, clenching and unclenching my hands. Because we'd felt utterly weak, because that's what little kids are. Utterly weak. All we really knew is that we didn't want to live through any more of the fighting and craziness and upheaval and emotional violence of our parents' first marriages. And of course, we knew there was nothing we could do, to stop it from all happening again. Nothing. So in the magical world of seven-year-olds, we invented a power that we didn't have: the power to keep our parents together just by proclaiming it, just by swearing a magical oath that we would do it, that no matter what, we'd fend off that ugly chaos that had wrecked our young lives from crashing back in, again.

Fairy tales aren't real.

But what about stories? What about the stories we tell ourselves? Are they real?

Does it matter if they are?

I sighed. A painful sigh, coming from the pit of me, the pit that had been dug out by the thunk of that word. Oath.

Was this really happening?

Was I really going to be sucked into all this Weekes-Flarey clan drama when what I really wanted—what I really needed—was to focus on my own life, my own story about Marion Flarey coming into her own as Fletcher's dynamic and successful and amazing young queen?

"I suppose I could try," I said resignedly. "Maybe I'll arrange a girl's night out with her. Maybe she'll talk to me if I get a cocktail into her."

"That might work," Candace said, nodding. "She'd open up to you."

I sighed again, but a silent sigh this time, because I had my doubts and I really didn't want Candace trying to argue me out of them. "Maybe."

A car passed on the road, its headlights sweeping over our windshield as it rounded the bend.

And you know what would have been really helpful at that moment? A fairy godmother. A fairy godmother who would actually help me out if I asked.

Right.

But Candace must have felt better, because she finally started her car, and we began to drive. Although she was quiet for a good ten minutes, which felt odd and unsettling. Because Candace and I had been butting heads for a long time, at that point. I wasn't used to this. To feeling like she and I were allies. Friends, almost. It was like finding a dress in the back of your closet that you'd loved at one time, and it had started to feel dated so you pushed it way to the back, you loved it so much you couldn't quite bring yourself to take it to Goodwill, but you also knew you'd feel silly wearing it. And then one day you notice it and take it out and look at it again and realize that fashion has circled back and this lovely, lovely dress that is so flattering on you no longer looks dated. It's retro. No, better yet, it's retro chic...

We passed through the town of Tibbs and turned onto the highway.

It's not much of a highway. A two-lane.

And suddenly I thought of something else. Another fairy tale, actually. Jack and the Giant Killer. Also an English story, but a different Jack, this time, than the beanstalk Jack. And there's this part of the story toward the end where Jack and a prince—King Arthur's son, supposedly, not that his royal lineage matters to the plot—reach a castle where a beautiful lady lives. They'd been looking for this particular castle because the prince had determined, prior to their setting out, that he was going to marry the lady living there. Only there was a problem. She'd been ensnared by a demon. And Jack ended up killing the demon and freeing the lady, so happy ending, yay. She ended up being a perfectly wonderful wife.

But the point is, while she was under the demon's enchantment, she was anything but wonderful. She was on the demon's side.

And it's not like I thought Mom was literally enchanted.

But the mind can do things. It can play tricks on people. It can pull you into a story that seems real, but it isn't, only you think it is, and you start doing things that are horrible and destructive, all the while thinking you are doing what is good and right. And then suddenly you wake from the dream and everything most important to you is in pieces on the ground.

I crossed my arms in front of me and gripped myself in a sudden hug.

That wasn't happening to Mom.

Was it?

I glanced over at Candace. She was lost in thought herself, now.

I couldn't talk about this to her. Not in that way. Not using ladies and castles and demon lovers.

We turned off the highway and crossed the valley and came to a four-way stop like you come to all the time in the little country roads around Tibbs, and Candace leaned forward and looked first right and then left before pulling into the intersection. "By the way, I had another idea," she said. "Have you thought about just asking RB if you could store your stuff at his place?"

I shot her an are-you-kidding look. Because first of all, we were finally figuring out how to get along, and here she was pushing that back into my face? And secondly: seriously? RB's place?

And by the way, in case I haven't mentioned this to you: I used to date RB. Yes, Quill's father. I dated him before Candace did. So there's some history there, too. And I would rather not have that history pushed back into my face, either, thank you very much.

"I guess not," I said, hearing a bit of an edge creep back into my voice. "Thanks for the suggestion, but I'm making other arrangements."

Not a total lie, right? Because Fletcher would be in town in two nights and we'd be on a date and I'd be able to ask him about storing my stuff at his house.

But leave it to Candace to keep pushing. "RB's got plenty of room," she pointed out. "You haven't seen his new place, right? It's pretty big. And you know how crammed we all are, trying to share our space."

"Drop it, please, Candace," I muttered. "I said I'm dealing with it. And I will. In my own way."

She opened her mouth, probably to argue about how storing my stuff in the home of my ex-boyfriend/father of her child was ideal in a thousand-and-one ways. But then she closed it again, maybe because she knew she wasn't going to win that argument with me. Not in a thousand-and-one years.

5

We were almost back to the dome when I remembered that I'd left my notepad back at the brewery. All day, during slow times, I'd been jotting down ideas of how Marion Flarey, budding businessperson, was going to transform the brewery from a modestly successful start-up into an eye-poppingly successful model for kombucha breweries everywhere, culminating in my being featured on the cover of Inc. magazine, which Fletcher would of course frame and hang prominently in the Booch4U tasting room.

And I'd planned to work on it some more that evening, and now I couldn't.

Darn it.

But maybe there was something else I could focus on?

For example. Candace had earned an associate's degree in business in only two years, right? Surely I could earn one in a much shorter time. Six months? Three weeks? Given that today, there were online options?

And I was pretty sure the ideas I'd jotted down earlier were brilliant. But it was possible that there were some gaps in my understanding of the ins and outs of running a business. And the last thing I wanted to do was champion an idea to transform Booch4U and learn too late that it was doomed to fail.

So, maybe, rather than continue brainstorming, I could grab a quick glass of Winchell's wine and retire to my bedroom in the camper, get online, and research my options for inexpensive but prestigious business degrees.

Great plan, right?

We zigzagged up the driveway—the dome sits on the side of a hill, so the driveway was built switchback-style—and I began unhooking my seatbelt in anticipation of beginning my highly productive work evening, and we pulled up in front of the dome and I shifted forward in my seat and reached for the car door latch...

And then, are you kidding me? Was that really RB's truck, parked in front of the dome?

Because okay. He'd been hanging around a lot recently, watching TV with the family or whatever, which was a major reason why I'd started to think that maybe he and Candace were getting something going, again. Which was fine by me, because despite our past—me and RB's—Quill was his son, and despite that in the back of my mind I was still a teensy bit upset that Candace had slept with my boyfriend, I'm a good person, and I could see that Quill worshipped his biological father, and I'd be a witch if I wasn't able to get over myself and be happy if Candace and RB got together.

I mean, I like RB just fine. Candace could do a lot worse than end up with RB.

It's just that I felt so awkward being around him.

So I considered skipping the glass-of-wine part of my evening plans. On the other hand, it wasn't like I'd let myself get sucked into hanging out with them. All I needed to do was make a beeline to the kitchen to grab a tumbler—yes, I drink Winchell's wine in water glasses, it's not like it's expensive wine and with a tumbler you can give yourself a generous pour, which is more convenient than having to go back and forth from the camper to the dome, if you want seconds. And it's not like I had to be up early the next day. I'd get my wine and make my excuses and be free.

I followed Candace to the dome, past RB's truck. The engine was making clinking noises like engines do in the summertime when they're still hot.

I kept my head down as I stepped inside and started across the room.

But so much for slipping in and out unnoticed. "Hey, Marion," RB called over from where he was sitting on the couch, next to Quill. "It's cool with me if you want to store your stuff at my house."

"Geez, Candace," I muttered to my stepsister. She'd beat me to the kitchen and was taking a bowl down from the cupboard for her nightly fix of sorbet. "I don't recall giving my permission for you to discuss my business with RB."

Candace swung the freezer door shut. "Chillax, Mayfly. RB just wants to help."

"It's okay, really, Marion," said RB, who apparently had excellent hearing.

Great. Now they were ganging up on me. So I opened my mouth because I was strongly tempted to tell them both to back off, but then I stopped myself. Because there was Mom, sitting on the couch as well, her legs folded up under her and her head down. Reading a book. Poetry of some kind, most likely. In addition to being a visual artist she devours poetry. And she was completely oblivious. But she'd seemed oblivious this morning, too, until she wasn't. So it was a good bet she wouldn't stay oblivious for long, now, if my sisterly scrapping with Candace escalated into obnoxious. And hadn't it been my suggestion that Candace and I exercise a bit more self-control? And wasn't I now a new woman: Marion Flarey, young queen, regal and aloof and above these petty squabbles?

"Thanks, RB, but I'm making other arrangements," I said primly and poured my wine and re-corked the bottle.

And I headed out to the camper.

• • • • •

Ah.

Peace and quiet.

I pulled out my phone and opened a browser window to start researching business degrees.

But after a couple minutes I put the phone aside. I'd had a long day at work. I needed a little relaxation time, first. I needed to clear my mind.

I picked up one of my fairy tale collections and started to read.

Ancilotto, King of Provino. By Giovan Francesco Straparola.

Straparola, by the way, is the father of the literary fairy tale according to my undergrad coursework. We're talking back in the 1500s (!) which is pretty wild, really, to think that a story over five hundred years old is still around, today.

Oh, and if you don't know the Ancilotto story but you're a fairy tale person you have probably read a version of it in The Orange Fairy Tale Book, where it's called The Bird of Truth. The setup is that a queen gives birth to beautiful children who are stolen from her by a jealous female relative. Jealous female relative then claims the queen birthed either cats or dogs (depending on the version). And the queen's formerly-loving king believes the lie.

What's interesting about the Straparola version is the appearance of the queen's children. They were born with long hair braided with gold thread, and with golden chains on their necks (which wouldn't come off btw) and with golden stars on their foreheads. And any time their hair was cut, precious gems would fall out.

I mean, obviously on one level that is ridiculous. But on another level, it has some sort of symbolic meaning, right? Maybe relating to the children's innocence, if you figure that being innocent is a kind of precious jewel. But the other thing about this story is that the queen was of low birth. Her old man was a baker. So working class, basically.

I'm sure she was pretty, but the real reason the king married her was because she prophesied that, if he did, she'd give birth to those miraculous children.

And I guess that made sense. What king wouldn't marry a commoner if she promised her children's hair would rain jewels? You could stop taxing people for one thing, which would make you extremely popular, I would think, and you'd never have to put the royal household on a budget. On the other hand, maybe there's something else there, something about the right reasons to marry versus the wrong reasons. Something like: don't marry the sort of person you're maybe expected to marry. Marry the person who is going to give you the richest future. Symbolically speaking.

And so, there you go. Because not so very long ago, I never even imagined I'd be with Fletcher. And here we were, together, in love, planning a future together. Well, not quite to the planning-the-future stage, but it was next on the relationship agenda, for sure.

And now I was planning to turn myself into the mother of the golden children, because my future business acumen would be the modern-day equivalent of hair that rained jewels, which gave me a surge of warm, marvelous feelings as I finished the story and sat with the book resting on my lap, sipping wine, and thinking about how gorgeous Fletcher was and wondering how many children we'd have and how we'd split our time between the stone house in Tibbs and his place in Manhattan.

And then I heard the camper door open and shut, and little footsteps—that would be Quill—followed by the sound of the stool being pulled out from where it was stored beneath the bathroom sink. He's small for his age and needs to stand on a stool to brush his teeth. And then, a minute later, he peeked his head around the corner.

I knew what he wanted.

A bedtime story.

"I brushed my teeth," he said, because that's a bedtime story prerequisite.

And maybe it was reading about the miraculous children with the jewels falling from their hair, but my mood had softened, and I wasn't sorry that the little boy wanted to spend time with me instead of watching more television in the dome.

Or that I'd have to postpone doing research on online business degrees until a little later.

I moved over a bit to make room on the bed. "Okay. Jump up."

I didn't re-read Ancilotto, though. It's on the long and complicated side, for one thing. And the more complicated the story, the more questions Quill would ask. He tends to interrupt a lot.

Fortunately, I had other books stacked on the bed beside me.

Yes, I sleep with books. So sue me.

"Let's read about the four brothers," I said. "There's a dragon in the story."

He nodded eagerly.

"Want to see a picture of it?"

Right. Like a seven-year-old would turn down that kind of offer. So I picked up my edition of Grimm that is illustrated by Elenore Abbot and turned to the frontispiece which is a scene from The Four Accomplished Brothers. There was the princess, in a low cut, sea green dress, shoulders bowed sadly, expression pensive yet serene. She's seated on the curled-up body of her captor, a rather Oriental-looking dragon with wings and fangs. Fire licks the air in front of his jaws.

"Her hair is very long," I said. "She'd better keep it away from the dragon's fire or—whoosh. Human candle."

Quill nodded because that was, of course, a perfectly logical observation. "How did the dragon catch her?"

"The story doesn't really tell. Probably she was wandering around without her retinue and the dragon pounced."

"What's a retinue?"

"Uh, her gang of friends."

"Do you have a retinue?"

Teagan.

But did having a best friend who was off working on a cruise ship somewhere count as a retinue?

"Not really," I said. "Only, kind of. I mean, I will have a retinue very soon, now, because my new boyfriend, Fletcher, has a ton of friends. So now they'll be my friends, too."

I started reading. It takes a while to get to the dragon. First comes the setup. Four brothers. Then—*uh oh!*—their father realizes he's too poor to feed them anymore. And he kicks them out of the house, which is brutal but, you know, we have to get the story going. And also, as he gives them the heave-ho, he (helpfully) tells them they have to learn a trade.

Thanks, Pops. That's better advice than anything I got from Winchell. If I recall correctly, Winchell's advice to me when I left for college was something like, "time well spent is time deposited in the savings account of life."

I think he meant, don't party too much. Hard to say.

Whereas in the fairy tale the brothers make good use of their dad's advice, although in a funny twist the first brother apprentices himself to a Master Thief. Which meant that as I was reading, I became aware that perhaps this story wasn't delivering the best moral lesson for a little boy. We'd read Jack in the Beanstalk the other day which meant I'd now exposed young Quill to story number two glorifying thieves, and we aren't supposed to hold thieves up as role models. OTOH, in The Four Accomplished Brothers, the thieving one ends up becoming the biggest hero, because thanks to his skills he's able to steal the princess away from the dragon.

In the world of fairy tales, thievery can sometimes turn out to be a very useful skill.

And hopefully, when Candace chatted with her son in the morning, Quill wouldn't announce that he'd decided to be a thief when he grew up.

Also, hopefully he wouldn't wake up in the night screaming from a nightmare about dragons.

But he seemed content and sleepy when we finished the story. He climbed down and went to the daybed on the other end of the camper where he and Candace slept, usually with Surprise curled up at Quill's feet.

And then Fletcher texted, yay, and then he phoned, and we had a nice chat, and then he said I should be getting my beauty sleep and I thought about saying I love you, but I didn't, but that was okay because the feeling was there. I could feel it and he could feel it. And then

Teagan texted and OMG, she had news, she was for sure getting time off next month. Which was amazing, she is my best friend, but she works on a cruise ship, and is saving money for med school, and hardly ever takes time off. So I hadn't seen her in nearly two years. And now she would have almost a whole month free, and could I meet her in Rochester (yes!) and she'd also be able to spend a week or so in Tibbs and she couldn't wait to meet Fletcher!

So naturally after that conversation I felt even more amazing.

And then her break was over, and she had to go, and I plugged in my phone and laid back and listened to the night sounds through the screen, the toads trilling in the ditch by the road.

I heard a burst of laughter from the dome. Candace and RB, it sounded like.

I wondered what they were watching that was so funny.

And I really should have stayed up a bit longer to start that online degree research, but at that point my brain was tired, and my eyelids felt all droopy. And it would be better to do the research in the morning, when I was a bit more rested and fresh.

6

The weather changed overnight. It cooled off and thick clouds came in, and when I first opened my eyes it was still pretty dark. So I rolled over and went back to sleep and then woke up again later and heard Candace clumping around.

I didn't feel as refreshed as I'd planned.

Nothing coffee wouldn't fix, though, right? Coffee and then I'd have (quick check of the phone) oh, at least a half hour, maybe more to do a little online business degree research before I had to shower and leave for work…

Plenty of time.

I set my phone back down.

The pocket door to the bathroom rattled closed. So Candace was in the bathroom, who knows how long she would be. And I needed to use a bathroom myself, which now meant I either had to wait or head to the dome.

I jumped up and threw on yesterday's jeans and tee shirt and darted to the door and stepped outside.

And stopped short.

Huh?

RB's truck? Still there? Still parked in our driveway?

I stood on the cinderblock steps. Because I really did not want to see RB. In the dome. On a Saturday morning, which meant he had spent the night. And if he'd spent the night—

Ugh. Don't even go there, Marion Flarey. Because even though I'd sort of forgiven him and Candace for sleeping together and getting Candace preggers, etc. etc., because after all that was, like, eight years ago and that really is plenty of time to get over it, Marion Flarey, in the back of my mind I wished I could really put it all behind me, and if I never had to see the guy again it would be so much easier...

And sure, it was Saturday, but shouldn't he be at work? Grappling with a pipe or something? Because he'd taken over his father's plumbing business when his dad passed. This was after RB had graduated from college—which btw makes him probably the only plumber in the country with a BA in European History, meaning that if he comes to your house to unclog your drain you could talk wrenches and fixtures, or you could chat about the root causes of Europe's Thirty Years War. Whichever you prefer.

But European History aside, the business was residential plumbing, and RB had more work than he could handle according to something Candace had said at one point. So no Saturdays off for him. And plumbers usually get going pretty early, don't they?

Also, I should have thrown on a sweatshirt. It was chilly and there was a stiff wind coming out of the west. It felt like rain, which meant things would be slow at the brewery, and Fletcher was probably still asleep in his hotel in Houston and he hadn't sent me his flight info so I had only a vague idea of when he'd be back on the East Coast, and I wouldn't be able to track his flight to make sure it hadn't crashed somewhere in a tragic accident that would leave me forever single. Again.

In other words, I should have turned around and climbed back into bed and waited there for the bathroom and then pulled a pillow over my head and tried to catch another hour of sleep. Because with weather like this, it would be a slow day at the brewery. I could just do my online business degree research at work.

I wondered if Candace and RB and Quill had made Saturday plans to do something together.

I guess I should have been grateful that she'd slept in the camper at least part of the night, instead of romping around on the couch in the dome with RB.

And then, sure enough, it started to rain. Big cold drops of water hit my hair and soaked immediately through to my scalp.

Gird your loins, Marion Flarey.

Gird your loins and march into the dome and pee and pour yourself a coffee and see if Winchell will let you borrow the truck today so at least you can drive yourself to work, instead of being carted around like you're twelve years old.

• • • • •

The dome was dark inside, the way houses that are surrounded by trees get on gloomy mornings.

It took my eyes a minute to adjust.

And then I saw RB. Sitting on one of the bar stools on the kitchen island.

Shirtless.

And okay. Fletcher was my love. And Fletcher was a very, very well-built and handsome and sexy man.

But RB wasn't bad looking, either. He'd played football in high school and lifted weights to get into shape, and even in the gloom all it took was about a nanosecond to see that he was probably still lifting. He wasn't, like, huge or anything but the muscles on his shoulders stood out and oh dear, those shoulders were the kind that would make any red-blooded American heterosexual female start to fantasize pretty much instantaneously about what it would be like to be horizontal, underneath, and hanging on. And he'd grown a beard while I was away, a full old-timey beard that looked pretty good on him. He had the right kind of face for a full beard. It made him look like he was a strong but sexy gentleman who'd time-traveled in from another age.

So yeah, I stopped short for the second time that morning, my breath catching in my throat.

Fortunately, RB was looking at his phone when I stepped in and didn't see me pause.

The screen door had gotten caught in the wind, but now it banged shut behind me.

He looked up. "Morning, Mayfly."

Mayfly.

I steadied myself. "Uh, hey, RB," I said and then beelined for the bathroom, while on the inside I was scolding myself to get the hell under control, Marion Flarey. Because of course what was going on was that I'd been expecting to spend last night with Fletcher, and subconsciously that had gotten me a bit revved up, if you catch my drift, and so naturally the unexpected glimpse of sexy male muscles had triggered a very natural, red-blooded American heterosexual female response.

But it was purely physical. It meant nothing. Nothing our Heroine, Honest and True, should find the least bit troubling or difficult to resist.

And Fletcher. Fletcher was perfect. And he'd been my teenage dream. The rich, gorgeous, smart, sexy boy who'd twirled me around the gym floor at the spring dance right after my fifteenth birthday. And then his wicked witch mother had separated us—see what had happened, there?—and my so-called fairy godmother blew me off for reasons I have yet to completely understand and so of course I thought I'd lost him forever. And so of course when we found each other again I was more than ready to make up for lost time.

RB, on the other hand, was none of those things. He was the kid from my hometown that I'd known since elementary school and then dated for a while in high school. After Fletcher. After my prince had been torn from my arms.

I finished my bathroom business and crept to the kitchen, keeping my eyes turned steadfastly away from the shirtless RB, and really, guy, I know it's stuffy in the dome but outside it's damn chilly and shouldn't you maybe get yourself dressed?

The coffee maker popped and hissed.

RB had made coffee.

Good. Coffee.

But also: geez, RB felt at home enough in the dome to spend the night and then get up and make coffee? And what was that supposed to mean?

"Hey, Marion?"

I jumped a bit and then quickly regained control and braced myself, because why shouldn't we have a casual conversation seeing that we were the only two in the room at the moment?

"Yeah?" I kept my eyes fixed on the mugs in the cupboard, picking my favorite (the one that says life begins after coffee) and then took down a second mug because I am polite and technically RB was a guest of my family's, even though apparently he felt as comfortable in the dome as I did.

"I was serious, last night, about you storing your stuff at my place," he said as I side-stepped over to the coffee machine. "It's really not a problem."

"Thanks for the offer." I poured our coffee. "But—"

"I'll help you move it, if you want. If that's the issue."

"Thank you. That's very generous. But as I said, I've made other arrangements."

Not precisely the truth. The arrangements weren't technically finalized. But it was close enough. And oh, phew, a movement caught my eye and through the windows in the front of the dome I glimpsed Candace and Quill heading over from the camper, Candace wearing her satiny black bathrobe with the huge orange poppies and her pink flip flops with the straps across the tops that look like feathery flamingo heads, and Quill in shorts and a little yellow slicker that would be way too hot later today. Both of them sprinting from the camper because the rain had begun to pick up.

And then Candace was bursting through the door and pausing to take in the scene while RB said, "Mornin.'"

He smiled at the two of them. Or maybe he was smiling at Candace.

"Why dontcha turn on a light?" she said as she scuffed across the room toward us.

The flamingos on her flipflops looked a bit bedraggled from the rain.

She flicked the light switch, and poof the kitchen was a glare of light, and RB maybe noticed finally that he was still shirtless, because he got up and went over to the couch and picked up his shirt from where it was draped over the back of the couch.

"Can we leave now, Daddy?" Quill hoisted a half-gallon jug of orange juice out of the fridge. "Are we eating at McDonald's?"

Fishing, I thought to myself. Good day to go fishing, with it raining like that.

"Yep," RB said, his voice muffled through his shirt. And then he'd pulled it on over those shoulders and he stretched, arching his back. But of course I only know how he looked because I caught a little bit of it out of the corner of my eye. I was *not* watching RB.

"We can leave right now, Quill, if you're ready," he said.

"Have him back by four, please," Candace said.

You know, I couldn't figure out those two. RB and Candace. Maybe they were basically like married people. Or maybe they put on an act when I was around. Like, maybe Candace had hung out with him in the dome before she'd turned in last night. You know, they'd cuddled and kanoodled and all of that on the couch or whatever after our parents had turned in. But then she'd slept in the camper, because it would be confusing to little Quill for her to be sleeping with RB so soon after leaving Garth. Only you'd think she'd have gone over to the RB for a morning hug, at least.

I went around to the other side of the kitchen island and took the stool where RB had been sitting.

The seat was still warm from his body.

Candace was pouring creamer into her coffee. "By the way Marion, I forgot to tell you." She yanked at the sash of her robe to re-cinch it. "Guess who I saw at the 7-11 yesterday? Pumping her own gas?"

Her own gas? That was significant, because—why? "No idea. Shari?"

Meaning Shari who we'd grown up with, who maybe now expected that someone else should pump her gas for her, being a bit of a snob.

But it wasn't Shari. "Fletcher's mom," Candace said. "Poor thing, she couldn't figure out how to use the credit card reader."

Fletcher's MOM?

Was it cold in there? Because I suddenly felt a chill pass through my entire body. I suddenly felt like an invisible shower of icy water had started pouring from the ceiling and I could now actually feel the cold driving the blood from my poor chilly extremities, and the hair on my arms was prickling.

"Did you know she was in town?" Candace was saying.

"No. Maybe." I cleared my throat to try to make my voice sound normal instead of coming out as a croaking noise. "And, um, so what?"

Candace shrugged. "Just thought you'd like to know. Has she been staying in the stone house?"

The stone house?

No!

It couldn't be!

She had a place in Westchester county. That's where she lived. Why would she be in Tibbs? She hated Tibbs. Fletcher's mom hated, hated, hated Tibbs.

"I, uh, I suppose she was in town on business," I muttered, wishing Candace had left the light off because I could feel that my face was warm, and no doubt Candace had noticed.

And sure enough, she snorted. Because my words were as ridiculous as they sounded. Nobody comes to Tibbs "on business."

"Where the heck is Dad?" I squirmed in my seat and looked up toward the master bedroom door in the back of the dome. I needed to get out of there. I needed to shower and borrow Winchell's truck and get to the brewery, and hopefully it would be slow there today so I could start my other project, but on the other hand Saturdays are often a big revenue day, because we not only get locals but also out-of-towners, people on their way through, heading west-ish to the Finger Lakes or north to the Adirondacks or south-ish to New York City. And it would be so nice to report the day's sales to Fletcher and know how happy he'd be that his girlfriend-slash-tasting room manager was running things so beautifully and profitably.

Ugh. Out of towners.

Like Fletcher's mom…

And here's the thing. I could deal with running into that old witch, I suppose. Even if I happened to run into her, one day, at the stone house. Which I supposed could happen. I suppose I'd always known, in the back of my mind, that it could happen, that one day I'd have to face her again and that one day might just happen here in Tibbs.

Although maybe at some point Fletcher and I could have a conversation about it. Because young queens have a right to assert ownership of their castles, and we all know what happens in fairy tales when evil mothers-in-law hang around making trouble.

Only it wouldn't be an easy conversation, because we hadn't been dating that long. So how was I supposed to bring it up? "Hey, Fletch, would it be possible to tell your mother to stay the hell out of Tibbs?" Right. That wouldn't backfire, not at all. Nothing could possibly go wrong if Fletcher picked up on my residual-yet-considerable hatred for his mother.

Maybe do it as a couples planning thing. "Hey, sweetheart. I was just wondering. Your mom bought the Tibbs house originally, right? Is it still in her name? Because I was thinking it would be nice to buy it from her so that, you know, it was our house. Yours and mine. Our private little getaway Tibbs estate, just the two of us. And we can easily afford to make her a generous offer since, thanks to my wonderful business acumen, Booch4U revenues have septupled and we are rolling in cash!"

Like I had the nerve to start talking to Fletcher about buying a house.

I hadn't even worked up the nerve to ask him if I could store my books there.

And then it hit me.

My books.

No way could I store my boxes of books in Fletcher's place.

Because it wasn't Fletcher's place.

It was HER place.

Why hadn't this occurred to me before?

No way could I store my precious books in a house where an old witch might come around and see them and cackle and carry them out into the yard and pour gasoline on them and burn them while dancing around and cackling even louder.

I looked over at the boxes stacked behind the couch.

Damn it.

Was I really going to have to eat my pride and take RB up on his offer?

Ugh.

RB was folding the blankets he'd used the night before and was stacking them on the end of the couch.

No. I couldn't store my stuff at RB's house. It was too awful to consider.

I jumped up and fled to the camper to douse myself with a hot, hot shower.

Only the idea didn't quietly douse itself like it should have. I finished my shower with my mind still arguing with itself. And I toweled my hair, and thought, forget the whole thing. I'd just leave my books in the dome. Easy answer, right? They'd just have to deal with it. Candace would just have to learn to look where she was going when she pranced around, carrying liquids in open-topped containers.

I dragged a comb through my hair and clipped my wet bangs back with a barrette.

Plus, don't forget: everyone knew that RB and I had history. It wasn't fair for them to ask me to put all that history aside and act like he was just another family friend. Like he was nothing more than my sister's boyfriend and my step nephew's father.

I heard the sound of Quill yelling happily and then RB's truck starting up. So at least he was gone. I wouldn't have to see him when I went back to the dome to arrange my ride to work.

I finished dressing and sat on the edge of my bed and unplugged my phone. Which was ancient and held a charge for only about twenty minutes at a time and also had a violently cracked screen. And OMG new phones are expensive, and although my expenses were now pretty low since I wasn't paying rent, I also had student loans and I had to pay my stepfather, Winchell, back for that money I'd borrowed from him earlier that summer, and what about a car? How long was I supposed to survive in that place without my own car, having to borrow Winchell's truck or beg a ride from my stepsister every time I needed to get somewhere?

And why were families so complicated? And why is it that even fairy tales are so often about families, even when like, in the version of Jack and the Bean Stalk by Joseph Jacobs, Jack ends up marrying a princess? Because it doesn't feel right, that ending. It comes across as an afterthought, tacked on at the end.

I mean, come on, there's no princesses at all in the entire story until that last couple of lines. And you know why? Because the story isn't about Jack and Jack's happiness. Not at all. The entire point of the story, the whole reason Jack risks life and limb, is his dear old mama. The story is about family. And yes, it's about how a young man becomes a thief, but the reason that's okay isn't because he's stealing from a murderous giant. The reason it's okay is that he did it to take care of his mother in her old age.

And yet here I was with all these qualms and everything about RB?

And so what did it matter to me, really? If it made my family happy and showed Candace and even more importantly my mother that I was perfectly fine doing whatever it took to keep them happy? What did it matter if I stored my books at RB's?

Why was I making such a big deal about it?

It meant nothing. Nothing.

I was bigger than that.

And it would only be temporary. It would only be for a few weeks, and it would give Fletcher and me some of the breathing room that all brand-new relationships need, after which we'd be on such a mature and solid footing that all these difficult conversations about his mother and the house and moving in together would come easily, and we'd laugh together and make our plans and my books would have their forever home at last.

And so I did it.

I slipped my feet into my sneakers and tied them, and I took a deep breath, and sat back down on the edge of the bed and sent RB a text.

hey. hope ok if I chng my mind. would luv to take up on offer to store boxes at ur house

I hit send.

Then quickly tapped a quick addendum.

only 4 a couple wks, tks

7

It rained steadily until early afternoon, and sure enough that put a damper on the Booch4U traffic, because who wants a refreshing glass of fruity carbonated hard kombucha when it's 64 degrees and the sky is as heavy and dark as old pewter?

Which was terrible for revenue but good for Marion Flarey, because I took full advantage of the slow afternoon to make considerable progress on launching my new business-savvy self.

And it was going to be amazing. Only I did reluctantly admit that getting a business degree might be problematic. And by "problematic" I mean insurmountably difficult. I couldn't go to night school—not when running the tasting room required me to, you know, actually work at night—and you would have thought that getting an online degree from a community college would be cheap as dirt, but you'd be wrong.

Thousands of dollars. Thousands and thousands.

So forget that plan. And anyway, I didn't need a degree. Lots of successful people run successful businesses without business degrees. You read about them all the time. Bill Gates, anyone? And on the other side of the argument you have people like Candace, who did get a business degree and what did she do with it? She works in the office of the Tibbs high school. Not very business-y. Not that I really knew what she did there. But still. I'm not taking anything away from Candace, it was a steady job and she seemed to like it fine. But Wall Street financial conglomerate board room, it was not.

So instead I reverted to my original plan. Because sometimes your first idea is your best, and don't second-guess yourself, girlfriend. I pulled out the notepad where I'd started jotting down notes. Telling myself that I was smart and resourceful, and I had access to the Internet. Surely I could come up with some terrific ideas for jump-starting Booch4U without having to first attend weeks of boring and overly expensive classes.

I reviewed my yesterday's ideas.

1. More Social Media.

Good one. Because the guy who'd helped Fletcher get the brewery going, Upton Munster, had done a bunch of social media for a while, but then he and Fletcher parted ways (remind me to tell you that whole sordid tale someday) and while in theory managing our social media fell equally to me and our brewer, Josh, and Fletcher, in practice we'd all sort of let it lapse. And everyone knows that social media is an inexpensive and effective way to build word-of-mouth and that word-of-mouth leads to customers and customers lead to revenues.

See? I didn't need a business degree!

I drew a little star next to Social Media.

Next up:

2. Survey.

I frowned. Because honestly, I'd completely forgotten what I was thinking, yesterday, when I wrote down the word Survey. So I looked at the word for a moment, got nowhere, completely stumped, decided to move to the next one, come back to Survey later.

3. Branding. Need Innovation, Excitement, No Boring Same Old Same Old.

Okay, now we're talking!

I looked around the tasting room. And it wasn't bad, for what it was. The space was a huge old barn, renovated of course and prettied up. So you had the barnboard walls and the rusted old farm implements suspended from the ceiling and the framed prints of happy-looking chickens and over by the seating area with the picnic tables on the fake grass, the cornhole boards were painted with black and white splotches like Holstein cows.

But hadn't this been done a million times before in a million different bars and restaurants and breweries?

And what did farms and barns have to do with hard kombucha? Hard kombucha is new and different and fresh. Not old and traditional, and it's certainly not made from cows or chickens.

And it was so dark. Did all that dark barnboard really speak to people who walked in? Did it make them think happy sparkly hip new adult beverage?

No.

No, it did not.

I put a star next to Branding and began adding a few more notes. Repaint. Fresh colors. Citrus? More light. Skylights. Uplights. Needs art—a lot of art. Some permanent. Also gallery?

"Oooh!" I said aloud as I wrote.

Local artists!!!!! Artsy vibe. Shelves for art.

Mom's chimes.

Wouldn't Mom be thrilled if we started selling her chimes out of the brewery?

Wouldn't that be richly conducive to a wonderful new era in Weekes-Flarey mother-daughter bonding? And Booch4U would get a cut? And Mom was selling some of her stuff for a lot of money, like over $500 apiece?

And see how a business degree would be utterly superfluous? In fact, if you think about it, what Booch4U needed was not a person with a business degree. It needed a person who was attuned to subtleties of style and creative energy. Someone who recognized that its current vibe reminded her of the murky start of a Grimm fairy tale. A dark, windowless hut, for example. It was a wonder we got any business at all. It was a wonder people didn't walk in and find themselves gripped immediately with a sense of gloom and foreboding and whirl around and flee. No. We needed to move more toward the French fairy tale end of the spectrum, with its balls and gowns and magic birds and golden apples. Not literally—I'd never propose a French fairy tale theme as the new Booch4U branding—but metaphorically.

I looked up from my work.

The sky, visible through the plate glass windows at the front of the room, had gotten lighter.

The rain had let up.

And sure enough, here came a car, our first customer of the day.

SURVEY! That was it! I remembered!

I was going to start surveying our customers. What flavors would they like us to make? What did they think of the décor? Would they appreciate a bit more natural light?

And OMG. Who knew being a businessperson would be so much fun?

I grinned to myself as I put the notebook back in the cupboard.

My phone buzzed and I took a quick peek while the customers scanned the chalkboard.

Two texts.

One from Candace.

i have an idea abt mom. can you talk

Ugh. No, Candace, I can't talk, and also I don't want to hear your ideas about Mom.

I texted back, *can it wait?*

Then swiped to the next text which was from Teagan, and it turns out her ship was in port in Jamaica for a few hours which meant that she was on a short work break.

So I poured some pints of 'booch, and then settled onto the stool behind the bar and texted Tea about my ideas to improve the brewery, and she texted back with the latest cruise ship hilarity. Apparently, some oldish divorced guy who owns a chain of grocery stores in the Midwest had proposed to one of Teagan's co-workers, and he wouldn't take "no" for an answer, so now everyone was helping this co-worker duck the guy. They had literally hidden her under a banquet table during breakfast. And the guy had brought a ring with him on the cruise, seriously? He was seriously wife-shopping, who does that?

And then Teagan had to sign off and get back to work.

And the customers ordered a second round, and then it occurred to me that RB still hadn't texted me back. Even though it had been over two hours since I'd texted him. And he was fishing with Quill. He wasn't working. So no excuses.

hey, I texted. *u there?*

Another handful of customers came through the door, and they hemmed and hawed and then decided to do flights of tasters. And I checked my phone. But there was no answer, and then the sun came out for real and we started to get seriously busy, and one thing led to another and I didn't look at my phone again until nearly closing time.

And how annoying.

RB still hadn't texted back.

• • • • •

The dome had a bunch of leaks in the roof, and Mom or Dad had set out a bunch of pails that afternoon to catch the leaks. The pails were still out when I got home, and the dome was deserted so I started collecting them and dumping the water, which was brown and filthy-looking, into the kitchen sink.

I was almost done with that lovely Weekes-Flarey family chore when Candace came in.

"What's with RB?" I asked her. And she asked me whaddya mean and I told her he wasn't responding to texts, and had she heard from him at all since he'd dropped Quill off that afternoon?

"I even tried calling him," I grumbled. "He won't pick up."

She shrugged. "He leaves his ringer off. Otherwise he'd never get a break from work calls."

"But Candy, he didn't work today." I set the last emptied pail next to the door. "He spent the day with your son."

"He forgets to turn it back on. But I wouldn't worry about it, if I were you. Just take your stuff over tomorrow morning. It's Sunday. He'll be home."

Ah hah. Told you. Those two have something going. How did she know he always left his ringer off? And that he'd be home tomorrow morning?

"Are you sure he'll be there?" I said, testing her.

"Thousand percent."

Double ah ha.

I felt my phone vibrate in my jeans pocket and thought there he is, finally.

But it wasn't RB, it was Fletcher.

Candace was watching me as I checked the screen, so I said "not him," and set my phone down and went to the freezer. But as I was scanning my microwaveable dinner options, I felt Candace touch my shoulder. "Can you talk?" she said in a low voice. "About Mom?"

I frowned. "Fletcher's about to call me. Can we do it later?"

And she made a face, but I ignored it and took my TV dinner with me to the camper for some privacy. And Fletcher and I talked for almost an hour. He told me all about his meeting in Houston, the brewery there was going to be fabulous, and that he'd made those dinner reservations for next week when we were meeting in Manhattan, and he couldn't wait for me to meet his friends. So that when I hung up, I felt soooo glow-y and in love, and thought to myself maybe I shouldn't worry about his mother, the witch. Maybe I was taking that all too seriously. Obviously he cared for me and was committed to me and all that. And I wasn't 15 anymore. I was 29, and had considerably more life experience, and as Winchell likes to say, bumps turn to bruises, but bruises turn to callouses. So why not pose a casual question the next time Fletcher and I talked, along the lines of: when you said back on that night you took me to the bar & grill in Cortland that the stone house was still in the family, what did you mean, exactly? Did you mean your mom still owns it and therefore might pull up one day on her broomstick and ask wtf are those boxes piled up in the corner over there?

And surely it was a rarity for Fletcher's mom to show up in Tibbs. She'd made her disdain toward our little town excruciatingly clear back when he and I were teenagers-in-love, and I'd sometimes go to his house after school (in the off-season only of course. He played football, basketball, and baseball, all three, and so most of the time he had to stay after school for practice). And so we'd go in and have to pass the witch, who would be sitting in the kitchen smoking her one cigarette per day—she'd light it and then put it out and re-light it an hour later. She'd be dressed in those super skinny-look designer outfits she favored because they showed off how skinny she was, although to me the look suggested more "insect" than rich/thin/available about-to-be-divorcee. Which I should know, being mayfly-ish myself, although I hope I am never quite that skinny. And Fletcher would lead us into the kitchen, and she'd stub out her cigarette and he'd kiss her on the top of the head, and she'd start complaining about Tibbs. The grocery stores were awful, the roads were awful, the restaurants were awful, how could anyone live in a place where there was nothing to do at night, and Fletcher there's a huge spider in the master bathroom please go kill it. And while she rolled off her litany of complaints, she'd fix her deeply eye-shadowed eyes on me, to make sure I was paying attention and was completely sympathetic to her misery, and being only 15 and terrified of her I'd smile and agree, pretending I could understand exactly what she meant, even though I'd never lived anywhere else, so how could I know what she was missing, living here in our little hamlet in the middle of nowhere?

And hadn't she noticed how beautiful Tibbs was, with its hills and trees and birds and sky and deer and peaceful spaces?

But I didn't say that out loud, either.

"Gawd I can't wait to get out of here," she'd mutter.

She was always drinking coffee, too. I wonder, now, if it was really coffee or if it was spiked. I bet it was spiked. I bet she put vodka in it.

At the time I was oblivious, of course, to the fact that she'd be moving back downstate. As soon as she got what she wanted, she'd be gone. And of course, what she wanted was a nice big monthly alimony-plus-child support check from Fletcher's dad.

Yeah. I was blissfully ignorant. Which meant, when it happened—when she got her divorce settlement and whisked away, taking her son with her—I was woefully unprepared. Which is why, now, the last thing I needed was to be woefully unprepared again, in case that woman suddenly reappeared and told Fletcher to get rid of that boxed-up crap in her house as if it were another spider in the bathroom.

Ugh.

I had to buy some time before I moved any of my stuff into the stone house…

Which meant I couldn't wriggle out of it. I would have to do what Candace had suggested. I'd have to drive over to RB's in the morning and dump all of my stuff on him unannounced.

Served him right, not answering my texts.

And Candace must've forgotten that she wanted to talk to me about Mom again, because she didn't come to the camper until really late. I'd long since finished reading Quill his bedtime story. I didn't even hear her come in. I was already asleep.

8

The tasting room opens later on Sundays.

Meaning that I had plenty of time to cart my boxes over to RB's.

I tried texting him one more time before I left. But he still didn't answer, which was even more annoying because now it was nearly 24 hours with no response.

And have I mentioned I was getting pretty sick of lugging boxes of books back and forth between the dome and the truck and the truck and various other temporary holding places? And miraculously nobody was around to help, either. Candace was sleeping and Mom was in her shop and Winchell was having a soak in the jacuzzi. I could hear the faint sloshing noises of him sloshing around, coming through the closed door of his spa.

• • • • •

It was a 15-minute drive to RB's. Not because his house was all that far away as the crow flies. Nothing in Tibbs is that far away as the crow flies. But like Winchell, RB had decided to build a house on a back road, which meant a lot of twists and turns and four-way stops, and not really any roads you could drive more than about 45 mph.

I knew where his house was because he'd taken me to see the land before we broke up. He hadn't owned it at the time. He had a house in town, one he bought right after he got out of college, because he'd always worked and he had money set aside to buy a house. But that was only temporary. His plan was to design and build a new place, and he'd already picked the site. A friend of his father's had promised to sell it to him. And he'd taken me there to show it to me.

So yeah, it felt a little funny driving up that road, again, knowing that I was going to see the house that he'd once described to me as his dream home. Our dream home.

I pulled into his driveway, which was gravel, like our driveway to the dome.

The gravel crunched under the wheels of Winchell's truck as I pulled in.

The property was on the downhill side of the road. It was a huge lot that, like most housing lots in that part of the country, had probably been a pasture a generation or two ago. So, other than the bit that had been graded to make a building site, the ground was uneven looking, with big hunks of stone sticking out here and there, and there was a pond over in the far corner by the wood line that been built by enlarging a natural spring. The pond had probably been used to water cows, but now it was heavily fringed by cattails and weeds. And nature was starting to reclaim the formerly-pasture, so now, except for the trimmed square around the house, the property was bristling with clumps of hawthorn bushes and nanny berry bushes and staghorn sumac and a few ash trees and a little grove of poplars taking hold not far from the pond, along with clusters of coarse-looking wildflowers. Joe Pye weed and milkweed and goldenrod. That sort of thing.

Unkempt and rough. Bachelor lot. So whatever RB and Candace had going on, it hadn't extended, yet, to her pressing him to groom his property. Their future marital home.

By the way, Fletcher's stone house was set in an enormous lawn that was always spectacularly well-maintained. Which now that I think about it couldn't have been Fletcher's doing. Perhaps his mother paid a crew to care for it?

I peered through my windshield at RB's house, and to complete the picture: it wasn't finished. There was no siding on it, yet. It was covered in white Tyvek sheeting.

Clumps of timothy sprawled against the cinderblock foundation like weedwhackers hadn't been invented, yet.

Okay, time out, because I should be fair to RB, here. He's a plumber. He spends all day, usually six days a week, working on other peoples' houses. So I guess I can understand that when you build a house yourself, thinking you're going to do all the work yourself, and then you spend six or sometimes even seven days a week fixing house-y stuff for other people, you get home and fall down on the couch with a beer and a microwaved pizza and tell yourself you'll get to the siding tomorrow.

I suppose that's what I'd do.

And, good news, RB's truck was there. Parked next to a metal-roofed carport that he'd put up so that when it snowed in the wintertime he wouldn't have quite as much scraping to do in the morning before he left for work, only there wasn't room under it for a truck because he was using it for storage. Lumber and a riding mower and a compressor, and other stuff that I couldn't tell what it was, because it was covered in blue plastic tarps held down on the edges by pieces of firewood.

I got out and went to the door, which of course didn't have a working doorbell. Nor a screen door. Just a concrete slab where maybe a stoop will go someday, ragweed and goldenrod sprouting up around it.

I banged a couple times on the door, yelling "RB! It's Marion!"

And the door swung open and there was RB and oh, crap.

Shirtless, again.

We have to stop meeting like this, RB.

Argh.

Ignore.

Ignore ignore ignore.

"Marion?" he was saying while I ignore ignore ignored that long waist and muscled arms, and although his legs were ever so slightly bowed it gave him a slouching cowboy look that I admit was quite appealing, and that soft-looking beard and those hazel eyes that I was somehow able to read so well...

Only what I was reading right now was that the guy wasn't exactly thrilled to see me standing there. And also what was that?

Why were those eyes darting back and forth?

Like he was hiding something?

"Geez, RB," I said. "I texted you, like, fifty times. Where have you been?" I paused a second, that quick, fake pause you give to sound like you're waiting for an answer but really you're not, really you are on a full offensive. "You say I can store my stuff here, and then you disappear off the face of the planet?"

Meanwhile, in the back of my head I'm thinking oh, crap.

He looks guilty and like he's hiding something and that can only mean one thing.

He's got a woman here, and it's not Candace. And he doesn't want me to know because he doesn't want Candace to know.

And sure enough, he was sputtering out a response which didn't make much sense. Something like "uh—meant to—busy. Work."

Right.

"Well," I said primly. "I've got my stuff. It's in the truck. But if now's a bad time—"

"No. Now is fine. I'll help you."

I turned and walked back to the truck, and a minute later RB joined me.

He'd put a tee shirt on.

"Books, I take it," RB grunted as he lifted the closest box.

"Mostly."

We made our way back to the house.

"We can just leave everything here, on the step," he said. "I'll bring it in the rest of the way. Less work for you."

Ah HAH.

He didn't want me in the house!

And as you've noticed, Candace and I don't always get along. But on the other hand, there was no way I was going to stand by and let RB brazenly two-time my stepsister. Even though it technically wasn't any of my business and I couldn't have cared less, personally, if RB was seeing someone else. But if Candace had the idea that she and RB had a future, and RB had a different idea, she deserved to know. And Candace is my sister. Which shows that even if we fight a lot, I'm still on her side. On things that really matter. So guess what, I was going to catch him red-handed and then I was going to march, metaphorically, back to the dome and tell my sister exactly what was going on.

"Oh, no," I said. "I wouldn't dream of making you carry it all in, RB."

And ah HAH!

Was RB's face actually turning...red?

Ah HAH.

He was caught and he knew it.

And he opened his mouth to argue but fat chance. He was caught.

HAH.

I pushed past him and pushed the door open with my hip and stepped into the house.

And the first thing I noticed is: no walls. The interior of RB's house wasn't finished, either. So instead of walls, the house was this cagey-looking jungle of bare 2x4s where the walls would be, someday.

Which meant that you could see every room from every other room. Which was good, because if I was keen-eyed enough, I'd soon detect evidence of the other woman.

"Where shall I set them?" I said sweetly as I stood there holding the box (which was winter clothes, by the way, not books. Let RB carry the books, hah) while I peered around, extremely keen-eyed, hunting for evidence.

"Uh—" RB said.

"Do you have a spare bedroom? How about we stash everything there?" I asked sweetly and innocently as I started walking toward the back of the house. The part of the house where the bedrooms would be.

"No, uh, living room is better," RB said. Trying to stop me.

Didn't work. I could already see all the way to the other end of the house, since as I said there were no walls, and of course I focused my keen-eyed attention on what was obviously the master bedroom, with

RB's mattress—no bedframe—pushed up against the wall and a massive antique oak dresser and a long oak bookcase under the window.

I slowed down as I reached the doorless doorframe, perusing the room's contents for any sign of a woman. You know. Bra tossed over the shade of the floor lamp, panties wadded up on the floor, a second phone charger dangling from an outlet by the bed, a forgotten pair of earrings on the bedside stand...

"The living room is better, Marion," RB was saying behind me, I guess from the living room where he'd stopped to deposit the box he was carrying. "Back here."

Then I noticed the second bedroom.

The spare room.

Someone was staying in it. There was an air mattress on the floor, covered with rumpled blankets, and a backpack on the floor. A big one, a hiking pack. It was open and there were clothes spilling out of it.

But they were men's clothes.

I stepped into the room, and there to my left, on the vanity of the half-bath: toothpaste and toothbrush—and a bottle of cologne.

I admit. This was not what I was expecting.

Difficulty computing.

RB had a male guest. Okay.

But why would he want to hide that he had a male guest?

Why was he acting weird about me coming into the house?

I retraced my steps, still carrying the box, and RB was standing in the living room, looking at me. A very odd look on his face, too. His eyebrows raised in almost a question but his face really tight. Like he was paying extremely close attention to my reaction.

"Over here," he repeated in a tight voice.

I carried my box back toward him. With my mind whirring like a computer hard drive, trying to find the file that would make sense of what I was feeling in that house.

"You have company," I said as I set the box down.

"Yeah. Out of town guest. Unexpected. Showed up yesterday afternoon."

He wasn't meeting my eye.

He was being evasive. Definitely.

"Anybody I know?" I asked, innocently and politely.

Okay. So you might have gathered, by now, that RB is basically a really decent guy. Meaning, in other words, that he is not the kind of guy who could outright lie to someone's face. Not in a million years. His style would be to avoid a conversation entirely rather than be in a position where he had to tell a lie. So instead of answering me, he choked and mumbled something and turned his back on me like he was suddenly in a big huge hurry to go fetch another box from the truck.

I stared at his back as he walked away.

And then—suddenly—I knew.

Call it women's intuition.

I knew.

In an instant, I was back in the spare bedroom, kneeling next to the backpack, looking through the contents.

Black brimmed cap with a Las Vegas Golden Knights logo on the front. A book, tattered, yellow cover, looked like it was a hundred years old, The World's Drinks and How to Mix Them.

And a tee-shirt.

I held it up.

The image on the front was a vintage Black Keys poster by Shepard Fairey.

"RB!" I yelled.

I needn't have yelled. He'd followed me. He was right there, standing in the frame of what would one day possibly be the door to the bedroom.

"It's Ace, isn't it," I said. "It's Ace. He's in Tibbs."

RB's eyes were cast down at the floor and he didn't answer.

My body was starting to shake. "I'm right, aren't I?"

And after a long, long pause, he nodded.

And—didn't see this one coming—I burst into tears.

9

Okay.

Not sure if I've gone into this with you before, but I have a brother.

A little brother.

Ace. That's short for Horace. Yes, despite the fact that my parents already had a Candace, when they had a son, that's the name they went with. Candace and Horace. Kind of like when families give all their kids names that start with the same first letter, only my parents matched up the end of the names instead. Lord knows what name they would have given a fourth child. Pumice, maybe. Or Bodice, if it was a girl. Or Solace, I suppose, which would have been appropriate and also poignant once two of their other three kids ran away from Tibbs.

And I could have used a little solace myself in that moment, because I hadn't seen Ace in seven years, because seven years ago, I did what all good fairy tale heroes do when they've been forced to live with evil stepparents and besides that, realize they'll never find their fortunes if they don't set out alone into the wide, wide world.

I set off. Left Tibbs, New York, and set off alone. And when I'd come back, earlier that summer, I thought I'd be staying for a day or so. Long enough to help the family look for a cat that had wandered off. But one thing led to another, and I ended up getting back together with Fletcher and now I was well on my way to my Happily Ever After with my prince.

While in the meantime I was temporarily living with my family, which was okay as long as it was temporary.

And in a lot of ways, it was like nothing had changed. Mom was still Mom. Winchell (who wasn't really evil evil, just kind of gross and annoying) hadn't changed much either, except for being a bit fatter and grayer, and Candace was also a bit heavier but really seemed to me to be even more herself than she had seven years ago.

But there was one missing piece, only until that morning I hadn't really thought about it. And because I hadn't thought about it, I didn't realize it was missing. Maybe I'd been too wrapped up in my own drama to wonder about him—about Ace, about where he was, about what had happened to him. I mean, I knew he'd moved out and broken off contact with the fam, but then so had I. And he and Winchell used to fight a lot. And Ace was one of those boys who grows up wild. He'd started running away while he was still in high school. And then one day, it must have been about three years ago, Mom called me to wish me happy birthday, and said he was gone, and she thought he'd left the state, nobody knew where he was, etc. etc. And I wasn't surprised. And besides, hadn't I done the same thing?

But now that I realized he was actually home—meaning back in Tibbs—and that he was alive, and safe—

I dunno. I just lost it.

He was my little brother. My baby brother.

I lost it.

RB put his arms around me and I felt his beard, soft against my face. "It's okay," he said. "Don't cry, Mayfly. It's okay."

"Where is he?" I snuffled into the shoulder of his tee shirt. "Where's Ace?"

He didn't answer, and for a moment that was okay. For a moment just being in RB's arms made everything feel like it was going to be okay. And his arms were so warm and strong and familiar then then—OMG! What was I doing? What were we doing? Standing there like that and OMG I was with Fletcher and RB was getting back together with Candace and OMG Marion Flarey, you're getting your wires crossed, here!

I jumped back and pushed him away. And he must have picked up on the weirdness, too. His eyes looked funny, lit for a split second by a flash of alarm. And my face felt hot so I quickly dropped back down into a crouch next to the backpack.

"I want to see Ace," I mumbled, my head down. "And I need a Kleenex."

"He's not here. He's gone out." RB's voice sounded husky. Not surprising. He's the kind of guy who gets emotional if anyone around him is upset.

I held up Ace's Black Keys tee shirt again. And I felt like I could see him, standing there in that shirt. How he'd loved that band! He'd run away to see them in concert right before his fifteenth birthday. We had no idea where he was, Mom and Dad put out a missing persons report. A horrible two days. The cops found him, finally. They picked him up the morning after the concert. He was sleeping on the sidewalk outside Madison Square Garden.

Anything could have happened to him.

RB and I were dating at the time. He'd been as worried as we were.

"I need to see my little brother," I whispered as I refolded the shirt and tucked it into Ace's backpack. "Where is my brother?"

Where is my brother?

I need to see my little brother...

I stood up and stole a glance at RB, and in his defense he looked pretty miserable. "Marion, I'm sorry. But I promised. He made me promise not to tell anyone he's in town." He paused. "He doesn't want to see you. He doesn't even want you to know. And I gave him my promise."

"I don't understand."

"Marion." Our eyes met and for a minute I thought he was going to help me. He was going to tell me where Ace was or when he would be back.

But instead, he shook his head. "I promised. I'm sorry."

"So that's it, RB?" I whispered, doing my best to remain calm while inside my guts were tearing into pieces. "You won't tell me anything? Why is he—what is he doing in Tibbs? Is he moving back? Is he okay?"

"He's in town for a wedding," RB muttered, wincing a little as he spoke. "He just showed up yesterday, Marion. He asked if he could sleep here. And that's it. That's all I can say. I've said too much. And please promise me you'll keep this to yourself."

I felt like I might start to cry again. "A wedding? What wedding?"

RB shook his head. And I knew what was going on. He'd made a promise. The last thing he'd ever do would be to break it. And here I'd caught him hiding my little brother from me and the rest of the family. And now he was in the middle of it. In the middle of a big, fat mess.

But so was I. "You have to understand," I said. "I wasn't there when he took off. I don't know even know why he left. I don't know what happened with him and my folks."

And my legs felt suddenly so tired and weak. Because it hit me, how broken my family really was. How my leaving Tibbs had seemed, at the time, like it was the right thing to do, but it hadn't solved anything. It had seemed like going out into the world to seek my fortune, breaking away, cutting contact, would somehow make everything better. And then I'd come back to Tibbs and reunited with Fletcher and I'd gotten the ridiculous idea that everything was fine. That somehow being with Fletcher would make it all work.

But it wasn't working. My family was broken and even marrying my prince charming and moving into his castle and becoming an amazing young queen wasn't going to fix it.

I sank down and sat on the floor and crossed my legs and dropped my face into my hands.

"Marion?" RB said, voice husky again. "Are you okay?"

"Just tell me this, RB," I said into my hands. "Tell me why Ace left Tibbs."

Because RB would know, wouldn't he? Even though RB wasn't the kind of guy who stuck his nose into other peoples' business, he was a family friend and, furthermore, he'd taken Ace under his wing when

Ace was a teenager, when RB and I were dating. He'd gotten Ace part-time work with the family plumbing business and generally served as a rock-steady role model. And it had helped Ace a lot, for a while. It was what Ace needed at the time to keep his head from becoming completely unscrewed.

I looked up at RB. "Just tell me what you know. Please?"

He shifted his weight, turning slightly away from me. "There was a huge blow-up. And he left. That's all I know."

"He must have said something. He must have told you something."

RB shook his head again. "No. I didn't see him before he left Tibbs, Marion. He didn't say good-bye."

Tears were streaming down my cheeks. "And what about now? What has he said? Does he know I'm home? Why doesn't want to see us?"

RB cleared his throat. "He says your parents want nothing to do with him."

Ugh. So Winchell had a temper. And Winchell's relationship with his son had become pretty volatile, even back in the day, while I was still around. So on the one hand, I could believe that maybe Winchell had said some words to his son that he shouldn't have. I never want to see you again, don't you dare come back here ever. Stuff like that.

But on the other hand, what could Ace have possibly done that would make Winchell want to drive him away for good?

And what about Mom? Mild, quiet Mom?

She wouldn't have given up on her son. Not for anything.

Not Mom.

I felt RB looking at me.

It felt like he was reading my thoughts.

Or my heart.

"Marion," he said, "maybe it's not that he doesn't want to see you. Maybe it's that he doesn't want to hurt people. He doesn't want to stir things up."

"But—"

"I've said too much. Please promise me you won't tell anyone."

Ugh.

I just wanted to think. I wanted to calm down, calm my stomach and my heart and think for a minute.

"Promise me," RB repeated.

I knew why he was saying that.

It was his honor code. He'd promised not to tell. And it wasn't his fault I'd found out, but now that I had, the only way for him to keep his promise was if I bound myself to it, as well.

"Okay," I whispered. "Okay." Because honestly, at that very moment, the only idea that could work its way up through my churning emotions was: *for you, RB. I'll do this thing for you.*

I looked up at him. "But—RB?"

He nodded, waiting for my question.

"Will you talk to him? Tell him that—that he should reach out to us—reach out to me?"

RB sighed. "I'll try," he said. "But Mayfly, you need to accept this. It's his choice."

I nodded. But my heart was crying out.

I wanted so much to understand.

I wanted so much to see my little brother.

10

I left RB's.

I didn't dare go home. I didn't dare risk running into Candace, because if she'd seen my face at that particular moment she would've asked a thousand questions, and next thing you know I'd be breaking my promise to RB.

So I skipped my shower. I drove to the brewery and let myself in the back door and went straight to the restroom. And my face looked as awful as I expected. My eyes were red-rimmed and my complexion looked almost green. Because of how my stomach felt. Sick.

I splashed some cold water on my face and grabbed a wad of paper towels and scrubbed the flecks of my ruined mascara off my cheeks.

I unclipped and reclipped the barrette I use to hold back my bangs, and made a smile-not-smile face at myself in the mirror.

I didn't look great, but it was better than ten minutes ago. A little color in my cheeks, at least.

But my stomach was still churning.

I went out and turned on lights and unlocked the front door, and fortunately we got a little business that day because it distracted me, and I needed distracting. Because behind the busywork of pouring 'booch and chitchatting with customers and bussing tables, there was a whole squirming pile of questions.

With zero answers.

• • • • •

Back at the dome after work.

Mom, curled up on the couch with a book. A three-inch thick hardcover, so poetry again, probably.

Candace on the couch next to her, sucking down her second helping of blackberry sorbet, ugh.

Quill climbing into Winchell's lap to watch TV.

I put a Lean Cuisine chicken curry in the microwave and sat at the kitchen island, feeling myself as a drifting piece of alien debris just outside the core orbit of Weekes-Flarey planetary bodies which made Ace—what? A drifting piece of alien debris that had exited the solar system completely and was now lost out there somewhere in empty space?

No. Bad metaphor. Because there are no fairy tales in space. Fairy tales are of Earth, they are about forests and towns and human beings.

And at that moment, I needed a fairy tale.

I needed a fairy tale that would explain what was going on and how I was supposed to deal with my lost baby brother. With my baby brother that had somehow been stolen from us.

I tossed my TV dinner tray into the trash and poured myself a bit of wine and slipped out the front door.

Nobody noticed me leave.

• • • • •

I sat on my bed, surrounded by books. Piles of fairy tale books.

But it was hopeless. I kept opening them randomly and reading bits of stories, hunting for some sort of clue about what do, but nothing spoke to me.

It was hopeless.

A moth had gotten into the camper. It swooped up and down in crazy loops over my head, up to the ceiling light and back down in front of my face, then landed on the page of the book in my lap and fluttered its wings, rapidly so it looked like they were trembling.

It was the same small, brown moth that Quill had captured on the camper steps.

But if the moth was a sign, I couldn't interpret it, either.

It flew up from the page, past my face, and perched on the ceiling next to the light, its wings now flattened and still.

I opened another book and scanned an English fairy tale called The Magpie's Nest, which is a "just so story" explaining why different species of birds build different kinds of nests. And moths fly like birds fly, so maybe it wasn't a coincidence that the moth had landed on this page.

But what did any of this have to do with my little brother?

Ugh. Maybe the message was "too bad, so sad, just like different birds have different types of nests, different people have different types of family, and if your type happens to be a Broken Family, Marion Flarey, you're just going to have to accept it."

I set the book aside and drained the last of my wine.

Maybe I should call Fletcher. Get his advice. Right? Even if it meant I wasn't exactly keeping my promise to RB? Or maybe I could ask his advice without letting on that I'd seen Ace, that he was in town?

But ugh, how much better it would be to talk to him face-to-face, especially about a subject that pricked my heart like a thousand needles every time I considered it. How I wished my boyfriend was there with me, in Tibbs, rather than out in the world, adventuring and conquesting. Home. Seated in his metaphorical throne which was right next to my metaphorical throne so that I could lean over and say, "m'lord" and he'd bend his head toward me and I could confide in him, tell him that something terrible had happened in my family and I had no idea how to fix it.

The camper screen door hinges made their springy noise, and then the door clunked, and I heard Quill's little footsteps patter down the hall.

He stopped short when he got to the bedroom and saw the books.

There were a lot of books.

"Are you reading all those stories?" he said in an awed voice.

"Not really. Sort of."

He leaned over the bed. "What about this one?" He pointed to one of the books that was laying open, a Grimm collection with color illustrations. "Can we read this one?"

Oooh boy. The plate that had caught his eye went with a story called The Elfin-Grove, about a little girl that is abducted by fairies. Of course, they were nice fairies. For the most part.

"Yeah, okay," I said slowly. "But, uh—you know the story is all made up, right?"

He nodded. "Uh huh."

I sent him to brush his teeth and moved books out of the way to make room for him, and a few minutes later he nestled up next to me.

The book was published in the 1930s and I caught a whiff of old-book mustiness as I started to read.

First, the set up: there's a troop of fairies living in a grove of fir trees. Most people can't see these fairies, but one day a little girl named Mary enters the grove and ends up staying there to play with them. And to her, it feels like she played for a day or so but it turns out to be seven years. Typical for people who go off with the little folk.

And of course that reminded me again that I'd been gone from Tibbs for seven years.

"So then what happens?" Quill prompted me.

I'd stopped reading.

"Sorry," I said, and found my place on the page and continued.

Mary was fine. She wasn't the least bit traumatized. She re-appeared and married her childhood sweetheart and had a daughter herself, who she named Elfie, because the little girl was a bit fey.

Only then the trouble started, because Elfie was befriended by the same fairies.

I turned the page.

The pages of that particular book are so thick they feel almost like cardboard, by the way, so there is a metaphor in there, somewhere, about how we used to give our books a lot more substance than we do, today.

But back to the story: we'd reached the page with the illustration, a watercolor by Grace Lodge, who you might know if you've ever seen one of the old Brer Rabbit books. Her paintings are quaint and old-fashioned and colorful. And so there was little Elfie, sitting on the ground with her legs folded under her striped skirt, bare feet showing. She's facing her fairy friend, Gossamer, who wears a fanciful cap and pointed shoes, and has translucent, butterfly-like wings. And Gossamer is presenting Elfie with a present. A rose.

But there's one other person in the picture. Elfie's mom, Mary. She's in the background, hiding behind a bush, spying on Elfie and Gossamer. Which is what sets up all the real problems of the story, because Mary tells her husband about the fairies, and apparently he's skeptical. Mary decides she needs to convince him by taking him to the grove.

A mistake. She'd promised Gossamer she'd never do that.

So all the fairies leave. Which causes the local trees and streams and meadows to dry up and become blighted. Not exactly a happy ending.

"So," I said, "the moral of the story is, if you make a promise to a fairy, you should always, always keep it."

Quill nodded, very solemn and serious.

Hah. So much for me being a good aunt and making sure he knew this was just a story.

"Can we read another one?" Quill asked, and then we flipped through the book and stopped at a black-and-white drawing from the story The Nose, which is about a soldier who eats a magic apple that makes his nose grow so long he can't stand up or go anywhere. His nose is too heavy. The drawing shows him on his hands and knees under the apple tree, looking down his rope-like nose with—I wouldn't say astonishment, exactly. He's in a bit of shock.

So we read The Nose.

Then Candace showed up and poked her head through the bedroom door.

"No stories about giants, tonight, Candace," I said quickly. "Just magic apples that make your nose grow."

"Into a long, long rope nose!" Quill chimed in. "But a little man in a red jacket helped! He gave them a magic pear."

I stirred nervously and Candace said "great," frowning slightly, probably considering whether Quill would be having nightmares tonight about rope noses and little men in red jackets.

"But he knows they're just stories, right, Quill?" I said brightly. "Night, you two. Sweet dreams."

I slid the pocket door to the bedroom half-closed and settled back against my pillows, looking absently at the pile of books on my bed.

Maybe the seven years thing was a clue…except that Ace had left how many years ago? Three? Four? So maybe that was it. Maybe he hadn't been gone long enough, yet. Maybe I just needed to wait. Maybe in another few years he'd return for real, ready to see his family again.

I frowned and re-adjusted my pillows. Because I didn't like that interpretation. Not a bit. Ace was here, in town, now. In Tibbs. Staying at RB's.

I didn't want to wait. I didn't want him to leave without me seeing him, talking to him. And where was he even living, now? Was it Las Vegas, maybe? Is that why he had that Golden Knights cap?

I heard Candace checking with Quill to make sure he'd brushed his teeth, and then the thud of his sneakers dropping to the floor as he climbed into bed.

Don't break promises to fairies.

No.

Don't break promises to anyone…

So was the message that I had to keep my promise to RB? And protect his promise to Ace?

So my little brother might be here in Tibbs, but there wasn't anything I could do about it?

My heart was hurting. My heart was hurting…

There had to be another answer.

More noises from the other end of the camper. Candace was running water in the little kitchen. It made a tinny sound as it struck the stainless-steel basin. I picked up another fairy tale book from the piles on my bed, but I didn't open it. I couldn't think with Candace still in the camper, rummaging around. Shouldn't she be heading back to the dome? To watch more of her beloved reality TV while scarfing down serving number three of that horrible purple sorbet?

I sat and listened, waiting for the sweet sound of the camper door.

But no luck. Instead, I heard her heavy footsteps clumping down the hallway toward my room.

She pushed her head through my half-closed door, and I braced myself for whatever was coming next. Something to do with what stories I was reading Quill, again, right?

But nope.

"Can you talk now, Marion?" she said. "About Mom? It'll only take a minute."

I sighed. "Okay, okay. What's your idea."

"Not here. Quill." She whispered as she tilted her head backwards, in the direction where Quill was in their bed. And still awake, apparently. "Let's go for a walk outside," she added in a louder, he-can-hear-this-one voice.

I sighed again. Because the only thing worse than another conversation with Candace about Mom was having to leave my warm bed to do it. Especially after the day I'd had. And besides, if we kept our voices low, Quill wouldn't be able to hear, even if he was still wide awake.

But as I opened my mouth to argue—something along the lines of how we could just shut the bedroom door and keep our voices down—something else occurred to me.

Candace would know why Ace had left Tibbs. Because she was living in Tibbs at the time. She was married to Garth and raising her baby, but she was still living in Tibbs.

So she had to know what had happened between Ace and Winchell, right?

And granted, it would be a tricky subject to broach. The last thing I needed was for Candace to somehow guess I was guarding a hot new secret about our little brother. But if I could just get her talking…

"Okay," I said, and got up and slipped my feet into my flip flops, and a minute later Candace and I were walking side-by-side through the dark, down the switchback driveway, toward the road.

• • • • •

Candace had turned on her phone's flashlight while we navigated the driveway, because as I think I've mentioned it is a gravel drive and washed out in spots. But she switched the light off when we got to the road. There was a half-moon high in the sky and I could see the pavement, a strip of pale gray, with dark trees leaning in on either side.

We were far enough away from the dome, by then, that there was no chance of being overheard.

"Okay," I said as we started up the road. "What's your big idea?"

"Two words," Candace said. "Private. Detective."

OMG. Figures she'd come up with that. Because that was so much like Candace. Let's turn this whole thing into a badly written television drama. It was almost enough to make me forget about Ace. "Really, Candace?" I said. "Spy on her? You think we should spy on her?"

"It would give us answers," Candace said.

I shook my head. "It's spying! That's wrong. Plus, private detectives cost money." And also, what would Fletcher think, if he found out that his future queen had hired a spy to handle intrigue at the court? I had a feeling it would not go over very well. I had a feeling that Fletcher would wonder what he'd gotten into, and was it really smart to make a match with this crazy commoner with her crazy family. "Anyway," I added, "we already have a plan, remember? I'm going to invite Mom for a girl's night out and get her to open up."

"I'm not asking you to pay for it. And I haven't exactly seen any progress on the girl's night out idea."

My bemusement gave way to irritation. And I was about to open my mouth to say something like, "It's only been one day, Candace, since we agreed to our first plan. Give me a break," when suddenly, I had an idea.

An inspiration.

A brilliant inspiration.

A brilliant inspiration for how to turn the conversation to Ace, without any danger that Candace would guess why I was suddenly curious about him.

"Anyway," I said. "If we're going to spend money on a private detective, I've got a better idea." I cleared my throat to make sure my voice stayed steady. "How about we hire one to look for Ace?"

Candace snorted. "Why would we want to do that?"

"Uh, because he's our little brother and nobody has heard for him for, what? Three years, now?"

"We don't particularly want to hear from him."

"Geez, Candace." I stopped walking and she did too. In that moonlight, her face was pale as a ghost's but her short, wavy hair looked pitch-black. "Why wouldn't we want to hear from our little brother?"

She didn't answer right away. There was a furrow between her eyes, and she opened and closed her mouth a couple times without any sound coming out. But then she finally spoke. "I really shouldn't tell you any of this."

"What do you mean?" I said, keeping my voice calm to hide the burst of dread that was rising in my belly.

"Because you might tell Mom. And Dad doesn't want her to know."

More secrets? Seriously? "Know what, Candace?"

"If I tell you, Marion, you have to promise you won't tell. Dad will kill me, if you tell."

Great. Twice in less than twelve hours I'm being sworn to silence on something relating to Ace. And also, why had I come back to Tibbs, again? I mean, I knew the answer. I'd come to Tibbs first to help my family find their cat but then, on a greater and more mysterious level, I was here so that I could be reunited with Fletcher. But OMG, would I ever, ever, ever be able to keep those two pieces of my life in their separate lanes—my crazy Weekes-Flarey life and my amazing Fletcher relationship life? And why did I feel like not keeping them separate was extremely dangerous? Like if I wasn't careful, my crazy Weekes-Flarey life was going to break into my amazing Fletcher relationship life and steal—steal!—my only chance for happiness and—

Stop it, Marion. Don't even go there. Your amazing Fletcher relationship life is safe. And it will stay safe.

"Promise?" Candace said.

"Okay." I felt her eyes on me. "I promise not to tell."

We started walking again. The trees along either side of the road were so black they were almost silhouettes, but overhead the sky was spattered with stars. Candace was silent for another minute as we walked, like she was still thinking it all over. Like she was still maybe wondering whether she should tell me anything.

"Also," she said finally, "don't blame Dad. It's not his fault."

"Candace!" I was starting to feel frustrated. "Blame him for what?"

"For kicking Ace out. All Dad wanted was to protect us. Protect Mom."

I should have grabbed a jacket. I shivered suddenly in the night chill. And what had Ace done? I mean, he'd been impulsive and careless at times. But had things been worse than I knew? And all the stories you read about angry, disillusioned young men shooting up schools or murdering their families? They now kaleidoscoped through my mind as I imagined the absolute worst. Ace had lost it. He'd threatened them. He'd threatened Mom. His drug use had gotten out of hand, maybe. Maybe he'd gone from smoking pot to the hard stuff, meth or something. Maybe my picture of him as a goofy, sweet little brother was completely wrong. Maybe he'd turned into something else. Some sort of monster…

I couldn't stand it anymore. I sucked my breath in, forcing myself to get a grip, to stop my imagination from running off into those dark places. "Candace," I said. "You're scaring me. Please tell me what happened!"

"He stole a bunch of money. Ace did."

"What? What money? From who?"

"From Dad." Candace kicked at the road a couple times, now, as she walked. Like she was kicking a pebble out of her way. "Their life savings."

Life savings? "What do you mean? Mom and Dad had money?" This was news to me. I'd thought that by that time they were dead broke. "How much money are we talking about?"

"A lot."

"How much is a lot?"

"Over a hundred thousand. Close to one-fifty."

I stopped walking again, this time out of pure shock. "Holy shit," I muttered. "I had no idea they had that kind of money."

"Neither did Mom," Candace said. "It was left over after the multi-level went under. But Dad never told her about it."

"Really?" I frowned. "Why not?"

"You know Dad," Candace said. "He can get paranoid. The feds had arrested the CEO and everything, remember? Dad was afraid he'd be next. Or that his money would get seized as evidence or something."

Yeah. That sounded like Winchell.

"And he didn't want Mom involved. Like I said, he was protecting her."

We started walking again. Me thinking that what Candace said made sense. Because as silly as Winchell is, in a lot of ways, I could see him wanting to make sure that Mom would stay clear of whatever trouble he'd blundered into.

"You know what else?" Candace said. "I also think the money was a pride thing, with him. He felt like he'd let us all down when the business tanked. I think he figured if he just stuck the money into an account and didn't touch it, they'd have a little for retirement. Like, it helped him save face or something."

I nodded, although inwardly I felt a little surprised. I didn't usually think of Candace being that insightful about other peoples' characters. But for the second time, her words made sense. It would be just like Winchell to hide a bunch of money, figuring that one day he'd announce to Mom that they weren't destitute after all, thanks to his careful planning. Winchell, the hero, saving the day.

"So then, what?" I said. "You really think Ace stole it?"

"Yep."

"How do you know it was him?"

"He admitted it, Marion."

He admitted it. The words hit me like a punch in the stomach. My goofy, sweet baby brother...

"And so what happened to it?" I said when I could talk again. "Sounds like Dad found out about it. Then what? Did Ace give it back?"

"No. I have no idea what happened to the money. I assume Ace spent it on drugs or something. All I know is they had a huge fight, Winchell told Ace he was going to call the cops, and Ace took off. And that's the last any of us ever saw of him."

Any of us. Except me.

We walked for a few minutes without speaking.

Something rustled in the undergrowth and I heard the faint hoot of an owl. And how could Ace have done something like that? The little brother I'd known was a sweet-faced boy. Mischievous but always kid-stuff mischievous. You know. Smoking a little weed, cutting classes, taking off to go to concerts when he was supposed to be grounded...

But maybe as he'd gotten older, he'd gotten into a different kind of trouble. The sort of trouble where he needed money to make things right.

"And Mom?" I said, still talking almost to myself, trying to make sense of it. "She had no idea?"

"Mom was out of town, at one of her shows. All she knows is that they had a fight and Ace ran away. But it wasn't the first time he'd disappeared. Mom probably figured he'd turn back up. But of course, he never did, because he can't, because he's a fucking thief and he doesn't dare show his face." Candace touched my arm. "We should get back."

We were almost to Effie's driveway.

We turned around and walked in silence again. Me, because my thoughts had drifted back to the relationship-with-Fletcher lane, and tomorrow was Monday and Mondays are my day off because the brewery's tasting room is closed, and Fletcher would be flying into New York in the morning, then driving upstate to Tibbs. Which would put him in town around two. He'd pick me up, we'd have hours and hours to spend together, and maybe I could talk to him—very carefully and discretely—about Ace. Ask his advice—

"So back to Mom." Candace's voice jolted my thoughts to a halt. "If the private detective thing is off, can you please just talk? Like, tomorrow?"

"I'll try. Fletcher's gonna be back in town."

"Ah. That's nice. You two are really getting along, sounds like."

I nodded, and despite all the weirdness that had dropped into my lap that day, a couple butterflies of excitement fluttered up through my stomach. "And guess what else?" I said, grinning to myself in the dark. "We've finally set up our trip to New York. I'm meeting him there a week from tomorrow."

And yeah. I might have been bragging a little bit. I might have been feeling a wee bit boastful about my well-off boyfriend inviting me to spend a night with him and his well-off well-connected friends in Manhattan.

And you know what happens when you brag?

Things backfire.

"You're going to New York?" Candace said. "Mom loves New York! Remember how she and Winchell used to take trips there back when they had money and how much she loved it, going to all the galleries? You should take her to New York!"

"What?" Her words didn't compute for a second, and then suddenly they did compute and OMG, really? "It's a couples getaway thing, Candace! I'm not taking Mom along on a couples getaway thing!"

"Oh, come on. That's not what I meant." We were walking faster, now, me giving her an are-you-kidding look that she couldn't see in the dark although I could see her head, because it was nodding vigorously, the way people nod their heads when they are positive they are being brilliant. "I meant some other time. You know how much she loves the city! And it wouldn't cost you anything. I'll pay for it, Marion. I'll pay for an Airbnb. She'd love it! And it would get you away from Tibbs. And give you time alone with her to bond."

"Right," I said, not very enthusiastically. "Good idea. I'll think about it."

And she must have gotten the message, because she grumbled something under her breath.

But she also let the idea drop.

• • • • •

There's a scenario you find in a lot of fairy tales, like one called The Three Children of Fortune, which starts out when three siblings leave home, one at a time.

And if it's true that scraps of fairy tales are still around—that fairy tales can still, somehow, catch bits of our lives the way an old, dried-up stream bed can still sometimes catch water and channel it and direct it, then: yes. You need to pay attention when a fairy-tale-like something pops into your awareness, intrudes into your life. Because if you notice it and pay attention to it, it can help you figure things out.

So after Candace and I had said goodnight and I'd crawled back into bed, I laid there, thinking about the Weekes-Flareys.

I'd gone out into the world. And Candace had gone out into the world.

We'd both returned. Candace, first, with her associate's degree and baby Quill.

And now I'd returned.

And Mom understood why we'd left. It's a good thing for your kids to go out into the world. A good thing. And Mom knew that.

But, Ace, on the other hand?

Ace was still out there.

Which, by fairy tale logic, meant that he had run into trouble of some kind. He'd been captured or was under a spell.

Which—more fairy tale logic—meant that either Candace or I needed to go out and find him and try to bring him back.

And it wasn't going to be Candace, obviously. It had to be me. And I had no idea how to do it. If Ace was a thief, and he'd stolen not to help his family but in an evil and selfish way, the answer wasn't to try to bring him back.

The answer was to let him go.

On the other hand, if I was going to bring him back, it would be a lot easier to do it now, while he was in Tibbs.

And I'd promised RB that I wouldn't tell anyone else that Ace was in town.

But I hadn't promised that I wouldn't sneak back to RB's house and talk to Ace myself…

11

Only I couldn't just sneak out and see Ace. Because RB's house was too far away to walk to, or bike to unless you were in a lot better shape than I was and also had a bike with tires that still had air. Whereas the one bike my family owned was leaning up against the back of the dome, looking forlorn and a bit rusty with weeds growing up through the spokes. Not exactly road worthy.

And I didn't have a car. I was completely dependent on Winchell or Candace to either chauffer me around or lend me one of their vehicles.

So the next morning, I sat at the kitchen island, ignoring the family as best I could while I sipped coffee and mulled my options.

Mom was making pancakes.

Candace, dressed again in her working-day finery—this time her top featured a palm frond and pineapple print—sat at the table across from her son, texting someone while also dumping flavored creamer into her coffee mug.

I frowned. Asking Candace or Winchell to drive me to RB's wouldn't work for a bunch of reasons which became all-too-obvious when I pictured myself telling either of them to wait for me in the car. Because I'd go to the door and knock and they'd naturally wonder who was opening it since RB was at work, which would lead to a bunch of pesky "who was that?" questions, which I'd have to answer by either being evasive or lying outright. Or suppose I took too long to come back outside. I wouldn't put it past either one of them to get impatient and follow me, eventually, burst through the front door and catch me red-handed in the act of talking to our supposedly missing baby brother. Plus, if even knowing Ace was in town made me bawl like a child, what would happen if I actually saw him? What would Winchell or Candace be able to read in my face when I got back to the car?

No. What I needed to do was to borrow Winchell's truck...which would also require that I tell a little falsehood, because obviously it was safer to claim I needed to run some random errand than mention I was headed to RB's—see pesky question problem, above—only the errand needed to be something that would take a long time and also discourage Wendell from suggesting that he could just give me a ride, instead. Which meant I should say I needed to run to Syracuse, since that was far enough from Tibbs to plausibly require me to be gone for a couple of hours...

Maybe I could say I'd just heard about a new volume of heretofore unknown fairy tales had been published and I wanted it so badly I couldn't wait the two days it would take to order it on Amazon. I just had to get to a bricks and mortar bookstore this very morning. Or I needed new socks and could not possibly wait one more day to get them, if I felt one more toe sproing through a hole in a sock tip I was going to scream, and the distress of my holey socks was also starting to impact my performance at work. Or I was desperately tired of my hair constantly falling into my eyes (not a lie, that part—it does get tiresome) and had booked an appointment in a distant salon because no Tibbsian hairdresser could possibly grasp the complexities of taming my flyaway bangs, let alone possess the skills to tame them.

Okay.

It might work. I just needed to have a second cup of coffee and bide my time until Winchell emerged from the upstairs bedroom...

I swiveled around in the bar stool and stood up.

Quill had polished off his first helping of pancakes, which were topped, that day, with sliced bananas and honey. "You know, you're the only one of us who Grandma ever cooks for," I said.

He gave me one of those bare-your-teeth smiles, showing he knew full well that he'd come into privileges of which the rest of us could only dream.

There was pancake mush stuck to his teeth.

Candace looked up from her phone. "Aunt Marion's right," she said. "When we were kids, we ate cereal for breakfast."

"Or Pop Tarts," I said. "And if we ran out, we had to walk to the grocery store and back ourselves, and it was uphill both ways."

Quill studied me for a second, caught on that I was joking, and then said, "Ha, ha," before digging back into his stack of pancakes.

Mom, over by the stove, poured more batter into the pan to start Quill's helping number two. "Okay, girls, stop telling tall tales. I sometimes made pancakes for you two on weekends."

"Right, Mom," I said, and Candace and I rolled our eyes at each other.

"And what are your plans for today, Marion?" Candace said, setting her phone aside.

And okay. I should have realized there was a scheming schemer reason she was suddenly so interested in my day. But, big fail, I said, "Date with my sweetheart," indulging myself in that sudden happy glow gals get when they are dating someone marvelous and yay! Here's a chance to talk about it. "Fletcher's back in town, finally."

"But that's not until later, right?" Candace countered.

And, uh oh. Why did those words alarm me? "Well." I turned my back on my stepsister and hurried over to the coffee maker. "He gets here early afternoon. I, uh, have a ton of stuff I need to do to get ready."

"But you'll be around? So you can watch Quill for a couple of hours?" Candace asked in a charming voice. If by "charming" you mean diabolical.

"Watch Quill?" I kept my back to her and grabbed the sponge from the sink, pretending to wipe up a non-existent spill on the counter. "This morning?"

"It's your day off, isn't it?"

I turned around then. Big mistake. Her eyes were narrowed accusingly as she waited for my answer. "Actually, I—"

But I broke off, unable to invent a plausible explanation for why I had the morning off but couldn't commit to watching Quill. "But, uh, Mom and Dad," I sputtered lamely because the best I could do was remind Candace that the grandparents always watched Quill while she was at work.

"They have dentist appointments," Candace said. "In Syracuse. It's their annual check-ups."

Syracuse? Dental appointments?

My coffee mug must have tipped a little because hot coffee splashed onto the skin at the base of my thumb. I winced and suppressed a little swear-word. Only not because of the hot coffee, even though it hurt. I swore inside because, oh, great. So much for borrowing Winchell's truck for my own errand. And now what was I going to do? I had no plan B, unless—

"If it's not convenient, Marion, don't worry about it," Mom said. She was back at the table and began cutting the second half of the banana, letting the slices drop onto Quill's pancakes while he reached for the honey squeeze bottle. The kind that is shaped like a bear. Have I mentioned my parents spoil their grandson? "We can take Quill with us."

I felt a flicker of hope. Good ol' Mom. She'd sensed that I was reluctant to babysit that morning and—and—

And Candace was glaring at me. A fierce glare that immediately doused my poor little flickering hope, killing it forever. "Seriously, Marion? It's too much to ask?" she said. "If Quill rides along to Syracuse, he'll have to sit around in a waiting room all morning."

I dropped my eyes and sidled miserably back around the kitchen island, only now Quill was watching me, too, his eyes, so big in his little face, so expectant. "I'm just, er—date—Fletcher—pressed for time—nerves?"

"They have coloring books in the waiting room," Mom said. "And Legos."

"Aw." Quill. Not so much a complaint as a sound that escaped him without his meaning for it to, and in spite of myself I stole another glance at him.

He'd stopped eating and his little head was bent.

Clearly, he was far from thrilled about the coloring books and Legos.

And then I had an amazing inspiration.

Effie.

Effie has a car.

And if Mom and Dad were in Syracuse and Candace was at work, all I had to do was dash up the road and borrow Effie's car.

And quick time-out. Because maybe I've told you about Effie. But in case it hasn't come up, she's the little old lady neighbor up the road who'd been my first best friend, in a way, when I was a kid and reeling and dizzy from being bounced from house to house and finally ending up in a crazy geodesic dome with a strange blobby stepfather and a mother who was hugely pregnant and then had a baby and then was holding a baby all the time, and a stepsister who was exactly my own age which made her seem in a bizarre way almost like a twin, but who was also as different from me as her father was different than my mother. And I was (naturally) my Mom's favorite daughter, and Candace was (naturally) my stepdad's favorite daughter, and our little baby brother was a further complication that I couldn't even begin to fathom—and something about all this felt…I dunno. Icky.

Or maybe everything felt icky and that was just a symptom.

Who knows.

And then, one day, I wandered off.

I was way too young to wander off. Way too young to be walking along a road alone, even if it was a quiet country road.

But nobody noticed I was missing, and off I went.

I remember it all so clearly. I was pretending I was a princess in a fairy tale. But not a Disney princess in a castle waiting for fate and princes to write my story for me. Not at all. I was a heroic princess, fed up with my evil stepfather, setting off to make my own fate.

It didn't feel like I was pretending, either. It felt real. I was in the story. I was the princess. I was setting off to escape the clutches of my family and seize my own destiny in my own two fierce little-princess hands.

I saw a mysterious path leading into the forest.

It would lead to an enchanted cottage, right?

That's what mysterious paths do.

And so you can imagine my astonished delight when after walking for a long, long time, I rounded a bend and came into a clearing and saw, for the first time, Effie's peculiar little house, its roof furry and green with moss and its wide, weather-worn porch, and its peculiar yard that instead of being dirt and weeds (like the yard around the dome) or neatly-trimmed green grass and neatly-bordered flower beds (like the apartment complex where Mom and I used to live) was a messy overgrown collage of fascinating treasures (a wagon wheel, the lid to a wooden chest, a pile of motorcycle helmets) half-hidden by a tangle of flowers and vegetables and berries and birdhouses and twisty little paths and hidey holes.

An enchanted cottage.

And then an old woman stepped out onto the porch, and grinned at me and waved.

I waved back.

I walked a little closer.

The old woman was barely taller than me. Her eyes were crystalline blue, and her hair was white, and her skin was soft and folded into soft-looking wrinkles.

She was missing a tooth. The gap showed when she laughed. So I considered the possibility that she was a witch. But in my little girl heart I knew that if she was, she was a good witch, and if she wasn't, she was almost certainly under a spell that made her look like a witch, because inside she was kind. I could just tell.

Plus, she knew who I was. "You're Winchell Weeke's new stepdaughter, right?" she said. "Marion, is that right?"

And then she told me her name was Effie and invited me inside. And her house was even more full of interesting treasures than her yard. I walked past the claw-foot table inside the door and down the front hall, staring at the shelves crammed with figurines and dishes and things I'd never seen before, things made out of brass and wood and porcelain, and then we were in her living room with its two enormous finial-topped bird cages.

And Effie's birds talked. They talked to me. Whole conversations. That's how I remember it, anyway, although I guess that probably didn't really happen.

And then Effie asked if I was hungry, and served me a butter and honey sandwich on a delicate-looking plate with pictures of flowers painted on it, and poured me a cup of tea that she made herself from leaves she plucked from her yard, and then we went outside together and picked berries and ate them right there, berries warmed from the sun.

And Mom showed up a little later to fetch me, all apologetic. I suppose Effie had phoned her. But I begged every day after that to go back and visit my new friend, again, and finally my parents relented, and soon I was spending more time at Effie's than at the dome.

And yes, sometimes her house had an odd effect on me. It made me forget things. I'd go home and tell stories about things I'd seen, things that had happened while I was there, and Mom and Dad would look at me funny and exchange glances and Candace would tell me I was making it all up. And then, sadly, I'd realize I couldn't remember the stories I'd told. One minute I'd be relating them something that had happened today in Effie's house and the next moment I wouldn't be able to remember anything except walking up her weed-choked driveway and sitting at her table, sipping tea and swinging my legs because they didn't touch the floor.

So when Candace challenged me, I'd get tongue-tied because I couldn't defend myself.

And maybe I was making it up. Maybe I'd imagined the whole thing.

Maybe Effie wasn't really a fairy godmother who could grant wishes.

And then I got a little older and I guess something shifted, because I fell in love with the gorgeous young boy who'd moved to Tibbs from downstate. And he was my true prince. But his evil mother took him away from me, and for the first time in my life, this whole granting wishes thing became serious, because my heart was breaking and if I didn't get my prince back, I was surely going to die.

And Effie did nothing.

I begged. Please, Effie. Please bring Fletcher back.

And she said "no."

And I realized that I'd been wrong about so much. That fairy tales weren't really about magic, they were about something else.

I suppose I became an adult that day.

I was fifteen years old.

And time passed, and RB asked me out and I said yes and for a time it almost seemed like it was okay to lose Fletcher. But then I started college, and RB and I began having silly arguments, and then he slept with Candace and she got pregnant and I lost it.

I decided that was it.

No more Tibbs. No more Weekes-Flarey craziness. Yes, I still talked to Mom once in a while on the phone. I missed her, sometimes. But I was making my own life, seizing my own destiny in my twenty-something hands.

And yet.

Here I was.

Back in Tibbs.

Back with Fletcher.

And Ace was in Tibbs, too. And I was actually thinking about whether I could patch the Weekes-Flarey clan back together again.

If it could possibly be patched...

And I had to try. And even if Effie hadn't helped me win back Fletcher, back in the day, surely she would lend me her car for a couple hours.

Quill was pushing banana slices around on his plate like he was full or maybe feeling a little knot in his stomach now, too.

"Well," I said, speaking slowly because I hadn't really had a chance to fully consider the Effie option, and maybe there would be some flaw in that plan, too?

"Marion," Candace said.

I looked back over at my stepsister.

"The other thing I was thinking," she said in a voice that struck me, now, as falsely bright. "If you could watch Quill, Mom and Dad could grab lunch together. And, you know, they don't get a chance to do that kind of thing very often these days." She stood up now and crossed the room to put the creamer carton back in the fridge. "They haven't had a lot of alone time since Quill and I moved in."

Okay. Boom. She'd now flashed me back, expertly, to our conversation from the other night, and this was obviously not a scheme to save little Quill from being bored for a couple hours, it was a scheme to patch up my parents' failing marriage.

No wonder Candace was so keen on it.

On the other hand...

"Okay." I nodded at Quill, whose little face instantly brightened. "I can look after Quill." "Only, how long do you think you'll be, Mom? I mean, er, what time is your appointment?"

"We were planning to run a couple other errands. Dad needs his eyeglass frames adjusted and I was planning to stop at the Dollar General on the way home. And we'll stop for groceries. You know how Dad likes to shop in the city, when he can, to stretch the budget." Mom dropped the pancake bowl in the sink and turned on the water. "We could be back by two. Would that be okay?"

"Sure. Take your time, Mom," I said. "Have fun. Enjoy your lunch."

And so, okay, I relaxed a bit. This would work. I'd just have to take Quill with me. Not to RB's. That was too risky. But I would take him to Effie's and, assuming she was there of course, I'd ask her to look after the boy while I borrowed her car, and—

"Oh, also, Marion?" Candace had taken a little detour on her way back from the fridge and now paused next to me, her voice low and her lips almost touching my ear. "This should go without saying, but under no circumstances are you to take Quill to visit Effie."

12

Candace left the dome first.

Then Winchell and Mom.

Leaving me alone with Quill.

So here's the thing. I admit that when I first laid eyes on the kid this summer, I wasn't exactly thrilled. Quill looks a lot like his dad. Actually, he looks exactly like his dad did when RB was Quill's age, seven years old, which also happens to be how old RB was the day we met. On the playground. When I fell off the swing and landed on him and broke his collarbone, whoopsie. And yes, I was over the guy 1000 percent. Plus I knew it would be a great thing if Candace and RB got back together and stayed together, this time, for good.

And I'd also become fond of my little nephew. Maybe, in fact, ever since my first night back in Tibbs, when I ended up reading him a bedtime story. It was a fairy tale, of course. And he'd loved it, and we fell into a routine. I started reading to him before bed almost every night. And it's true that once I became a grown-up I started studying fairy tales intellectually instead of losing myself in them as stories. I even started a master's degree in them, because I believe they teach timeless lessons about human nature and problem-solving, and maybe I should devote my life to them except, unfortunately, being a fairy tale expert—surprise, surprise—pays less than being a barista. But they are damned entertaining little stories. So it was fun to enjoy them again through the eyes of a kid.

This was different, though. It wasn't bedtime. I really needed to get to RB's house, and at the moment, Quill was not a cute little kid, snuggling up next to me, asking cute questions about fairy tales.

He was a Major Impediment to my Plan.

I started by giving myself a little time to think. I reminded Quill he had to go brush his teeth. And because he's a good kid he immediately scampered off to the camper.

It was going on ten o'clock.

I reheated my second mug of coffee in the microwave.

I didn't know how long Ace would be in town. Heck, it might already be too late. He might already have left. In town for a wedding, RB had said. Had the wedding already happened? Was Ace, at this very moment, flying through the sky on silver wings, thirty thousand feet above the Midwest plains, lost to his family—lost to me—forever?

My stomach tightened.

I needed to get to Effie's. And I needed to get there today.

Somehow.

Only if I took Quill with me, after Candace had specifically forbidden it, my only option would be to ask him to lie. Take him for a walk and casually end up turning into Effie's driveway while saying, also casually, "So, Quill, by the way, honey, let's not mention to Mommy what we did today."

And I could argue that it wasn't the worst lie ever told. And I could argue that it was a white lie. Or anyway very, very pale gray lie.

And seeing that Quill had asked to go to Effie's, he'd probably go along with the lie, which means I wouldn't run the risk of getting caught. Except there's a problem with lies. Even when they seem like they'll work, at first, something always goes wrong later and uh oh. Like in The Three Little Men in the Forest, where the wicked stepmother has her servants cast the beautiful queen into the river and then tells the king his wife died in the night. Her plan seems flawless, right? But it falls apart because the queen isn't dead, after all. She's been transformed into a singing duck that swims around in the river and—even worse—also talks to a kitchen servant. Which means that inevitably the lie is found out (it doesn't take long, only three days) and the evil stepmother is sent into the forest to be devoured by wild animals.

Not that I'm defending the wicked stepmother. She had no business tossing people into rivers. My point is that the singing duck is the key to the entire story, because no matter how perfect a lie might seem, traces of the truth are always left behind, and those traces sing and speak, and if there happens to be someone around who can detect the traces of the truth, the liar quickly finds herself in deep doodoo.

And Quill is a seven-year-old kid. And seven-year-old kids don't always have a nice, tight filter on their thoughts. I could see him spilling accidentally, dropping some comment about Effie's budgies. Or, even worse, asking questions about Ace. Which would be a major singing duck, because Quill couldn't possibly remember Ace. He was only three when my brother disappeared. So if he suddenly started talking about his long-gone half-uncle?

Singing duck.

I had only one option.

I had to sneak out to Effie's, borrow her car, and get to RB's and back.

Without Quill knowing I was gone.

Fortunately, I had a magic tool at my disposal.

The television.

13

It seemed like it would work, at first.

"Hey, Quill," I said when he returned from brushing his teeth. "Wanna watch a little TV?"

"Ya hoo!" he yelled and ran over to the couch.

Because this was a treat, you see. The trick and the treat. Because normally, Quill is not allowed to watch TV during the day when he could be playing outside. Mom's old-fashioned that way. Country mama, if you know what I mean. Kids are supposed to interact with the 3D world, not screens.

She's probably right, of course. But this was an extraordinary and unusual circumstance.

Quill picked up the clicker and navigated to the Cartoon network in approximately one nanosecond.

I walked over and stood behind him for a minute. "Oh wow," I said. "New Looney Tunes! Cool!"

He didn't answer.

The clicker dropped from his hand.

It had worked. The spell was cast. Little Quill was entranced. Immobilized. Oblivious to everything except the bright figures leaping and chattering across the screen.

"Be right back, k?" I said.

No answer.

I waited another minute just to make sure. Just to see if he'd even turn his head or acknowledge that he'd heard. But no. Quill might as well have been one of the courtiers in Sleeping Beauty after the good fairy touched everyone with her wand and put them all into a 100-year-long coma-like state.

I mentally high-fived myself. WTG, Marion Flarey. Way to find the power of fairy tales in everyday things and weave your story exactly the way needed to get what you want.

And with Candace at work and Mom and Dad in Syracuse, no danger that anyone would show up to wake the kid with a kiss.

I tiptoed away.

I closed the screen door very, very softly.

I tiptoed down the front steps to the driveway.

I broke into a trot.

Trotted trotted trotted down the driveway to the road.

Trotted trotted trotted, out of sight of the dome.

Ugh. Out of breath.

I slowed to a walk.

Reminded myself that one of these days I was going to have to get back into shape.

And ugh, I'd left my phone back in the dome, and what time was it?

I reached Effie's driveway, which twists through the forest and is gravel but overgrown with wildflowers, butterflies on the wildflowers, bright blue bird darting through the air, black and yellow bird darting through the air, all so pretty pretty pretty but don't have time to stop today, don't get distracted, Marion Flarey, don't let a pretty bird lure you away from your task.

I reached the clearing and there was the barn, door open, Effie's old lunking car parked inside. Pointing out, toward me with its dusty headlights like big, dull eyes.

I started up the path to her house.

And, as if knowing she had company, she met me at her door.

She held it open.

"Hi, Effie," I said. "I came to ask you a favor."

"Of course, dear," she said as I stepped inside.

I could hear her budgies chirping and churring from the other room.

And of course I expected her to shut the door and follow me. So when I realized that she had not—that she was still standing back at the entrance—of course I turned around.

And looked past her.

And there was my little nephew, climbing the steps onto her porch.

Gah!

"And you must be Quill," Effie said as my little nephew stepped through the doorway.

14

Yikes.

Okay.

So much for my fabulous plan. So much for my fabulous plan and my magical, television-induced enchantment.

Both had failed rather spectacularly.

Quill had somehow broken the spell.

And, rather obviously, he'd followed me.

Argh.

"Nice to meet you, Quill," Effie said.

He stood without answering, staring at her. The mysterious Effie that he'd heard so much about. He probably expected her to vanish suddenly or sprout wings and float above us toward the ceiling.

Then he stopped staring at Effie because he noticed what was around him. Because at kids-eye view, the first thing you see when you step through Effie's front door is a little table. An unusual table, with feet carved into eagle talons holding onto glass balls and legs that morph into huge bird wings at the top, so the glass tabletop is held up by the spread wings. Effie and I used to pretend the table was actually an enchanted eagle, which is why the table is covered with figurines of wild sheep. So, you know, if we ever managed to break the enchantment, the eagle could have a quick snack before returning the favor by granting us a wish.

Then, as you step a bit further into the house—still at kid's eye view—you find yourself walking past a long wooden bookcase, also elaborately carved, this one with sprays of apple blossoms and flying doves with garlands in their beaks. The shelves are crammed with knickknacks, so that at first glance a reasonable adult might think, OMG, I've lost my way and stumbled into a crazy flea market, help. Only if you look a little closer, you see that the objects aren't junk. They're either unusual or visually striking or both. And most of them are pretty old. I suppose she collected most of them when she was living in Europe. Back in the late 50s and early 60s.

In other words, they were the kinds of kooky-looking things that fascinate little kids.

And Quill was no exception.

"Quill, you can look, but don't touch," I said. "Some of that stuff is valuable. Breakable."

"Touch whatever you want, Quill," said Effie. Which was a bit annoying but of course served to remind me that when I was Quill's age, I was allowed to touch whatever I wanted.

"What's that?" Quill pointed at a large brass thing that looked a like a legless throne, only the seat of the throne was hollowed out—the seat looked like a flat-bottomed dish. Dark and heavy and patinaed and ancient-looking.

Figures a little boy would gravitate toward that when there were perfectly lovely bisque figurines of pirouetting fairies right next to it.

"It's called a diya," Effie said. "It's a brass lamp."

"It doesn't look like a brass lamp," Quill answered, his brow knitting.

I agreed with him. It didn't. At least not like the brass lamps you see in the pictures of the Aladdin stories.

Effie picked it up and handed it to him. "It's heavy," she warned, and sure enough the weight of it made his hands sink. I saw his grip tighten to keep from dropping the thing.

"Whoa," he said, looking at the diya and then back at Effie. "Is it real?"

"Yes, it's real. Shall we light it?"

He looked at me. Like it was up to me to give him permission. Then he looked back at Effie. "Is it magic?"

"Of course not!" I yipped and stepped forward, stepping between them. "Effie?" I said quickly. Partly to divert the conversation away from topics that might get back to Candace in the form of singing ducks, because I was already in enormous trouble and if Quill came out of this with stories of magic lamps it was off to the forest to be devoured by wild animals for Marion Flarey. And partly because I didn't have a lot of time, and I needed to get to RB's and back before Mom and Dad returned to the dome. "I have a favor to ask."

But Effie ignored me. "Possibly," she said to Quill. "But there's only one way to find out. Let's get some lamp oil."

She started toward the kitchen, Quill close behind.

Oooh boy.

Now, to be clear, Effie does not have supernatural powers. I know, I know, I came home from her house when I was a little kid with all kinds of crazy stories, and yes, I believed at one point in my life that she could wave a wand and solve all my problems. And yes, odd things had happened in her house when I was little, or I'd believed it at the time, and yes, she sometimes seemed to have ESP. Only what that really means is she's one of these people with such a keen understanding of human nature that she can guess your thoughts. And all the "magic" we did together when I was little was all the "let's pretend" variety. Which I adored because Effie was the only grown-up I'd ever known who would actually play with me—really play, like other little kids would play. And for a lonely little girl on a lonely country road, whose mother had plucked her up and set her down in a blended family and then almost immediately produced a baby who now took up all her time—well, finding a peculiar old lady with a peculiar house who seemed to love having me around—it was pretty marvelous.

And Candace used to visit Effie too, at first. Only for Candace, the experience never clicked in the same way. She was never as willing to let herself go. Because even though she was the same age as me, she always seemed older. And so at some point she decided that visiting Effie was silly. She became interested in boys and to my astonishment began to need a bra when I was still flat as a barnboard. And she'd roll her eyes when she saw me reading fairy tales or when I asked for fairy tale books for Christmas or begged my parents to take me to a bookstore so I could spend my allowance.

She'd outgrown the silly stuff.

And so even though, by then, I knew better than to mention the strangeness I encountered at Effie's, in Candace's eye I was still ridiculous, because she'd outgrown fairy tales and I had not.

And I suppose, as far as Candace was concerned, I was now indoctrinating her child. And so, yes, I should have grabbed Quill's hand at that very second, made up an excuse like OMG, I think I left the stove on, we have to go! And escaped.

But instead, I followed Effie and Quill to the kitchen.

Effie bent down and began rummaging through the cupboard below her kitchen sink.

I cleared my throat. "So, uh, Effie? I have a favor to ask. Could I borrow your car to run a quick little errand?"

"Of course, dear," she said. "And here's the lamp oil!"

She stood up.

In one hand she held a greasy-looking, rectangular oil can.

She extended the other hand to me. She was holding a key. A car key.

Must be she also kept her car key in the cupboard under the sink?

I took the key and cleared my throat. "And, uh, also, would it be a big inconvenience if Quill hangs out here while I'm gone? I won't be more than, uh—" I did a quick mental calculation. "Maybe 45 minutes or so?"

"I wouldn't mind a bit," Effie said. "Would you mind, Quill? You can help me feed my birds."

Right. Like a seven-year-old boy would want to go anywhere, when he was about to test a possibly magic brass lamp and then meet Effie's talking birds.

15

So the first thing I noticed when I got into Effie's car—a huge old Buick, originally maroon but now faded to a purplish gray—was that the registration and inspection stickers had expired.

Nine years and eight months ago.

Good thing I could get to RB's via back roads.

Second, the car started right up. Which made me wonder if perhaps she was still driving it despite its woefully out-of-date paperwork.

The car was so big that as I drove, picking my way along those narrow country roads, it felt like I was taking up way more than half of the pavement. Like if I met an oncoming car, I'd have to pull off the road to give it room to get by.

Not exactly the hippest ride.

But it got me to RB's.

• • • • •

And RB's truck wasn't there.

A relief.

Because although I was pretty sure he'd be at work, considering it was a Monday morning, there was always a chance he'd be home.

I pulled into the driveway and parked.

My heart was hammering.

I sat for a moment in the car.

A long moment.

A long moment of doubt.

Because what if I was making a huge mistake? What if Ace wasn't there and I was setting myself up for a huge disappointment? Or what if he was but he was a completely different person, no trace of the kid brother I'd known when I was growing up—what if he'd evolved into some sort of nasty character, some sort of shifty criminal or toothless zombie meth head?

Or what if he was riddled with guilt and shame over stealing the money from the family, and seeing me would bring it all back, and he'd resent me and slam the door in my face and that would be the end of it, he'd be gone forever?

What if he was scared that if we found out he was back in town, Winchell might make good on his promise to call the cops? Which would, naturally, freak him out?

Or how about this: what if I didn't recognize him? I mean, ticking off the math in my head: he was 16 years old the last time I'd seen him. He was 22 now. From a boy to a man, you know?

I considered turning back. Taking RB's advice and letting it go. Let Ace decide to come to us if he wanted to, but if not? Let it go.

But something wouldn't let me leave.

I got out of the car.

I walked slowly to the house.

I banged on the door.

I heard someone's footsteps.

The door opened, and I was looking at the face of my little brother.

• • • • •

Lanky, still. He hadn't filled out all the way, yet. But wow! The last time I'd seen him, he was this gawky, awkward kid, his cheeks peppered with zits and his upper lip covered with pale fuzzy stuff he was trying to pass of as a moustache.

And now he was a grown man.

And have I mentioned his face? He has one of those faces that reminds me of a faun. Sort of delicate yet masculine at the same time.

So that, if Ace wasn't your brother, and he stepped out of a forest dressed in green and said he'd been watching you for years and was madly in love with you and would you please marry him and join him as his queen to rule his magical kingdom, I promise. You'd go in a heartbeat. You'd be instantly madly in love with him.

And so you understand: the second I saw him, it was like the story of the stolen money vanished from my head.

I was looking at my little brother. And I love my little brother, so much.

"Hey," I whispered.

We stood there for another couple of seconds. Him not speaking but OMG what was going through his eyes. Shock, at first, as he realized who I was, then a flash of something else that might have been alarm and then something that might have been sadness.

And then he said, "Mayfly."

And we fell into each other's arms and I was wrapped up into the sweetest little brother hug.

We stood like that for what seemed like twenty minutes. I could hear his heart and I could feel the wetness from my eyes soaking into the sleeve of his shirt.

We stepped apart.

His eyes were wet, too.

"I was here," I said. "I stopped by yesterday. And don't blame RB. RB didn't tell me anything." I paused. "I saw the backpack and I guessed it was yours. And RB told me you didn't want to see us, he told me to let it go. He didn't break his promise to you."

"It's okay, Marion." Ace's voice cracked and he gave an almost imperceptible shake of his head. "You don't have to apologize."

I wiped my eyes. "Can we talk? Is it okay if I come in?"

He nodded. "I'm sitting out back, on the deck."

• • • • •

The deck appeared to be the only part of the house that was actually finished. The wood was still bright and fresh, and there was a big gas grill and a set of Adirondack chairs.

We sat down and were quiet for a minute while we looked out over the brushy overgrown pasture, and beyond that, the typical landscape you see everywhere around Tibbs: the woods and then a distant forested hill and beyond that the top edge of another forested hill, the furthest one blueish because of the damp summer air and soft-looking, like it was painted onto the sky with watercolors.

I let the scene flood my eyes, hoping it would calm me down. Because I needed to be calm. I needed to figure out what to say to my little brother.

I noticed a book on the table between our chairs and suppressed a gasp. It was one of my books. An annotated collection of classic fairy tales. A book you read if you want to actually think about fairy tales versus just be entertained by them.

I gestured at it. "Enjoying the read?"

"Yeah. I hope you don't mind," he said. "I was bored and RB's books..."

He trailed off, but I knew what he was thinking. RB's books were all 800-page history tomes.

"I don't mind at all," I said. "Interesting choice."

And by the way, I don't remember Ace being into books when he was little. Although I used to sometimes read him bedtime stories, the way I read to Quill, now. Until he got too old for them and announced he didn't need bedtime stories anymore...

I glanced over at my little brother. He was looking straight ahead, out over the wooded hills.

"So," I said. "RB says you're in town for a wedding."

"Yeah." Ace nodded and I got the feeling he was relieved that I was making normal small talk instead of what he knew I was thinking. Like where have you been and why did you steal that money and wow Ace you really made a mess of things, didn't you. "Remember my friend, Jaco?"

I considered his question. "Vaguely. Blond kid, kinda hefty?"

"Yeah. He gets married next Saturday."

"You in the wedding, then?"

"Yeah. Best man." He wrinkled his nose briefly. "Had to rent a tux."

I smiled in spite of myself. The thought of my little brother, a grown man, wearing a tux. "I bet it looks great on you."

He gave an absent smile, and then his chest rose and fell as he took a deep breath. "Mayfly, I'm sorry to sneak into town like this. I thought it would be best if you guys—the family—didn't know."

You guys.

Ace picked up a vape pen from next to my fairy tale book and took a pull and exhaled. A puff of white smoke floated up around his head.

I'm not one of the "you guys."

"Whatever happened, Ace, I want you to know that—"

"Dad told me not to come back," he said, cutting me off. Then he laughed a short laugh. "'Horace. Get out and don't come back.' And words are words."

Didn't I know it.

Two turkey buzzards came into view, circling against the bright blue sky. And without my intending, my mind immediately jumped to the thought that crap, that was a sign. Turkey buzzards mean something is dead, and the buzzards are circling us. There's nothing to do but let it go. Mourn and let it go and let nature clean it up.

I pushed the thought away. "No, Ace," I said. "Words aren't always words. They are sometimes mistakes. Dad was angry. He has a temper. But he couldn't have really meant it. Not really. Not for good." I'd stopped myself from watching the buzzards. "You were Winchell's favorite. He loved you more than me, more than Candace, even. I'm sure that whatever happened, you guys could find a way to—"

"That's not how I remember it," Ace interrupted. His voice sounded a little clipped, now, a little hard, and he stood up, and when I looked over his beautiful, delicate faun face was tight.

Tight with pain.

What the hell had our family done?

"Want a beer?" he said. "I'm gonna have a beer."

"No thanks," I answered, because even for me drinking in the morning is a bit too much and also, oh crap. It wasn't even noon. And Ace had been one of those kids who started, you know, "experimenting" with alcohol and stuff when he was still pretty young. Nothing too awful, as far as I knew, but he was smoking pot by the time he was in seventh grade, and the word around town was that he was dealing a little here and there when he was in high school. And smoking pot is legal in more and more places today, but back then it wasn't, and he and Winchell used to have huge arguments about it. Because Winchell was really worried about Ace running a drug op out of his house.

The civil forfeiture thing.

Which makes Winchell the world's biggest hypocrite, by the way. Everybody knew that he'd been a huge pot dealer when he was younger. Hell, he'd paid for the dome with his pot business. And sure, he'd gotten too paranoid in the end and had gotten out of it. But it was still damned hypocritical of him to yell at his son because he'd found a joint in his room.

Ace came back, holding a bottle of beer in a koozie. "Sure you don't want one?" he said.

I shook my head and he sat back down, and I considered what to say next. Because obviously this was uncomfortable, but I wasn't sure if I'd get another chance and if there was any way to fix this mess, I was going to figure out how to fix it.

"Can I ask you, though, Ace? Because I know a little bit about what happened. Candace told me. She said you and Dad got into some sort of fight."

Ace sighed. "Sure. Ask away. Dad said I took a bunch of money."

The buzzards had disappeared behind the house, but they were back now. They'd caught another thermal and wheeled back overhead. But I looked away, again, because I had an idea. If Ace had taken money, maybe money could fix it. You know. Ace could offer to pay it back.

But he must have figured where my thoughts were going, because before I could suggest it, he sighed again. "It was a lot of money, Marion."

I suddenly wished I'd accepted Ace's offer of a beer. Because maybe it would have given me a shot of courage. Because I wanted, now, to ask Ace directly. Ask him if he'd done it. Because that's what Candace had said. She's said he admitted it.

But I didn't need the beer, because he'd guessed what I wanted to say.

"No, Marion. I didn't do it."

My heart jumped.

He didn't do it?

My little brother wasn't a heartless thief, heartlessly robbing his aging parents, after all?

But Candace had sounded so sure!

"Okay." My voice came out just above a whisper. "If you didn't do it, what exactly happened?"

And I sat, holding my breath, waiting for the magical story that would explain how Candace could be so sure that Ace was a dirty rotten thief who pocketed my parents' life savings, while Ace could sit there and say he hadn't done it.

He tipped back his head and drained his beer, then pulled the bottle out of the foam koozie and turned the bottle in his hand like he was studying the label.

"It's stupid, really, Marion. I found this slip. The receipt for the withdrawal. I didn't even know what it was. It was a slip of paper. I stuck it in the pocket of my jeans."

I frowned. This didn't sound much like a magical story. "What do you mean, you found it? Where?"

"It was on the ground. By the driveway." Ace shrugged as he spoke. "I didn't look at it. It was, you know. Litter. All old and faded. I picked it up and stuck it in my pocket and forgot about it. Then—it must have been week or so later, maybe longer—and Dad starts acting really weird."

I rifled through my memory banks as Ace spoke, trying to remember what I'd been up to when this had happened. It was the year I moved to Denver. I'd lived in Denver for three months, then moved back. Dumb idea, moving to Denver, but I'd dropped out of my master's program and my loans were coming due and I was trying to find a job that would help me get ahead, and a friend of a friend had opened a restaurant and said I could work there, as a hostess. And Mom used to call me from time to time. So I tried to remember if she'd started to seem different, on the phone.

I wondered if Candace was right. Was it possible Mom had no idea what had happened?

"And what about Mom?" I said. "Did you ever talk to her?"

Ace stood up. His face looked tight, again. "Nope. She was at one of her art shows in Buffalo or someplace. Dad was yelling and screaming about how he'd found the receipt and 'where's the money, Horace,' and when I kept saying I hadn't taken it, he said that was it, he was gonna call the police. So I was, like, 'ok, bye' and I grabbed a backpack and left." He shook his head with a rueful little smile. "I had a lot of practice at taking off, by then."

I wanted to say what was in my heart. I wanted to ask my little brother, "but you really didn't do it, right? You really didn't steal the money?"

But I couldn't bring myself to ask him.

I mean, he'd said he didn't steal the money.

I had to believe him, right? And the way he sounded? The way he looked?

I did believe him.

I did.

"Anyway, what's done is done," he said, and I heard the pain in his voice again. Which of course made me think: *no*.

No.

He didn't steal the money, or if he did, there was some sort of explanation. It was a big misunderstanding. There has to be a way to fix this.

Ace stretched and yawned and pulled his tee shirt off over his head. Which is when I saw that he had a tattoo on his left shoulder. It was an ace of spades playing card, only the bottom half was melting. The top of the card was solid, but the bottom was twisty and dripping and collecting into a pool of melted playing card stuff.

"Sure you don't want a beer?" he said.

I shook my head. "Nice tat."

"Like it?" He turned as he spoke to show me his other shoulder. It had a tattoo as well. A Salvador Dali clock, meaning a clock that was also melting, like the playing card. "Ace on the left, Horace on the right," he said, his face breaking into a quick grin. "Get it?"

And I did. It was his two names. His nickname, Ace, and his real name, Horace, which means timekeeper.

"The artist, Clayton, is a friend of mine back home," he said. "Back in Vegas. He's really well known. Clayton Starr. Ever watch Ink Master? Reality show? Clay won a couple seasons ago."

"Vegas, huh? That's where you're living, now?" I remembered the cap I'd seen with his backpack. The one with the Golden Knights logo.

"Yep. Been there a few years, now."

He went in to get another beer and I checked my phone, which gave me a little jolt because I saw the time, and I really, really needed to get going.

But I wasn't ready to give up, quite yet, on the hopes that I might be able to fix this, somehow. Get Ace reconciled with Winchell. Because it was only money, right? Even if Ace hadn't stolen it, even if he'd only borrowed it or something.

Ace was Winchell's son.

There are things that are more important than money.

He returned, tucking his new beer back into the koozie.

"So, uh, how long will you be in town?" I asked casually.

"Dunno. The wedding's next week. And I'm between jobs right now. So, you know. I'm taking it easy."

"What do you do?"

"I'm a cook." He saw the surprised look on my face and grinned again. "I know, right? Grew up on microwaved TV dinners, and I somehow figure out how to cook shit."

"No kidding!"

"Yeah. I'm actually thinking I might apply to culinary school. You know. Make a real career out of it."

See? That's what happens when you don't see your little brother for seven years and instead of a gawky teen, he is now an actual adult. It turns out he is more mature than you are, even. And sure, I was one thousand percent committed to my new career path as Fletcher's successful business partner, but something about the idea of my little brother, finding a job he loved and now planning to go to school for it?

I felt a slight tinge of wistfulness.

But then something else occurred to me.

Another brilliant inspiration, in fact.

So brilliant that it would save my little brother while also impressing the hell out of my darling Fletcher.

"Ace!" I breathed, sitting up in my seat. "I run a tasting room. It's a brewery, we make hard kombucha. And we're doing really well, only I've been looking for ideas about how to build the business—and we should hire a cook! We should hire you! There's a whole kitchen, brand new. They put it in when they renovated the barn. You could run the whole thing! It would be fantastic!"

Ace's eyes became alert for a split second. Of course they did, because the idea intrigued him. And I was thinking OMG, this is it. I'll keep him here. Keep him in Tibbs. And he'll work for the brewery which means we'd see each other. I'd have my little brother back. And sooner or later, I could figure out a way to talk to Winchell, to clear things up between him and Ace.

And guess what? Two birds with one stone: Fletcher would be so impressed. He'd see what a keen business partner he had, as Marion Flarey keenly and astutely rolled out a keen and astute plan to open the kitchen and create new revenue streams and—

"Oh, Ace! It would be perfect. It would be so much fun!" And suddenly I thought I might start to cry again. Because my heart suddenly felt all full, and hurt so much with all my wanting.

Wanting my little brother to stay in Tibbs and wanting my future with Fletcher to be perfect. Beyond perfect.

And Ace hadn't jumped on the idea, but he also hadn't said no.

Time to close the deal, Marion Flarey. "Tell you what, Ace. You could start this week. You could start now. A consultation. You're in town a few days, right? You can stop by, look the kitchen over, let us know if we need to make any changes. Help us do a menu."

"I dunno, Mayfly," he said. There was a little frown between his eyes. "You won't tell anybody I'm in town, will you?"

I shook my head. "Of course not." And I wouldn't. I could have the entire conversation with Fletcher without ever revealing that Ace was actually in Tibbs. "I'll set it all up," I said. "You can make a little money and we'll get to hang out!" And if I got him to stay in Tibbs for a little bit longer, and he liked the brewery and we offered him a job, he'd stay. And I'd have my little brother back.

I felt so good, all of a sudden. "I'll talk to my boss about it today," I said, grinning and thinking, as we hugged good-bye: wait until Ace realizes that my boss is Fletcher Beal.

But no time for that, now. I was becoming more and more aware of how nervous I was feeling about getting back—I had to get back to fetch Quill from Effie's ASAP or I was gonna be in huuuuge trouble.

I stood up. "I have to run. I have a situation back at the dome and—just promise me you'll do it," I said. "Promise me you'll take the job."

And Ace shook his head and gave me a half-smile. "We'll see," he said. "It could mean more trouble for me than it's worth, to show back up around Tibbs. But I promise I'll think about it, at least."

16

I hustled back to Effie's, driving as fast as I dared in that enormous brown sedan with its squishy suspension that made it feel like I was sliding every time I took a turn. Thinking as I drove that I sure hoped Effie had acted like a normal, boring human being while I was gone, that she and Quill had spent their unsupervised time doing normal things like feeding Effie's budgies and drinking mint tea.

And not trying to catch elves or something.

Right.

I was nearly at her driveway when I realized I'd forgotten to ask Ace for his phone number. And how stupid is that, Marion? Stupid, stupid, stupid. Because how was I supposed to get back to him about the brewery gig? Other than going back to RB's—and we've seen how hard that is, to pull off—or asking RB for it, which would be tricky unless I confessed that I'd talked to Ace, and RB wouldn't be too happy about that.

Damn it, Marion Flarey.

And it was too late now, to turn around.

I backed Effie's car into the barn and went up to her house.

She and Quill were sitting at her kitchen table. They'd been eating cookies. There were crumbs on the table and one sugar cookie left on a plate, and I thought, phew, all they did was eat cookies, no magic stuff.

But then Quill said, "We fed the budgies. Did you know they like watermelon?"

"Nice," I said, feeling a slight twinge of uneasiness.

"They talk," Quill added, then looked longingly at the last remaining cookie on the platter in the middle of the table. Effie nodded her okay, and he smiled and grabbed it, and took a bite. And then after he'd chewed and swallowed, he added, "An' Thumbelina told me a secret."

Two of Effie's budgies talk. Billy Beg and Thumbelina.

"What secret?" I said, trying to sound natural.

Quill and Effie exchanged looks. "I can't tell you," Quill said, smiling suddenly. "It's a secret."

So: great. Here I'd been agonizing over asking Quill to keep a secret from his mom, and didn't he turn around and keep a secret from me?

Only maybe I could turn that to my advantage. Oooh! "That's right!" I said in a quick, bright voice. "If you have a secret, you can't tell anyone. Good for you. Don't tell me! I don't want to know!"

"But I can tell you what it's about. It's about my Uncle Ace. Can I have some more tea, Effie?"

WHAT?

"Uncle Ace?" I gasped. "Do you even remember your Uncle Ace?"

Effie poured a bit more tea into Quill's cup as he munched his cookie and nodded at me. "Thumbelina told me about him."

"Effie," I said to Effie. "What is this about?"

"You'll have to ask the bird," she said. "Tea?"

She poured some of her tea into the third cup at the table. And she had that look she gets. Ugh. That mischievous, now-we're-gonna-play-a-game look.

The glint in her eyes that I'd loved so much when I was Quill's age.

But not anymore. Now I knew that look meant something else. That my life was about to get a lot more complicated. Like when the cat, Surprise, disappeared and instead of just helping, Effie turned it into a fairy tale game, sending me on a crazy quest to find The Pot With the Golden Star in order to get the cat back. She tortured me with that one for weeks.

Although, in this case, it appeared to be less of a complication and more plain old bizarre-ness.

Or at least, a weird coincidence. Because nobody in the Weekes-Flarey household spoke about Ace.

Ever.

And Effie wasn't going to be any help.

"Uh, finish up your cookie, okay, Quill?" I said. "We have to get back to the dome."

Tell you what.

I'd been looking forward to my afternoon with Fletcher for days and days.

But never more so than I did then, because more than anything I needed to get away from my nutsy family and hang out with someone halfway normal for a little while.

Get me out of here.

Get me back to my castle and my prince.

I finished my tea and stood up from the table.

Quill was still finishing his cookie.

"I'm going to go say 'hi' to the birds," I said. And I sounded grumpy. Because I suspected Effie knew that what I was really going to do was ask the birds about Ace. And it didn't seem very dignified, to be begging a bird to talk to me.

Effie keeps her budgies in her living room, in two huge cages. Which—Effie being Effie—aren't the sort of cages you'd find in your neighborhood big box pet supply store. They're huge, they're on legs, and they're gorgeous, with wires curving up and joining at the top in elegant spires topped with fancy finials. Who knows where she got them. They're more like pieces of art than cages.

I visited the cage with the two male budgies first, because one of them—the green, which also happens to be the original color of wild budgerigars—had been my favorite when I was little. Billy Beg. And yes, he was still alive. They can live 15 years or more. And he talked, and what kid wouldn't fall in love with a talking parakeet?

Billy Beg was a really friendly bird, too. He came right over to the side of the cage when he saw me.

"Once upon a time," I cooed to him.

"Once upon a time," he said back, and then, "I love you!"

"I love you, Billy Beg!"

He touched my finger with his beak through the cage, his clawed feet clasped around the wires.

Then I went to the other cage, the one with the three females. Blanche, who is a blue, but the blue is really really light, so pale she's almost white, except for a little sky blue that shows around the base of her tail. Another green, like Romeo. And the yellowface, Thumbelina.

"Good morning, Thumbelina!" I said. "I love you!"

"I love you," Billy Beg said from his cage.

Thumbelina just hopped from one perch to another and looked at me.

Like she did every time I tried to get her to talk.

I glanced over my shoulder.

Effie and Quill were still in the kitchen.

"Hey," I said in a low voice. "Tell me the secret, Thumbelina. What did you tell Quill? How do you know about Ace?"

Nothing.

"Ace," I said. "Ace."

But she just hopped onto her little swing and cocked her head and looked at me like I was—I dunno. An alien species, I guess.

Sigh.

And what time was it, anyway? It had to be after one?

"Quill, honey!" I yipped. "We gotta get back to the dome! I need to start getting ready for my date, and—we have to get back!"

17

You know, one of the reasons I would vastly prefer to be living in a fairy tale instead of this Stupid Reality that we're all stuck in? Time, in fairy tales, is a great deal more cooperative and easy to deal with. Sure, heroines might get stuck someplace for days or longer. Years. But as a reader, you get through the stuck period in only a sentence or two. So in, say, East of the Sun and West of the Moon, when the youngest daughter marries the White Bear who is in reality a bewitched prince and then breaks her promise to him (there goes that promise-breaking thing, again! Which always leads to disaster, ugh) and he disappears and she has to go hunt for him, she walked "for many and many a long day," per the Andrew Lang version. But it's a story. So for the reader, that "many and many a long day" is over in an eyeblink. Because the reader doesn't need to live the tedium of wandering around for weeks or months, on foot and then by horseback and then on the backs of the South and North Winds. Wandering and wandering and asking yourself if maybe setting off on this stupid journey was a really dumb idea, and you may well not survive, and also guess what? There's no guarantee you'll even find what you're looking for.

For the reader, it's a couple of sentences and boom, you've arrived at the happy bits where the heroine outwits the long-nosed troll and wins her prince.

And the reverse is true as well, in fairy tales. If you need some extra time, you have it. As long as it takes the pretty daughter to reach the castle where her prince is confined, he's still not married to the troll when she gets there.

She's got time to save the day.

Whereas, while I trotted with Quill back to the camper, all I could think was OMG what if I get there and Mom and Winchell are back already and want to know where we've been and I will need to lie to them because if I tell them we were at Effie's, Candace will find out.

But, thank goodness, we got back and phew! Mom and Winchell weren't home, yet. And that was great only oh, crap. What if they're lollygagging in Syracuse and Fletcher gets here and I'm still stuck on babysitting duty? Then what do I do?

"Are you hungry?" I asked Quill as we reached the pseudo yard between the end of the driveway and the dome's front steps.

"Nah," he said.

Of course not. Effie's cookies.

"I need to take a shower and stuff," I said. Thinking to myself maybe I could park him in front of the television again, but second thought maybe that wouldn't be a good look if Mom and Dad did roll in before I was done with my shower.

But did I have any other options?

"Hey," I said. "I just had an idea. What if you pick one of my books in the camper, and find a picture, and write a little story about it?"

I looked at him hopefully.

But my hopes were dashed. He looked decidedly unthrilled. "Like they make us do in school?"

"They make you do that? Write about a picture in a fairy tale book?"

"No. It was a book about polar bears." He rolled his eyes.

"I see."

Why weren't Mom and Dad home?

I swear I could feel the minutes ticking away as we stood there.

"Well," I said, "I can't, uh—Grandma wouldn't really like it if you were watching television now because, you know, it's a nice day and everything, and, uh, Quill—"

"Can I use one of the boxes in the camper to make a house for Surprise?"

Okay. So he meant the boxes Candace had used to pack up my books, when she'd moved into the camper after leaving Garth. So, poetic justice. If I needed one of the boxes to amuse her son, and if that meant some of my books would now be stacked on the floor next to her bed? So what.

"Sure," I said. "Great idea. Surprise needs a house."

We went together to the camper.

"And also, Quill?" I said. "You know what you said earlier? About secrets? Let's not, uh, mention to anyone that we went to Effie's today. Okay?"

"Okay," he said. "I won't tell. Don't worry, Aunt Marion."

Worry? Me, worry?

Of course not. That little snag of something catching in my guts? That wasn't worry.

Right.

Because that Candace, she's a shrewd one. It would be just like her to figure out what I'd done. She'd smell it. Just like the giant, fee fi fo fum, smelled the blood of an Englishman.

Fee fi fo fum. I smell that you've been up to something, Marion Flarey.

But I couldn't worry about that, now.

I had a date with Fletcher. I needed to get girlfriended up, and I needed to get business partnered up, too, because tonight I was going to propose that Fletcher hire a consultant to get our brewery's food business launched and in the air.

So I helped Quill unpack one of the boxes of books—stacking them very, very neatly and out of the way along the wall under the little table that served as the camper's eating nook—and he promised me he knew how to safely use big people scissors, and then I scooted into the bathroom and showered.

A long shower because I had to shave my legs.

And then I wrapped myself in my towel and did a few extras, like pluck a couple strays that had sprouted beneath my brows.

I peeked at Quill. He'd found some markers somewhere and was now drawing faux windows on the outside of the cat's new house.

I picked my dress. Well, okay, I was already pretty sure which one I was going to wear. A pale lace dress I'd picked up, recklessly, from the clearance rack at Marshall's that spring when I was single and unemployed and hadn't an inkling how much my life was about to change.

And tonight would be my first time wearing it.

I put it on, then walked to the other end of the camper to borrow the big people scissors from Quill so I could clip off the tags.

I brushed my teeth, and tucked my bangs back with a barrette, and dusted my eyelids with a touch of blushy eyeshadow and touched my lashes with a bit of golden-brown mascara and looped a simple gold chain around my neck.

Excellent. Elegant, sophisticated, just right for my wonderful new role as Fletcher's beloved. And also his valued business partner.

I wondered what he had planned for our date. Maybe he'd whisk me off to a fancy restaurant in Syracuse, where we'd sip wine and eat dishes that were only two bites apiece and made of ingredients I'd never heard of before.

Or maybe he was planning to eat in. To cook for me! Fletcher and I, seated across from each other at the massive oak table in the stone house dining room...the meal something simple but incredible like grilled salmon and roast fingerling potatoes...our faces flickering in the light of stately taper candles, cool summer air wafting in through the screen as the sun sank behind the trees and the little birds sang themselves to sleep.

Or maybe he had something truly exotic and mind-blowing in store. "Marion," he'd say. "I've got a surprise for you. How would you like to take the rest of the week off? I've got a private jet waiting on the tarmac at Hancock International. Have you ever been to the Caribbean? Josh will fill in for you at the brewery and I've canceled all my meetings this week and—"

OMG.

A whole week in the Caribbean?

Nothing but me and Fletcher and crystalline beaches and azure skies and pineapply cocktails topped with tiny paper umbrellas?

Maybe I should find the box where I was storing my bathing suits? Because I'm ready for anything and everything except I'm not sure which box has the bathing suits in it, although if he says Caribbean, he'd know I have to pack, right? And surely my bathing suits are in one of the boxes I kept here in the camper and not in the boxes I took to RB's.

Hopefully.

Or, never mind! I can buy a suit when we get there! What was I thinking? Hah.

I gave myself one last check in the mirror. And, granted, I'm not going to be plucked off the street and offered a modeling job. But generally, men seem to think I look fine. At least, I've noticed that if I'm out in a bar they tend to sputter over to me and ask to buy me a drink, not that that's a very good measure since a lot of men would probably buy a fence pole a drink in a bar if they thought it would talk to them.

And happy day. I heard Winchell's truck in the driveway. Mom and Dad were home.

And Quill had finished his project. He held the box up and I admired the door he'd cut out from the front, and the lovely windows and the way he'd drawn a fringe of grass along the bottom of the house walls all the way around. "Surprise will love it," I said. "Grandpa and Grandma are home. Why don't you go show them?"

And he nodded and then I bent down and whispered a reminder. "Just remember, Quill. Not a word about Effie."

And he nodded, and I felt a little flicker of anxious guilt because as I said, lies have a way of being found out.

But then I heard another car and peeked through the slats of the shades.

Fletcher's Audi, which is a vintage Audi, in case you want to picture the scene, meticulous of course, but because it's old not pretentious, because Fletcher is one of those people who grew up with money but doesn't flaunt it.

I grabbed my purse and a shoulder wrap because it can get chilly in the evening in Tibbs, and also on planes, so I needed to be ready in case this turned out to be an impromptu trip to the Caribbean.

I shut the camper door behind me and descended gracefully across the packed dirt that passed for our lawn and hopped into Fletcher's car, filled with the deliciousness of knowing that I was about to spend a full 24 hours with this amazing man who leaned toward me and planted the most delicious, sensuous, tender kiss on my lips as his fingers touched my chin and dropped down to brush my neck...

And then he pulled away and his expression changed, and I felt a small shot of alarm.

"Everything okay?" I said. Because he looked so serious.

"I'm so sorry to do this, Marion," he said. "It's the St. Louis location. The operations manager quit, today, without giving notice. I have to fly out first thing in the morning. But I booked the flight from Syracuse so we'll have tonight together."

"Aw!" I said, trying my best not to sound too terribly whiney, despite the fact that once again my prince would be setting forth to conquer instead of dallying with his princess. "Crap." Also, so much for that fantasy jaunt to the Caribbean. "What time's your flight?"

"5:50."

He'd have to leave for the Syracuse airport at an absolutely ridiculous hour. Cursed St. Louis operations manager. But I put on a brave face. "That's business, though," I said.

"I'd hoped Urban could step in, but he has his hands full in Massachusetts." He pressed the Audi start button. "Oh, and Shari and Alden have invited us to dinner. Is that okay? I thought that would be fun."

My stomach, which was already halfway to my knees, sank a little further. Because not only were we not headed toward an impromptu meal in a luxury hotel on an exotic beach? We weren't even going to a decent meal in a respectable restaurant somewhere near Tibbs. We were headed to a couples night with Shalden—the nickname they earned in high school because their faces were stuck together so much they had clearly begun to merge into a single entity.

Did I dare raise an objection? Oh, Fletcher, I'm sorry but I would so much rather have these few hours alone with you, not pretending to be fascinated by all things Shalden?

But before I could formulate a calm, reasonable, business partnery style response, Fletcher reached over and touched my shoulder, and I felt a shiver of Anticipation of That Kind swirl through my body and settle down through my belly toward my thighs...

And what did I care how we spent our evening, as long as I could be next to my prince?

"Sounds great," I said as we turned from driveway onto the road, and I meant it.

• • • • •

Shalden—I mean Shari and Alden, I really need to stop calling them that—live in this house that is, you know, fabulous. Which is saying a lot for any house in Tibbs, but it's the truth. It's known locally as the Moreland house. It stands out because the style is Gothic Revival.

Fun fact: when Gothic Revival was big, back in the mid-1800s, the style was considered appropriate for country estates. Not cities or towns. And originally, old man Moreland had built his house as a large estate near Tibbs, not in Tibbs. But then Tibbs grew—not much, it's still a tiny town—and ran into the Moreland property, which was later subdivided to create a string of smaller lots along the street, on either side of the house.

And over time the house fell into disrepair. Because, first, the flush of land speculation that had driven the local economy played out, and then the opening of the American west sucked a lot of the money in that direction. So Tibbs was no longer a place where entrepreneurs made fortunes mining stone or cutting timber, because they all wanted to go to California and mine gold. And during the 1920s and 30s and 40s, wealthy downstate people would summer in places like Tibbs, but then even that ended, because along came trains and planes and cars, and wealthy downstate people could summer anywhere they wanted, and Tibbs is a beautiful spot but it's not, like, white sand beaches or purple mountain majesty. It's more like: quiet and quaint and oh, look, a deer.

So by the time I was a kid the Moreland house was empty and had a No Trespassing sign tacked to the front door. And the wood of the siding was showing through the faded, cracked paint, and the shrubs around the foundation had grown up so far they covered the first-floor windows. And we used to dare/double-dare each other to go up and knock on the door on Halloween, and every other year or so some overly-hormoned teenager would break in and spray paint the walls and smash Jack Daniels bottles on the living room hearth, and then get caught and the adults around town would tut tut, and say the place was dangerous and should be torn down, or else registered as a national landmark and some fairy godmother would then wave her wand and restore it to its former state of Gothic Revival glory.

This was the house that Shalden bought.

And restored.

To its former state of Gothic Revival glory.

Also, now you see why my fancy theories about fairy tales seem to make sense one minute, and then the other minute they are obviously complete malarkey. Because if anyone deserved to live in a gorgeous Gothic Revival house it wasn't Shari Williams Drysdale. I don't care that she has impeccable taste and probably deserves staggering mounds of credit for rescuing a gorgeous example of civil war era American architecture. I mean, the place has a tower. And yes, you have to be careful with towers. Banishing yourself to a tower can be an enormous mistake. But Shari Williams Drysdale wasn't banished. She was married to her high school sweetheart who ended up being a successful salesperson (medical device sales, whatever that meant) and, of course, incredibly handy. He'd done a lot of the restoration work himself. And they had three beautiful children.

Banished, my ass. They were living in their castle, happily ever after. Seriously. They didn't even call their living room a living room.

It was the Grand Room.

I was going to spend my lovely date night with Fletcher in the Shalden Grand Room.

18

Shari invited us to admire her newest fabulous piece of furniture.

"It was a pulpit, originally," she explained.

We were standing on the tiled floor of the Grand Room, and at her prompting began admiring the thing-that-had-been-a-pulpit.

It was a massive, curved cabinet-looking thing with Gothic (of course) arches carved deeply into the face, set in a corner of the room, angled so that there was space to stand behind it.

And then Fletcher and I followed her directive to step around it, so we could see how Alden had turned the once-a-pulpit into a cocktail bar. He'd mounted a set of gleaming glass shelves that Shari had stacked with glassware and stirrers and pitchers and shakers, and on either side were cubbies that I suppose were once used to stash Bibles and prayer books and vestments, but were now bristling with bottles of top shelf spirits and liquors.

"Lovely," I said, aware that Fletcher's hand was resting on the small of my back. Isn't it funny how noticeable that is? Even when it's such a light touch. And just like that, I didn't mind a bit that Shari was bragging about her "cost five figures" Gothic pulpit. I even added another compliment. "And Shari, I love how it matches your décor."

Because it did. The Shalden had loaded their home with Gothic-inspired furniture. The enormous, dark, carved pulpit-turned-bar fit right in. But I was with Fletcher, and we had our own castle that we'd be living in together, one day, and it would be a jillion times more beautiful than this, just you wait.

"We should have martinis, don't you think?" Shari said, and we agreed since you might as well have martinis if you're in a house with a brand-new bar and all that martini-making equipment lying around.

Alden went to get ice—the pulpit-bar lacked a refrigerator, he said apologetically—and Fletcher and I found a seat on the Shalden's Gothic reproduction sofa, which was quite comfortable since it was made in the 21st Century, not 150 years ago, because décor can be tasteful and livable both, don't you agree?

"The fish is new too, isn't it?" I asked after we'd settled into our seats. I pointed at the enormous, glossy trophy mounted on a wooden plaque over the fireplace. "It's a Halibut, right?"

Shari rolled her eyes. "I guess. Alden caught it in Alaska. Last winter. Guy trip. Alden?" she called in the direction of their kitchen. "Is that trophy thing a Halibut?"

But it was. I knew because both of its eyes were facing us. Because that's what Halibut do. They start out as babies looking like normal fish, but then as they grow, one eye migrates from one side of the head to the other, so that the fish ends up with two eyes on one side. That way, they can lie flat on the sea floor without one eye being against it. Which is where they live. Flat against the sea floor, looking up at sea life and seaweed and water swishing around above them.

And yes, if you haven't ever looked at a Halibut, quick go to the Internet, because you'll see that the two eyes on one side of the head also gives this fish a sort of goofy wall-eyed look. One eye points one way, one eye points the other. Like they are clowning with you.

Alden had returned with the ice. He stood behind the pulpit, stirring a pitcher of martinis. "Shari wasn't too crazy about the mount. But it was either the Halibut or I go back out this year and bag an elk." Shari made a face and Alden began pulling glasses out of the ice bucket—he'd stuck them upside down in the ice, to chill. "Or maybe a snarling brown bear. That would look fantastic over the fireplace, don't you think, Fletch?"

"Why 'either or', Al," Fletcher said. "There's plenty of room on that wall for both. Think big!"

"Very funny, Fletcher." Shari wrinkled her nose. "Don't encourage him."

Alden stepped around the pulpit-bar and brought Fletcher and I our martinis. "Speaking of thinking big," he said. "We have some news. Want to tell them, Shari?"

Of course, she did.

• • • • •

So I'll spare you the long version, because Shari got interrupted twice. First by the Shalden's six-year-old. They'd hired a sitter to look after their three kids so most of the night the kids were off in some other part of the house or out in the yard, being supervised by a teenager. But the six-year-old had some question for Mommy and ran into the living room—oh, sorry, I mean the Grand Room—and climbed into Shari's lap and mumbled something the rest of us couldn't hear, and then she resolved it somehow and sent him back to the sitter, who stood the whole time at the other end of the room, looking nervous and apologetic.

Then another interruption: pizza delivery. For the kids.

But between the interruptions, we learned the Shalden had put an offer in on a house downstate. "Alden will be able to take the commuter train to the city," Shari said. "Less than an hour commute."

I suppressed my astonishment.

Shari and Alden were leaving Tibbs?

She showed us pictures of the listing on her phone.

"No more flying out of Syracuse in the dead of winter," Alden said with a satisfied smack of the lips. "Forty-five minutes and I'll be at the home office. And you can get work done on the train."

"So you'll be leaving Tibbs?" I heard myself say. Stating the obvious. But to be honest, I was a bit unnerved. Despite the fact that I found the Shalden a bit annoying, they were also the only people in Tibbs who were serious candidates for a couples friendship. Because Fletcher and Alden were obviously friends. And Shari might be full of herself and overly perfect and a bit of a know-it-all, who had also by the way tried to warn me away from Fletcher at one point, have I mentioned that to you? Because she knew Fletcher was still married and didn't realize his wife was having an affair and their divorce was imminent. Meaning, I suppose, that she was trying to protect me. Her heart was in the right place.

And it's nice to have couples to do couples-y things with. I'd even begun considering trying to be friends with her. Especially once I was feeling the effects of a martini on an empty stomach, combined with how it felt to nestle up next to Fletcher on the Shalden's Gothic-restoration sofa. So I felt a twinge of disappointment as I realized that my vague vision of me and Fletcher meeting the Shalden's for drinks, inviting them to the stone house for barbecue and lawn games, that sort of thing, had now suddenly gone poof and disappeared.

Fletcher was swiping Shari's phone, looking at pictures of the property. "View of the Hudson, eh?" he said. "Nice."

"It's a big house," Alden said. He was slouching in an upholstered parlor chair across from us. The chair had a throne-like look because of the height of the carved wooden back. And it seemed to me that Alden didn't sound particularly cheerful. Like maybe, to Alden, "big" wasn't an entirely positive characteristic.

"We need the room," Shari responded, confirming my hunch that there was a teensy bit of strife in the Shalden household around the decision to buy a multi-million-dollar home overlooking the Hudson River.

"Shari's been bugging me for months about wanting a bigger place." Alden stood up. "Ready for another?"

And for some reason, I noticed that mounted Halibut again. And—you know how my mind works—a fairy tale suddenly sprang up in my mind. The one about the fisherman who caught a talking Halibut. You know that story, right? He hooks big fish, fish says, "Please let me go," fisherman being a good-hearted fellow with a natural aversion to the idea of slaughtering and cooking a talking animal says, "Sure." And lets him go.

But then the fisherman's wife gets involved and—also understandably, in my opinion—demands that the fisherman extract a boon from the talking fish in exchange for sparing its life. Because of course if you do a good turn for a talking animal, you get a boon. That's how it works. The fisherman's wife did okay, up to that point.

But then she gets greedy. The fish grants her first wish, but then she makes her husband go back and ask for a nicer house. Gets it. Becomes dissatisfied with the nicer house. Asks for a castle, etc. And this goes on, with the fish getting more and more annoyed at each request.

Until fisherman's wife finally oversteps. She demands to be made God. At which point the fish becomes furious and uses his magic to put the fisherman and his wife back where they started, in their original hovel.

So you have to admit it was pretty interesting to sit there in that beautiful Moreland house and realize that Shari was all about wanting a bigger, grander one. With that mounted Halibut on the wall above us the whole time, one of his two eyes pointing clownishly toward the ceiling but the other pointed down at where we sat.

Like he was watching us.

"Shall we fire up the grill?" Alden said after he'd made our second round of drinks. "Anybody hungry?"

19

"That was one big fish," I said to Fletcher in the car, after we'd left the Shalden's.

"One big, fugly fish," he said.

That made me laugh. Because first of all, I felt amazing. Because turns out, I was wrong when my first response to Fletcher, when he told me what he'd planned for the evening, was disappointment. Because if it had been just him and me in a secluded booth somewhere, we'd have had our hands all over each other all night, which would have been fun in its own way, but you know what else is fun? Sitting inches away from a sexy guy who keeps looking over at you so that you blush because you know what he has in mind, and then his leg moves and you feel his muscley thigh touch yours and you can't breathe for a second, but it's all completely discreet and secret. I mean, talk about a build-up.

I was goo. My insides had been transformed into nothing but goo.

And we were headed toward his house, the stone house, our future castle. And sure, he'd have to drop me back at the camper at something like three in the morning on his way to the airport, but I was long past caring about lack of sleep or stupid operations managers who quit without giving notice.

I was in heaven.

The fugly comment also made me laugh because Fletcher was right. Halibuts aren't pretty fish. They aren't tropical-colored like clownfish (you know, like the cartoon Nemo) or delicately spangled like rainbow trout or fiercely beautiful like swordfish. The Shalden's halibut was mottled browns and ochres, the color of sea bottom because when halibut lay on the sea bottom, they are trying to blend in. So they are the color of shadows and dappling and rocks and old dead seaweed fronds and other things we'd rather not think about, including (hahahahaha) watery piles of fish poo. Of course since the Shalden fish was a mount, it was coated with a finish that made it shiny, and the taxidermist had painted it as prettily as possible, given what he had to work with. But it was still a fugly fish. Even without considering those goofy eyes.

And then, because I was feeling gooey and relaxed and we'd had wine with dinner after our martinis, I threw caution into the wind and jumped enthusiastically into my favorite topic. "And you know what's really funny?" I said. "Alden caught the same sort of fish as in the fairy tale The Fisherman and his Wife, and Shari is doing just what the wife did, pining away for a bigger house."

"Not sure what you mean," Fletcher said. In a vague-sounding way, which in his defense was probably because he was paying attention to the road. Sometimes in the summertime, the little valleys around Tibbs can collect mist after the sun sets and the air starts to cool. And it was that kind of night. When the road sank down and followed a creek for a few minutes, the air became suddenly white with layers of mist, some layers thicker than others. And deer sometimes run into the road. So he was paying attention to that, as he should have been.

So I waited until we got to a place where the road left the creek and rose to a higher place and the air cleared. "It's just interesting, the way fairy tales can erupt into our normal, everyday lives."

Fletcher chuckled. "If you say so."

And I didn't mind him teasing me. Who minds being teased, when you're in love? On the contrary. It was like a challenge, to get him to understand what I meant and what I have noticed about the world. "Do you know the story? The fisherman fairy tale?" And without waiting for his answer I continued. "It's about a marriage where one partner is greedy and pushes the other partner to go along. And didn't you notice that Alden wasn't as enthusiastic about the new house as Shari was?"

I watched Fletcher to catch his reaction, and in the light from the dashboard I saw him shake his head slightly. "I guess I didn't notice that, no," he said.

"You didn't?"

"A lot of people get off on owning big houses," he said. "Alden's doing really well for himself. Why wouldn't he want a nicer place?"

"Right." But I felt a bit nonplussed now, because if Fletcher's perception of the Shalden dynamic didn't gibe with mine, it would make it hard for us to have this conversation. And also really? He hadn't noticed?

Although on the other hand, you can't expect your Significant Other to have a mind that is 100 percent in lockstep with your own 100 percent of the time. Therefore, so what if Fletcher lacked enthusiasm for my fairy tale theories? Or that I sometimes felt like fairy tales had somehow brought us together, because as I may have told you it was Winchell bringing me a rose like the father in Beauty and the Beast and then later a vase of prematurely dying roses that made me put two and two together and realize that Fletcher was my prince? Fletcher didn't need to know my theories. He was perfect in every other way. And maybe he'd become more sympathetic to my ideas over time. Relationships are a marathon, I reminded myself, not a 100-meter dash.

And besides, I had something else I wanted to talk about.

"So Fletcher," I said. "Remember what I texted? That I had something big to tell you?"

"Oh yeah. That's right."

A car had caught up to us, and he watched it now, in the rearview mirror, then slowed down to let it pass.

"I've been thinking about the brewery, and ways to make it generate more revenue," I said proudly, and sure enough he glanced over, obviously intrigued that I was taking that kind of initiative.

"Yeah?" he said. "Like what?"

"Well." I settled myself back into my seat. "I have quite a few ideas. Like maybe we should look at the tasting room décor. Make it a little brighter. You know, brighter colors, more light. More in keeping with the style of our 'booch."

"Okay," he said again, only more slowly this time. "That'll cost some money, though."

Right. I knew that. Of course I knew that. Granted, the cost of redoing the décor hadn't been the first thing that popped into my mind. But how expensive could it be? "Sure," I said. "For paint and stuff." But I felt a bit less certain as I spoke, because the tasting room was enormous, and I hadn't thought about how much the other things would cost, like putting in the skylight.

"What else?" Fletcher said.

I decided to abandon the décor idea. "We could start serving food. We have a huge kitchen."

"That's a possibility, sure. Assuming we could get a decent cook. And it would need to be marketed."

"Fletcher," I said triumphantly. "Guess what. I can get us a cook. My little brother is a cook, and I know for a fact he'd be interested in taking a look at the kitchen and doing a little consult on our menu."

"Whoa. Hang on a second," Fletcher was waving his hand at me and looking back and forth between me and the road. "Your brother? You mean Ace?"

Okay. So that was a weird response. Of course I meant Ace. I only have one little brother.

"Yes, Ace," I said. "I found out he's been working as a cook, and he's quite successful. In Vegas. So isn't that great? What do you think? Could we offer him a job in Tibbs?"

"Marion. Are you kidding me?" Fletcher snorted. "Not on a bet!"

So you can probably relate to what it feels like to be in a new relationship with a guy you really, really like, and how you're watchful when you're around him, because you're just starting to get familiar with him, so you can't know for sure how he might react to things. That's the stage I was at with Fletcher. And crazily, I had somehow upset him. And I wasn't ready for that. So it surprised me but also felt a bit like a stab of something in my gut. Fear, I suppose. Like: OMG. I just said the wrong thing.

But how could bringing up my little brother be the wrong thing?

"I don't understand," I said, my voice sounding unsteady in my ears, because I was in a bit of shock, to be honest.

"Look, Marion, this is a business."

Oh. So he was thinking this was just me, doing a favor for a family member? Was that why he'd reacted that way?

"I get that," I said. "But if he's qualified and everything, would it really hurt to have him come work for us? And he says he's looking into culinary school—"

"Marion," Fletcher interrupted. "I get that he's your brother and you want to help him. But hiring a felon? That's not the way you run a business."

A felon?

I felt that icky stabbing in my gut again.

"What do you mean?" I said, my voice now definitely shaky. "Ace isn't a felon."

"You get what I mean."

"No," I said slowly, "I don't get what you mean." While meanwhile my mind was racing to try to figure it out. Was this about the thing with my family, about Ace stealing money from my parents? But how would Fletcher know about that? And I'd believed Ace when he said he hadn't done it, although to be honest in the back of my mind I still felt uneasy about the whole thing, like maybe there was more to the story, and Candace was certainly convinced that Ace had done something awful. "Ace isn't—I mean, he used to smoke a little pot—"

"He was a dealer, Marion. He dealt drugs."

Ah, okay. That was what this was about. And I was in college by the time Ace got involved in all that, so I didn't have first-hand knowledge, but I cringed a little at Fletcher's words, because there was some truth in them. Not that my little brother had been a big-time dealer. It was more like pooling funds with his buddies and divvying up little baggies of pot for their personal use. But dealing and possession were two very different things under New York State law.

On the other hand, it was a long time ago. Fletcher wasn't being entirely fair. "He was 14 years old," I said quietly. "I'm sure you didn't always show terrific judgment when you were 14 years old."

We'd reached the last leg of the drive, the long uphill stretch to the stone house.

"And that's only the start of it," Fletcher said as the Audi shifted gears to climb the hill. "What about the break-in? He burgled our house. He wasn't 14 when he did that."

A chill passed through my body. "I don't know what you're talking about," I gasped. "What house?"

"Mother's house. The stone house."

My brain wouldn't compute. "What do you mean?"

"Your little brother. He stole a bunch of shit. Jewelry. Stuff he could fence."

"Oh my God," I whispered. "What are you talking about, Fletcher? I never heard anything about this."

"Well, next time you see your little brother, maybe ask him about it," Fletcher said, his voice tight. "I was in the middle of a deal for my dad and had to drop everything and jump on a plane. And Mother—she was a mess. The doctor had to give her a sedative to calm her down."

And my brain was going oh, Ace. Oh, Ace. What have you done? Because you said you didn't steal Dad's money but now this? And no wonder you ran away. And no wonder you don't want anyone to know you're back in Tibbs…

We turned into the stone house's crescent-shaped driveway, and Fletcher parked and turned off the car. But he wouldn't look at me. He kept his face straight ahead.

"I'm sorry," I whispered. "I didn't know." And then I swallowed hard, because something else had hit me.

Something about his mother.

How she would never give up a grudge.

How she must hate our entire family. Because even though we were her neighbors, we had never been her friends. She was from a different world and hadn't really lived in Tibbs that long. And how violated she must have felt, when she learned her neighbor's son had broken into her home and stolen her jewelry. Fletcher's mother loved her jewelry as much as she had hated living in Tibbs. Having a bunch of her jewelry stolen from her house? No wonder she'd needed sedation. She'd probably had the meltdown to end all meltdowns.

Ugh.

All I wanted to do, now, was curl up into a ball and cry...

But then I felt Fletcher touch my arm, and I looked over and he was finally looking back at me. "The point is," he said, and his voice was now calmer, less chilly, "now you know. So you can understand, right? I would never want him around with the brewery. I could never trust the guy. You understand, right?"

My eyes felt suddenly wet. "And you're sure it was him, Fletcher? Because—I mean, I know he was a bit wild. But are you sure he was the one who—"

"I'm sure." He was still looking at me, his eyes steady. "He returned the stuff he stole. He brought it to the house. Handed it over to me, personally." He paused a moment. "We dropped the charges."

"Oh, God."

"He was a month shy of his eighteenth birthday. We didn't want to ruin his life."

"I had no idea."

"Hey." He reached over and touched my shoulder. "I'm sorry. I thought you knew."

I shook my head. "I was out of touch with everyone for years," I said. "I mean, I know something went down—but Ace was—he and Winchell butted heads a lot."

Fletcher's hand was warm on my shoulder. "Yeah. And he's your brother. I get it. You want to help him." He leaned toward me, and his arm moved behind me, and he pulled me toward him. I felt how much he was trying, now, to comfort me. How sorry he was that I was upset. "And if there's a way I can help him, just let me know," he said. "I'm here for you."

Wasn't that nice of him? "Thank you," I whispered.

"But please don't bring him into the brewery."

"Of course not," I said. "I understand."

And then it was done.

Fletcher pulled me even closer, and his lips found mine.

And then we got out and he led me through the front door and up to his bedroom.

And for a couple of hours I forgot entirely about my little brother.

My little brother and the big mess he'd made...

A mess I was going to have to clean up, somehow.

But how?

20

Fletcher dropped me off at the camper that morning on his way to the airport. I crawled into bed and finally dozed off again, until something suddenly woke me. Somebody yelling. Make that shrieking. Okay, yelling. But it sounded like shrieking because of how violently it jangled in my ears, and what the hell time was it?

Candace. It was Candace, shouting.

Shouting at Quill?

I reached out to feel for my phone, couldn't find it, rolled over and sat up and yeah, it was Candace all right.

Outside?

I tried to make out what she was saying.

Too late. I could still hear her voice, she was still going on, but it was a normal-voiced scolding, now, not a top-of-her-lungs hysterical eruption.

Damn.

I'd never heard her yell at her son. Not ever. And she sounded really, really mad.

What could Quill have possibly done to make his mother that mad?

Ugh.

I found my phone, under the covers, and damn it. I'd forgotten to plug it in when Fletcher dropped me off. It was down to five percent charge.

It was 5:30. Fletcher would be boarding his plane…

I'd had only a couple hours of sleep and it was a workday, and what the hell was Candace doing at 5:30 in the morning out in front of the dome yelling at her son?

I plugged my phone in, and flopped back down, and pulled a pillow over my head.

She was still at it. That scolding tone and words I couldn't make out.

Shut up, Candace.

I need to sleep.

• • • • •

So I got a little more sleep. But thanks a lot, Candace, waking up at dawn to the cacophony of you, yelling at your kid, isn't exactly conducive to restful slumber. On the contrary, even after I drifted off, I had that lingering sense that something was wrong. And my dreams turned strange. Whatever had happened at 5:30 a.m. with Candace yelling began to seem unreal and began to merge into my dreams, which had water with things swimming in it, but the water was dark, murky, and I couldn't see what was swimming in it except that suddenly the surface moved and swirled and bubbled like hot oil and I glimpsed something long and slimy like an eel only it had the head of a dragon. Not just any dragon, either. The dragon from the Elenore Abbot illustration in the story about the thieving brother.

Sigh.

I pushed the dream away and opened my eyes and checked my phone.

It was nine o'clock.

Late enough that Candace would be at work, and at that point coffee would be as useful as another hour of sleep.

I slid my bedroom door open and paused because the other end of the camper was so still and dark.

The shades were down. Quill was in bed, asleep, with Surprise curled up in a ball at his feet.

I tiptoed past them and closed the front door as noiselessly as I could.

Ugh. Candace's car was still parked out front.

My spidey sense began to tingle.

I considered reversing course and tiptoeing back into my bedroom to hide.

But I had no reason to be afraid of Candace.

Right?

• • • • •

Okay, maybe I had a little reason to be afraid of Candace.

Because she was waiting for me in the dome, and her eyes were as mean-looking as two spinning buzzsaw blades.

"What. Have. You. Taught. My. Son."

Her words were also as mean as spinning buzzsaw blades. And, oh, crap. Of course. She'd found out that I'd taken Quill to Effie's. "Um, calm down?" I said weakly, feeling my face get hot and taking a step backward toward the door while thinking to myself, here it goes. Here's what you get, Marion Flarey, for trying to cover things up with a lie.

The duck had sung.

But then Candace pointed across the room in the direction of the couch and the flat screen television.

I had no idea what she was pointing at. And she must have noticed that I looked confused, because she barked at me. "Marion, open your eyes. Mom's wind chime!"

Okay, so that was what she was pointing at? The big, sapphire wind chime Mom had set aside in the dome so she could ship it to her customer? This cleared up exactly nothing about anything. "Uh, so?" I cleared my throat. "What about it?"

"I caught Quill with it this morning. He was sneaking down the driveway."

The uneasiness I'd been feeling ever since I'd heard Candace yelling suddenly tightened into something a bit more definite. A knot of definite worry.

"He was stealing it," Candace snarled. "Those stories you've been reading him. You've been teaching him that it's perfectly fine to steal things. Do you deny it?"

I felt my eyes jerk from the wind chime to Candace's face. And so, okay, rather than cave to her accusations, even though maybe there was a teensy bit of truth to them, I became defensive. "They're just stories, Candace," I said, my voice sharp now, and louder. "What the hell are you accusing me of, exactly?"

A movement caught my eye.

Mom. She'd stepped out of the master bedroom and was standing on the balcony, above us.

And I felt a little twinge because hadn't we promised Mom we wouldn't bicker? And here we were, going at it again, and—

"You're normalizing criminal behavior!" Candace's voice bit like teeth, bit through my thoughts. "Do you know how much that piece is worth? Six hundred and fifty dollars."

"That's retail," I said sulkily. "That's not what it cost Mom."

"Oh my God. You're not taking this seriously, Marion!" Candace's face was now red with fury. "My son stole it. He STOLE it. And not only that, do you know where he planned to take it?"

Uh oh. Was that the sound of the second shoe dropping? "No idea?" I said weakly.

And with that, the volcano blew. Candace's voice became a near-shriek. "To Effie's! You took him to Effie's! After I expressly told you NOT to! You're crazy, do you know that, Marion? You're crazy and you're deluded, and you are a BAD influence on MY SON. And you're to stay away from him from now on, do you understand? No stories. No being alone with him. No talking to him—I don't even want you TALKING to him EVER AGAIN."

And I forgot that Mom was there. I forgot that I'd told her that Candace and I wouldn't fight any more.

I lost it. "Me? I'm a bad influence?" I yelled, my voice almost as shrieky as my stepsister's. "And have you ever taken an honest look in the mirror, Ms. Steal-Your-Sister's-Boyfriend and then get preg—"

"GIRLS!"

I looked up at the balcony.

And the look on Mom's face was terrible. Terrible.

I felt the color drain from my face.

What had I done?

I looked at Candace and her face was as white as mine.

"I'm so sorry—Candy—I'm so sorry," I said, my voice cracking. "You didn't steal RB, it wasn't like that, I never should have said that." I turned and took a step toward my mother, toward the balcony, a step that felt almost like I was falling because of the way my legs wanted to crumple, holding my hands out toward her, palms up. "Mom—I'm so sorry."

"I can't stand this," Mom said.

She was shaking.

And she looked old to me. Tiny and old as she stood there, looking down on us. My mother, who had never seemed old, who had always looked so petite and fresh and like she had somehow some core of fundamental peace and contentment in her soul. Like she had a place inside her that was safe and protected, a place she drew on for refuge no matter what indignities she had to endure, her ridiculous husband, her near-poverty, the family squabbles that kept breaking out around her ears...

It had gotten to her.

I dropped my arms.

I felt like I was going to be sick.

"Do you girls have any idea how hard this is on me?" Mom said. "How exhausting this is?"

I have never, in my entire life, felt smaller and meaner than I did in that moment.

And Mom came down the steps and walked past us both, without saying another word.

• • • • •

I gave her a good long time, this time, before I followed and knocked on the door of her workshop.

Silence.

I tried the latch. It was unlocked.

I stepped inside. She was seated at her work bench, working on one those chimes she makes—the expensive ones, the bell-style chimes. She was surrounded by wire and lengths of brass chain and a stack of her wind chime clappers—the peculiarly-shaped clappers that reminded me of little clay-red femurs—and a smaller stack of the unglazed clay disks that she uses to mount the clappers.

"Mom," I said, my voice small and tentative.

She didn't answer.

I watched her work. First, she threaded wire through the holes in one end of each of seven clappers, and then wired them to seven little holes around the rim of a clay disk. Then she got up and went to her shelf and picked out one of her glazed bells. She sat back down and passed the end of a length of chain through the hole at the top of the bell, and then through a short piece of metal pipe, and then through the hole in the middle of the clay disk, and then she attached the last link of the chain to a big brass washer to keep the chain from slipping back through the hole. So that when she held the chime up by the chain, the disk slid up inside the bell, and the clappers were now suspended inside it, almost hidden, except that as she carried the chime over to the shelf where she stored her finished work, I could hear the clappers clank musically against the bell as she moved.

She was completely engrossed as she worked.

She'd forgotten I was there.

Had she forgotten I was gone, all those years I was away from home, away from Tibbs?

"Mom?" I said as she sat back down and picked up a piece of wire and a clapper.

She looked up at me, then back down at her work.

"I missed you, you know."

She didn't say anything. But I felt that she was listening.

"I've been thinking. About how I was gone for so long. And you know how I'm going to New York next week? Would you like to go along? I could get an extra day off, leave a day early. We could go together. We could spend the day together in the city. Two days, because Fletcher isn't getting in until the afternoon."

She threaded a piece of wire through another clapper. "You know I can't do that, Marion. Who will watch Quill?"

"Dad can watch him. We'll work it out. If he has deliveries Quill can ride with him. Or we can get RB to watch him or Candace can take a personal day. We'll work it out."

She looked up at me, finally.

And her expression had changed.

Her eyes, that had looked so dull and sad, had brightened ever so slightly.

"We could visit some galleries," I said.

A thoughtful look crossed her face. "I used to sell my work in New York, years ago."

I nodded quickly. "I know! Have you thought about doing that again?"

Her turn to nod. "I have, to be honest."

"Wouldn't that be great, Mom?" I said. And in my voice was everything I suddenly felt in my heart. That I wanted to be with my mother. To spend time with my mother. To somehow start making up for all those years that I was so far from home. And sure, my trip to NYC was supposed to be my getaway to spend time with Fletcher. But having Mom along wouldn't interfere with that, right? Mom and I would have our day together and then she could head back to Tibbs or she could hang out the next day while I had my mini-break with my boyfriend and then we could travel home together. "So what do you think?"

She nodded again. "It might be fun. But you need to work things out with Candace."

"Of course," I said, thinking to myself that I'd also have to mention this to Fletcher. Although he'd be fine with it. I'd just tell him I was coming down a day early, to spend a little time in the city with my mother. He wouldn't mind. "I can do that, Mom. I can work things out with Candace."

21

Right. Work things out with Candace.

More like, negotiate a tentative cease-fire. Because she was pretty mad at me. So although she was fine with Mom going to New York, she wasn't close to forgiving me for corrupting her son. So we avoided each other as much as possible. Avoided looking at each other, avoided talking to each other, avoided being in the same room as much as we could. In the mornings, I loitered in the camper until she'd left for work. And at night, instead of spending any time in the dome I went straight to my bedroom and shut the door.

And I read, and listened to the sounds of the television wafting through the evening air from the dome to the camper.

And then I'd hear Candace escorting Quill straight to bed. Do not pass Marion Flarey, do not collect your bedtime fairy tale.

And eventually I would fall asleep surrounded by my pile of books.

Only I wasn't sleeping very well. I was waking up in the middle of the night and smelling the cool night air as it drifted through the screen above my head, listening to the sounds of night animals—coyotes singing, racoons chattering, and the summer's first tree crickets had started their high-pitched ringing calls. I'd tip my head back and see the stars in the gaps between the dark treetops, and once in a while I'd see a satellite, a single point of light sweeping smoothly through the visible bits of sky.

Candace was wrong to blame me for Quill. I hadn't taught him to be a thief. I hadn't done anything wrong. I'd read him stories. Millions of people have read Jack and the Beanstalk without deciding it was okay to steal.

And I wished Fletcher was in Tibbs instead of St. Louis, and I wished my little brother wasn't a criminal, and I wished that my trip to New York City was tomorrow instead days away, still.

Although I guess I understood why Candace was so sensitive about her son and thievery. Because she'd been around when Winchell caught Ace. And that had probably left a mark, psychologically speaking. And maybe she was thinking wow, what if it's genetic? What if Quill is taking after Ace and he's going to morph, like Ace did, from a sweet, innocent little boy into a devious young man who does drugs and runs away and steals from his neighbors.

And maybe from his parents?

Because who was I kidding? He must have had something to do with Mom and Dad's money going missing, right? If he'd stolen from Fletcher, he'd probably stolen from them.

And then lied to me about it.

Oh, Ace...

And then I'd turn the light on and read some more, because there was no way I was ever going to get back to sleep, thinking thoughts like those.

Night after night, that long, long week.

And then finally it was Saturday, and the trip was tomorrow. And I was able, thankfully, to sleep in until nearly ten, because I really needed to be rested for the trip.

And I thought the camper was empty because of how quiet it felt when I slid the bedroom door open.

But it wasn't empty. Quill was there.

And the scene just about broke my heart, because he was seated on the day bed with one of my fairy tale books opened up in front of him, only when he heard me coming, he shut it and shoved it under the covers.

I recognized the book. Hans Christian Andersen. Illustrated by Arthur Rackham.

The boy jumped down from the bed and darted toward the door.

"Quill," I said. "Wait a sec."

He stopped and looked back at me.

"I have a question for you." I glanced through the screen, guiltily I suppose, to make sure Candace wasn't stomping toward the camper from the dome. "Why did you do it? Why did you have Grandma's wind chime?"

He shook his head. Meaning either "no, he didn't want to answer," or maybe "no, he didn't know why." Maybe my adult-person question implied he would have an answer, and how could he possibly have an answer? And he had a look on his face that only little kids get, eyebrows raised and eyes looking scared and hurt—the look kids get when they realize they broke a rule, but they don't understand it as a rule, so they don't show any guilt. Only pain.

I felt bad that I'd bothered him about it. "I'm sorry," I said. "I won't bug you about it anymore. Never mind. It'll be okay."

And his face changed, again. The confused, pained expression was replaced by a more set look. Stubbornness setting in. And defiance.

Which would have been striking even if it weren't Quill. But it was, and now the little boy who was the exact duplicate of a young RB now had a Candace look on his face. "It was pretty," he said suddenly, in a voice that had a hardness in it I'd never heard before. "It was a present for Effie."

"I figured that," I whispered, feeling my breaking heart break even more.

Because I understood exactly what had happened.

Quill had been pulled into a story. A story about taking something beautiful—a treasure—to make a gift to a mysterious old woman who lived in a house with magic lamps and talking birds.

He'd been pulled into a story and had tried to play out the part.

And Candace was right. It was my fault. Being around me with my fairy tales and then, worse yet, leaving him with Effie that day? Everything that is wrong with me, with my world, had begun to work on the boy, as surely as if it were an enchantment.

But it didn't mean Quill was bad. It didn't mean his mother should be upset with him.

Only how could I make Candace understand that?

"Quill. I know this is hard," I said softly. "And I promise I'll help you if I can."

He nodded. But his expression didn't change.

"I'll start by setting things right with Effie," I said. "I'll get a wind chime from Grandma. I'll buy it from her. And I'll give it to Effie. I'll tell her it's from you, a present from you. Okay?"

He considered this for a moment, his brow furrowed.

Then he nodded again. Assenting.

"I can't do it today. It will have to be next week, after we're back from New York. And it won't be the big one you picked out, because Grandma had already promised that one to someone else. But it will be just as pretty. And Effie will understand that it's all you. I'll explain that it is your idea and your present. I promise. So she'll have her present, without having to take something from someone without their permission, which is wrong. Okay?"

He didn't answer or respond.

He pressed the button on the screen door latch and flung the door open and ran down the steps.

I stood for a moment, watching him run toward the dome, only instead of going in, he ran past the door and disappeared.

Was he headed to Mom's workshop?

I rubbed my forehead.

I had to get to work. I had to brave Candace in the dome and remind Winchell I needed a ride and get myself to work.

I'd done all I could do for little Quill. At least for now.

22

When I was growing up, I didn't realize how close Tibbs was to New York City.

And in a way I suppose they aren't very close. Although it depends on how you look at it. If you drop pins on Tibbs and New York, and then zoom out to a full view of North America, the pin icons will overlap. Or touch at least. But if you consider the distance from a human point of view—well, it's a bit like in a fairy tale when little Jack or Hans or whoever grows up in a cottage with his father who is a woodcutter or a miller, and he sets out by foot and walks for days and days, winding through forests and clambering over mountains and swimming across rivers before he gets to the city. He covered maybe a hundred miles as the crow flies. But it's like he left one world and entered another.

And I suppose he's different when he gets to the city because the trip itself tested him somehow, or hardened him, or he picked up tools or allies on the way.

And sure, cars chop the travel time down to only hours but there's not really a direct route. You wind around a lot. You spend a lot of time in "are we there yet" mode.

Not out loud however because your mother is sick of that joke and might get annoyed.

And we didn't drive all the way into the city, either. We parked in Middleton and took the Metro-North into Hoboken and from there caught another train to Penn Station. Which put us in Manhattan without needing to find a place to park, which is a big plus. And who needs a car in Manhattan? But switching from car to train and then, after we reached Penn Station we were on foot, walking—it stretched the trip out. And each shift in mode seemed to mark a stage in the journey. So that I could feel, as we drew further away from Tibbs and closer to the city, that we were passing through some sort of test or some sort of hardening—me and my mom, two boon companions, drawing closer and closer to some adventure that we didn't yet understand. But that I hoped would be a relaxing adventure involving a bit of bonding with my mother followed by an idyllic and very sexy interlude with my prince.

And then we were in Manhattan. A different world than Tibbs. The air that smells bitter from car exhaust and dank from sweat and mold and urine, the light that is so different, filtered by the heavy air and reflected off buildings, diffuse and pale, and the air jangling constantly with the noise, too. The traffic, the honking cars and so many, many people jammed in the streets and walking in and out of shops and talking on their phones, and pigeons pumping their heads as they walked to get clear of our feet.

The Airbnb was in Chelsea.

A bit of a walk. And it took me only about a half a block before the straps of my backpack started to dig painful tracks into my shoulders. And why, why, why did I bring so many changes of clothes? And cosmetics? And shoes? I could have survived with two tee shirts and a stick of deodorant, right? Marion Flarey, you idiot.

And Mom, meanwhile, was walking really fast. Apparently, the straps of her backpack didn't hurt her a bit. It was bizarre, to be honest. She was almost skipping.

It was also my first clue that letting Lana Flarey loose in New York City might have unintended consequences.

But of course instead of paying attention to Mom, I was noticing, in addition to my increasingly sore shoulders, that a blister had begun to form on my right heel, and another was threatening my left instep.

"Shall we get some coffee?" I said when I caught up with Mom at a streetlight. But she didn't seem to hear me. She stepped out into the street even though the walk sign hadn't come on yet, blending perfectly with the natives who also didn't seem to care, much, about traffic laws.

I gave up trying to get her to stop. I focused instead on gripping the sole of my flats with my toes to keep them from sliding as much, in the hopes that perhaps when we reached our Airbnb, the blister would be just an inflamed, red, popped, blister, not an inflamed, red, popped, blister that was also bleeding.

She led me right to the address, too. I felt like I was following a bloodhound. Even though I'm the one who booked it. Which made sense, as I thought it over afterward, because she and Winchell used to spend a lot of time in New York City when they were younger. As you'd expect. They were a couple of counter-culture sorts, and my mom being an artist and everything. They'd leave me and Candace to babysit Ace and spend a long weekend in Manhattan. Right up until Winchell's MLM went under and they were broke. So of course Mom knew her way around. But it was impressive to see it, to see how she didn't need to think about it, she could just navigate the street v. avenue grid. She always seemed to know right where she was relative to where she wanted to go next.

We looked up at the face of the building. Then I slid my backpack off and found the slip in the front zippered pocket where I'd jotted down the building pass code.

And then we ascended a flight of dark, narrow stairs, and found the door to the apartment, and I punched in another code, and held the door open for Mom.

So she went in first. And it was funky. I mean, from a layout standpoint the apartment had been cobbled together from goodness knows what sort of space. To enter the apartment, you made a little jog one way then the other way, around a couple of corners. It had the feel, almost, of a passageway, dark and crooked. And the apartment itself was basically two big rooms, but the rooms weren't aligned, so it was like two big boxes that had been connected as an afterthought by knocking down part of the wall between.

She was standing in the second room when I caught up with her.

"An artist lives here," she whispered as she looked around.

Because yeah. That's the other thing. I'd picked a place owned by an artist. Not an artist you'll ever hear of. Nobody famous. It was one of those artists who live in New York, have lived in New York since before it got too expensive and still keeps a place there no doubt because of rent control, and has spent her life doing art and probably teaching here or there and has exhibitions once in a while but you'll never hear of her. And her apartment was full of art, pieces she'd done at various times in her life as she experimented with different media, paint and textiles and sculpture, and also art she'd collected. You could see at a glance that she'd traveled all over, collecting as she traveled.

"Do you like it? That's why I picked it," I said, setting my backpack down on the nearest of the two beds and opened it to paw through my stash of toiletries. I was hoping I'd been smart enough to pack Band-Aids.

But then I realized Mom hadn't answered and hadn't moved from where she was standing.

And I did a double take, because I realized tears were streaming down her face.

"Oh my God, mom," I said, rushing over to her, putting my arms around her. "What happened? What's wrong?"

She shook her head but didn't speak.

She felt small in my arms. How can it be that your mother, who was once so big, can feel suddenly so small in your arms?

"What's wrong?" I repeated. "Don't you like the place?"

I was thinking, darn it. She hates it. It's messy and chaotic. I could have booked one of those places that was dolled up to look like a boutique hotel room. Instead of a place that looks like it was someone's home.

But she pulled away, breaking out of my arms, and took a tissue from her pocket and wiped her eyes. And all she would say was, "The apartment is beautiful. It's amazing. It's—" She broke off and screwed her mouth into what passed for a smile. "But Mayfly. We're in New York. Let's go out and see New York. Please?"

And in a funny way, I knew then: whatever had been bugging my mom, bringing her along on this trip had been the best possible thing I could do.

But was it also the worst?

23

So you know how I told you that when we walked from Penn Station to our Airbnb apartment, Mom was moving so fast I could hardly keep up?

Well, guess what. It wasn't much better when we left the apartment and began to explore. Except this time, I was wearing sneakers, and had padded my blisters with Band-Aids. So at least I wasn't in agony as we walked.

And by the way, everything they say about Manhattan is true. The streets of that place are like the zap-zone of a psychic Tesla coil. You might not feel it in the same way you'd feel it if you stuck your finger in a light socket. But if you pay attention, it's there, a peculiar energy field, humming around you, penetrating you.

And it can make you a little crazy. I mean, depending on who you are. It didn't make me crazy. It just made me feel a little high, like the high you get when you've had just the right size cocktail.

But my Mom, on the other hand? Let's just say I was sorely tempted to yank her into a bar and force her to have a drink, just to calm her down. Up one street, down the other, in and out of shops. All in Chelsea or thereabouts. The bloodhound thing struck me again. I swear she stopped outside of restaurants and sniffed the air like she could tell what was on their menus. And just when I was certain this was completely random, don't we end up at the Whitney Museum of American Art. She darted inside and paid our admission fees. It was a bit of a respite from the street, at least. And so I was following her around, me not looking at the art so much as looking at my mom, looking at the art. And thinking to myself, there you go. Mom's an artist, and she's got her life in Tibbs, in the dome, with Winchell. And she goes to her shows, of course. Several weekends every summer she loads the back of Winchell's pickup with her wind chimes and a tent and a table and drives herself off to a show in Syracuse or Rochester or Buffalo or one of the little cities in the Finger Lakes. And I realized, for the first time, that those shows were probably a second life for my mother. She probably had artist friends that none of us had ever met. She probably went out to dinner with them after shows, and discussed the festival biz, and compared notes, and who knows? Maybe they went to museums or galleries together.

And I also realized that I was making this up. Making up a story about my mom and putting her into it. But the story made sense, because as I trailed her, watching her wander through the museum, stopping here and there to look at a piece, stepping forward to read the notes on the little plaque mounted next to it, I saw a completely different person than the woman I was around every day in Tibbs. A stranger. And from time to time she'd turn to me and make a comment. "Nice line here," she'd say, tracing a line in the air in front of a painting as she spoke. Or "look at that use of color." And it was like, okay. We're bonding now, right? And isn't that why we are here, together, on this trip? Mother and daughter? To bond?

Take it, Marion Flarey. Take in what you're seeing here today and tuck it away to think about later.

After a couple hours of this she asked if I'd seen enough. And of course my answer was "have you seen enough?" because clearly, she was gulping this experience like she'd been crawling on her hands and knees through hot sand for days and had just reached the proverbial oasis with its cool, dark, sweet spring.

"For now," she answered. "Let's go back outside."

Which is how we came to the High Line, which—if you've visited New York City recently—is a long skinny public park built on what used to be a section of elevated rail. It's very pretty, all landscaped with native grasses and wildflowery-style flowers, and the whole length is festively populated with a mix of strolling locals getting their outdoors time and tourists snapping pics of the skyline or the street life below. And there's also art installations along the trail, so again I was following my mother and watching her as she paused in front of pieces of art.

"Having fun, Mom?" I said to her as I caught up again.

"I am." She gestured out over the view that spread around us, the skyscrapers and rooftops rolling endlessly in every direction. "We are literally elevated. We are literally above it all."

Wow. She was right. And she was doing a story herself, about us and what we were doing. Which was very cool. "That's so true," I said, and we grinned at each other, and for the first time I started to feel like maybe this mother-daughter-bonding thing might work out like I'd planned. "And isn't it marvelous, how they preserved the rails?" I said. "And how they've landscaped it so that you feel like you're walking down abandoned train tracks? And they've done the landscaping to look like that, too. Only its idealized. So it's like we're standing in an Impressionist painting."

"I was thinking the same thing," Mom said.

I grinned. Because OMG that felt good. Because you know we are an awful lot alike, me and my mom. Kindred spirits. And sometimes I think that the most important thing in life is to find someone who really gets you. Know what I mean? Like, when you find someone who really gets you, that's when you maybe feel like you're not completely alone. At least for a couple moments.

We walked a bit further.

And I was thinking about how we should do dinner. So when Mom slowed down again, I pulled out my phone and started searching, using the map thing. Search for restaurants near you.

Which means that I didn't notice, at first, that something else had snagged her attention.

Only this time, it wasn't art.

It was Poetry Man.

24

He was standing on the High Line, in a little spot where the walkway opened up. Near some benches. And I suppose he was Mom's age, maybe a little older. He was wearing jeans and a Doors tee shirt, and his long graying hair was braided in a tight ponytail down his back.

And he was reciting poetry. Reading it off a little Moleskine notebook. With a Folgers can on the ground in front of him so people could give him tips.

I would have walked right by him without noticing, probably. But then I realized Mom had stopped and was listening to him.

I looked up from my phone.

The poem was political, in a cry-of-the-people sort of way. Something about our naked and impoverished being crushed under the wheels of the gilded technology machine, and the best minds of his generation having their howls stifled behind the glass screens of their smartphones, an allusion to the Ginsberg poem because why not, right?

I stood off to the side and browsed some more restaurants, until the poem seemed to be over. The five or six other people who'd stopped to listen clapped politely and someone dropped some coins into the coffee can.

I tapped Mom's arm to get her attention. "Are you hungry? There's a bunch of places near here that look pretty good."

"Yeah," she said. "I could eat, I guess."

I did a double-take. Because she wasn't really answering me. I mean, she was. But her voice had gone distant, again.

And she was looking at the poet, who was thumbing through the pages of his notebook.

"That was wonderful," Mom said, in a voice loud enough to carry.

And I did another double-take. Because I got the distinct impression that she didn't mean the poem, exactly. She meant the guy.

"Sure," I said. "So. Shall we get something to eat? I've found some options."

But OMG. That did not work. She was not listening to me. My mother was actually—OMG—she was making eyes at the poetry guy.

And worse yet, he was making eyes back, and OMG. Did he just wink at her?

"Come on, Mom," I said, my voice sounding unnaturally high-pitched. "If we go now, we won't need reservations."

Pretty smart of me to come up with justification for swift action, don't you think? Even though we hadn't actually picked a restaurant yet. But I knew she wouldn't realize that.

And yep: "Sure, honey," she said, but then she pulled out a bill and dropped it in the can.

A five-dollar bill.

Sheesh.

And they were smiling at each other. So I smiled at the guy, too, but my smile wasn't so much a smile as fearsome eye contact that shot a message that he could hopefully read that was along the lines of: careful, bud, she's married, and she's got a daughter chaperone and said daughter isn't about to let her married mother be seduced by some street performer who measures his income stream by how many lattes he can now afford at the nearest Starbucks.

I touched her elbow, trying again to break the spell.

And it worked. To my relief, we were moving again.

But unfortunately just breaking the spell wasn't good enough.

Because a little later we reached the northern end of the High Line. By then, the Hudson River had come into view, and—my mistake—I stopped a couple times to take pictures of it with my phone. And then I brought up food again. We weren't far at that point from the Gansevoort Market, which supposedly has a lobster bar, and Mom loves lobster.

"We could get lobster rolls," I said.

And then I saw him.

Poetry Man.

"Hi, again," he said as he walked up to us. "Enjoying the park?"

He was talking to Mom, not me.

"It's beautiful," she said. "It wasn't here, the last time I visited the city."

"My name's Alan," Poetry Man said, holding out his hand which of course Mom took, and did he just hang onto it a beat longer than he should have if it were an innocent handshake?

"I'm Lana," Mom said.

Okay, now I was seriously beginning to freak. Because this was supposed to be a mother-daughter getaway bonding experience that would segue easily and seamlessly into an idyllic interlude with my sweet prince charming.

It was not supposed to devolve into a mother, out on the town, spreading-her-wings-and-meeting-men type experience. Which meant that I had a decision to make. Either stage a major intervention of complete rudeness, which unfortunately might backfire by making Poetry Man seem like a more pleasant companion than The Daughter, or play along for a bit while working on my ulterior motives, which was to find a way to get rid of Poetry Man for good.

"Lobster rolls," I said to Mom, trying to get her attention focused back on lunch. "Or if you want to walk back south there's a place on 20th that's supposed to be good."

"Your work is amazing," Mom said to Poetry Man.

"I can tell you're a true lover of verse," Poetry Man replied.

Emphasis on the word lover. Right? I wasn't imagining it, was I? Because now I was no longer hungry. Because instead of hungry I was feeling a little sick to the ol' stomach.

"I'm on a Merrill kick right now," Mom said, ducking her head in a charming, shy, flirty kind of way.

OMG. What was she, reverting into a twenty-something former self that she should have retired, for good, decades and decades ago?

"Sandover?" Poetry Man breathed approvingly in response, and Mom lifted her eyes to him again and nodded, meaning that OMG this was getting worse by the second. Now they were talking a language I couldn't even follow? Sandover? What is a Sandover, please? What are you two even talking about?

"Eden tells a parable of fission," Poetry Man was saying in a solemn, formal, I'm-now-quoting-poetry tone of voice, because that's how poetry men try to seduce people's unsuspecting married mothers. "Lost world and broken home, the bitten apple stripped of its seven veils."

Okay, now we've moved to broken homes and stripping? Can ya get any more obvious with your subtext here, fella?

Yep. It was time to whip out the rude. Because somehow, some way, I needed to pry my mother's eyes away from this guy's face.

"That is lovely," I said in a voice that communicated the exact opposite, i.e., you are making me want to vomit. While I simultaneously gave Mom's elbow a little yank. "Nice to meet you, Alan. Good luck with the poetry. Mom, we have to get going, we're gonna be late."

"Sure, hon," Mom said, blinking.

I started walking, my hand still on Mom's arm to make sure she was moving again, too. "We'll try the place on 20th, okay?" I said. "The internet says it's uncomplicated but high end."

But to my horror, Poetry Man hadn't gotten the message. On the contrary. He'd fallen into step next to us. "I'm going to a reading tomorrow night," he purred. "It would be wonderful if you ladies could come."

Right. Like he wanted me along.

"I don't think—" I started to answer, but before I could finish Mom smiled and said, "why, as a matter of fact, Marion has plans tomorrow night, but I'm free."

Argh!

"Here," Poetry Man said. "I'll put the location in your phone if you want."

Noooooo!!!!

Too late. She'd stopped walking and was unlocking her phone and handing it to him. Me, meanwhile, tensing up, thinking: this is a ruse for Poetry Man to steal her phone and no way was I gonna let that happen, I was coiled and ready to pounce, I'd grab his ankles and pull him down, I'd scream bloody murder, I'd—

He handed the phone back.

It was opened to maps. He'd dropped a pin.

"I'll be there about 9," he said.

"We'll see." I shot ice cubes at him from my eyes. "We really have to get going, Mom."

And finally, finally, he got the message. Hopefully.

Unfortunately, my mom had also gotten a message. "I love New York City," she said dreamily as we reached the stairway that led back down to the street. "Nothing like this would ever happen in Tibbs."

OMG.

This is not how this trip was supposed to go.

25

I woke the next morning with this weird mix of feelings chasing themselves in circles inside my belly.

Because on the one hand, I'd been looking forward to this day for weeks. Ever since Fletcher had first floated the idea of us meeting in New York. Meeting on his turf, in his kingdom, surrounded by his people.

But on the other hand, how could I possibly leave Mom unsupervised with that Alan person preparing to pounce?

I tried to talk myself out of feeling worried. Maybe the Poetry Man encounter wasn't as sinister as I thought. Maybe I was imagining things. Maybe Mom was capable of innocent flirtations. I mean, she and Winchell had been together for 21 years, and sure, he wasn't my idea of a prince charming, but they'd always gotten along. And I'd never have thought their marriage was in serious trouble if it weren't for Candace putting weird thoughts into my head. And what did Candace know, anyway? It's not like she had any solid evidence that Mom had strayed.

I should do a better job telling Candace to skip the innuendo and stick to facts. Either that or ignore her altogether.

I heard the creaking of bedsprings and looked over to see that Mom was sitting up in her bed.

"What time do the galleries open?" I said.

"Mid-morning, most of them." She stood up and walked barefoot to her backpack to get a change of clothes. "You know," she said, "you don't have to go with me if you'd rather have the day to yourself, Marion."

"Of course I'll go with you, Mom! I want to go with you."

"What time are you meeting your boyfriend?"

"He'll text me when he gets in. It'll be late afternoon. Uh, Mom? I was thinking. Do you want to join us tonight? To go to dinner or whatever?" I paused to steady myself because I was completely winging this, and if Mom said yes, I'd need to give Fletcher a heads up that I'd invited my mother along on our date. And so much for my marvelous evening of alone-time with Fletcher in the city. But maybe some things are more important than alone time with boyfriends. And he would understand, right? "I hate to leave you all alone. And wouldn't you like to spend some time with Fletcher? Get to know him a little better and—"

"Oh, Marion!" She smiled and held up her hand, signaling me to stop. "That's very sweet but I wouldn't dream of crashing your date."

"It's not crashing, it's—"

"I'll be fine, Marion," she interrupted me again. "I have plenty to do to keep myself occupied."

OMG.

Occupied? As in by conducting a dalliance with Poetry Man?

"Mom," I tried again. Really desperate, now.

"I plan to drop in on that poetry reading," she said, confirming my worst fears.

So that I yipped, "Oh! Mom. No!" And it came out louder than I'd expected, and I instinctively clapped my hand over my mouth. "Sorry," I said, feeling my cheeks burn hot. "But Mom, that man, Alan. I don't trust him. He's—"

"Marion Sadie Flarey," she said, straightening her body slightly, indignant. "You cannot possibly think that I am unable to look after myself for a few hours in the big city."

"But he—his—"

"He flirted with me, Marion. So what? It happens, you know. Even to old ladies."

"You're not an old lady." I heard myself say the words and it struck me, as I did, that I was now arguing to my mom that she was young and presumably attractive enough to be out there in the singles marketplace winning boyfriends and influencing people.

I mean, whose side was I on?

"The thing is," I said, "I'd like to spend more time with you. Hey, I know, maybe Fletcher and I could meet you at the reading!"

"Oh, come on, Marion, don't be ridiculous. Fletcher doesn't want to be stuck listening to amateur poets prattle on for hours and hours. And neither do you. You'd both hate it."

She had a point, there. But I wasn't ready, yet, to give in. "But this weekend is supposed to be our mother-daughter thing. I can't abandon you!"

"You're not abandoning me. We agreed we would hang out for a day and then you'd have your date with Fletcher. Go on your date, just like we planned, and tomorrow morning we'll head home, just like we planned."

What could I do?

She can be stubborn.

It runs in the family.

That doesn't make it any easier.

26

Six hours and Lord knows how many galleries later—I lost count—I did the thing.

I left my Mom to her fate and went back to the Airbnb to shower and change.

I'd packed four possible outfits, so it took me a bit of time to make my choice. But ultimately, I decided on a skirt and a scoopy rayon sleeveless top that seemed perfect for a steamy summer night in Manhattan.

And rayon droops and clings so nicely.

And Fletcher picked me up a little before four o'clock in—get this—a private car. He texted me that he was outside, and I went downstairs and out into the street, and there he was. Standing next to a big, dark car that looked like a cross between a limo and a sedan. And he opened the back door and I got in, and he slid in beside me. And there I was, sitting on the smooth black leather, inhaling the scent of leather mixed with Fletcher's cologne, and part of my brain was going holy crap, I'm in a private car with my boyfriend in New York City, and the other part of my brain is going: *Marion Flarey. You are leaving your mom unattended and now she's going to start a passionate affair with Poetry Man.*

Fletcher pulled me into his arms, and we kissed, the sweet softness of his lips reminding me all over again what a lucky gal I was.

"Ready to have some fun?" he asked.

"Am I ever."

But almost instantly, the woozy deliciousness bubbling up inside me got whacked aside by the disturbing inner image of Poetry Man, kissing my mother the way Fletcher had just kissed me. I sat back and smoothed my skirt and murmured, "I'm a little worried about Mom, though," wondering as I spoke how much I wanted to get into any more Weekes-Flarey craziness, considering that the last conversation we'd had about my family hadn't gone terribly well.

"Oh?" Fletcher leaned forward and gave an address to the driver through the little sliding window between the front and back seats, then turned back toward me. "What's going on with your Mom?"

I hesitated, because what was I going to say? *I worry that she might start an extramarital affair?* So that, what, Fletcher would think my mom was some kind of ho? *She's gotten involved with a street performer?* Like we were a couple of rubes, next I'd confess we'd lost a hundred bucks at three card monte?

Best to just let it drop. Pretend I hadn't said anything. But then Fletcher picked up my hand, and as the car pulled out from the curb, he prompted me to tell him more. "Isn't she enjoying the city?"

Okay. Maybe I could go at it sideways. "You know how much she loves poetry," I ventured slowly.

He didn't know, of course, but he said "sure," the way people do, agreeing they know something as a way of accepting a story's underlying assumptions.

"So, yesterday we met a guy about her age, and he invited her to a poetry reading. And I guess she's going. It's tonight." I paused, and to be honest part of me was hoping Fletcher would turn to me and say, "Poetry reading? I love poetry readings! We should meet her there!"

But of course he didn't. Because first of all, while I was talking, he got distracted by something he saw through the window and dropped my hand and turned his head around like he was watching something or someone as we drove. And then he gave his head a shake and settled back into the seat and put his arm around my shoulder and pulled me toward him again, because in the back seat of a private car in

Manhattan you don't need to be strapped in by seatbelts on the other side of the car. So you can snuggle. And then he said, "I'm sorry, Marion. What were you saying?"

"Oh, it's nothing. I'm sure it will be fine. But I feel a bit strange, knowing my mom is going out on her own, like that."

"Oh. She'll be fine," Fletcher said.

"I'm sure she will. Only to be honest, I feel like she's in a vulnerable place, right now. She's been acting a bit strange, lately. And being here, in the city, has had an odd effect on her."

Fletcher may or may not have been paying close attention. Because instead of answering, he turned his face to me and lifted my chin and kissed me again.

It took me a couple moments to get my breath back and re-collect my thoughts.

"I just hope the guy doesn't take advantage of her," I said when I could think again.

"She's a grown woman." Fletcher smiled. "I'm sure she can handle herself."

And there. See, Marion Flarey? You're all worked up over nothing.

Your Mom can handle herself.

Don't let your crazy family and their goofy problems steal your chance at happiness. Ever, ever.

I re-nestled myself into my boyfriend's arms. "Where are we headed?"

"First stop, a drink with a couple of my friends." Fletcher's hand caressed my shoulder as he spoke. "Then dinner. Just you and me."

My insides started to turn to goo again. "Sounds like perfection," I whispered.

And anyway, I could always check in with my mom periodically by text. And as long as she responded in a fairly timely fashion, I would know that she was, er, engaged in licit activities.

Right?

• • • • •

And the evening was magical, naturally.

Starting with happy hour on a rooftop patio with Fletcher's friends, drinking wine, listening to their chitchat, while right there in front of me was the skyline including, yes, the Empire State Building.

Of course I felt a little shy, so I didn't talk much myself, except once when someone asked Fletcher how business was going and he mentioned Booch4U and said I was running it for him. Which was, like, wow. Running the place for him? Like, not just managing the tasting room but running the whole thing? What a feeling. I was more than a girlfriend, I was a partner! A business partner! And isn't that exactly what I'd wanted?

And their chitchat was interesting, life-in-the-big-city stuff. They compared notes on places to eat, where they'd had good food and where the service was terrible. And one of the couples had just come back from a trip to Thailand so they were full of stories about the amazing food, and the amazing snorkeling, and how nice the locals were. And then they shared gossip about other people they knew, this person was getting a divorce and that person had a cancer scare but it turned out to be nothing.

I sipped wine and checked the time and then texted Mom.

Who texted right back.

Two galleries want to exhibit my work!

Wow.

I texted back *omg that is so great!* and then considered how to pose my next question.

I decided: just be direct, Marion.

what are you up to now?

Back at the apartment. Resting. Did a lot of walking today.

Okay, then. So far, so good. And maybe she'd tired herself out. Maybe she was so tired that she'd decide to stay in and go to bed early, rather than head back out, later.

"More wine, Marion?" Fletcher asked and I nodded and held out my glass. And wow, he was handsome and was I really here? Did I really have a whole evening ahead of me with that sexy man who was now leaning in for another kiss, right in front of his rich Manhattan friends, and I take another sip of wine and did I mention that's the Empire State Building over there?

I mean, did you see that?

It's the Empire State Building. With the late afternoon sun turning the air all golden and shimmery like we're standing in front of a painting layered by golden, shimmering paint…

• • • • •

Fletcher's favorite New York City restaurant turned out to be a farm-to-table type place. And the food was incredible. We ordered cocktails (Fletcher's was the most expensive Old Fashioned I'd ever seen and mine was purple because one of the ingredients was plum shrub, and was garnished by a fresh hibiscus) and then the server brought us each an amuse-bouche (mouthful of scallops ceviche topped with some sort of crazy fragrant foam) and then we had appetizers (fire-grilled oysters and chicory and chervil salads, we split both dishes) and then a bottle of wine even finer than the wine we'd drunk with his friends on the rooftop, and then our entrees.

I had the skate. Fletcher had the most expensive steak I've ever seen.

By then I was loopy from all the alcohol and drunk on love because of how Fletcher kept reaching out and touching my forearm with the tips of his fingers.

I admit it. Don't tell Candace, but, for a little while, I completely forgot about Mom.

Until I got up to visit the restroom and like a jolt it hit me that it had to be after nine, right? Because this had not been the sort of meal that goes by at exactly rapid-fire pace.

So I took my bag with me to the bathroom, and when I sat down in my stall, I pulled out my phone and tapped another quick text to Mom.

how's it going

My phone buzzed a minute later as I rinsed the soap from my hands in the massive white and black marble sink.

I'm at the reading! Some of the work is quite good.

Ugh.

I pictured her in some low-ceilinged place below street level that smelled like stale beer and sweat, with peoples' faces lit orange by faux candles on the table, and a little stage in front where thin, earnest-faced students stood up one by one, reading impassioned verse about the environment or love or the emptiness of modern life. And the picture started to evolve in my mind so that it looked like the scene in Funny Face where Audrey Hepburn does her interpretive dance, and my mom—in the picture—was now dressed completely in black, slim black jeans and black mock turtleneck, and her hair pulled back in a tight ponytail, and she was seated at a little table with Poetry Man who was looking down at her with an expression on his face just like the wolf when he sized up Little Red Cap...

Argh!

I looked up at myself in the mirror.

Was it too late to ask Fletcher, outright, if he would please take us to a poetry reading?

But she's a grown woman, Marion. And she'll be fine. And maybe Poetry Man is hoping to get laid but he didn't strike me as a serial killer sort although isn't that the thing about serial killers? They never seem like serial killers to their victims?

And what would Candace say if she found out that instead of bonding with our mother on this trip, I'd helped her begin a florid and life-changing love affair?

I put my phone away and retouched my lip gloss and squared my shoulders and started back to the table.

Fletcher looked up as I threaded toward him, and oh, the look in his eyes as I slid back into my chair.

Now I was Little Red Cap. And Fletcher was licking his chops.

"Shall we go back to my place for dessert?" he said.

Leaving no doubt what he meant by dessert.

• • • • •

Fletcher's place was on the Upper East Side. One of those narrow little streets you find when you wander a block or two away from Central Park, where the trees along the sidewalks lean inward because that's where the light is brightest. Brick, attached homes with arched windows and decorative cast iron metalwork. Although technically it wasn't Fletcher's place, it was his father's. His father lived there when he was in the U.S. and not Europe or Japan.

"Home sweet home," Fletcher said as we walked up the steps.

He took me on a quick tour. First the formal part of the house: the front sitting room, the dining room, the library. All high ceilings and dark polished wood, the walls with their wainscoting and crown molding, the floors hardwood, layered with thick, plushy rugs. Furniture all the stately sort that looked like it was more for posing than for sitting. Cross your legs and smile for the camera, dahlink. Then the kitchen with its granite counters and glass cabinets and huge copper pans hanging on the wall, ready for a celebrity chef to stride in with a catering crew to whip up some fabulous meal that would be, of course, a fusion of something-something and something-something else.

It was all so beautiful. And there were lights on sensors in every room so that as you walked through, they turned on automatically. The light would come up slowly, which combined with the soaking silence and desertedness of the house made you feel like you were walking through a space that had been sleeping and was only now waking as you entered and would fall asleep again in a few moments, as soon as you left.

And then up a flight of stairs, and there was a media room, one end three rows of leather club chairs facing a huge white screen, the other end a pool table.

And then Fletcher's room.

On the fifth floor. And the entire wall and a section of the roof had been replaced by glass. Big panes latticed with wrought iron, giving that end of the room a Victorian greenhouse feel.

"This was a terrace, originally," he said as we stood in front of the glass and gazed out over the glittering uptown skyline. "The couple who owned the house before Dad bought it enclosed the terrace to enlarge the room."

And the furnishings in this room weren't old-fashioned. Exact opposite. Chic modern.

Including a California King platform bed.

And now, I am going to shoo you out and shut the door...

27

I opened my eyes.

What time was it?

The sky, through the glass wall at the other end of the bedroom, was a bright pale orangish color that would have meant dawn in Tibbs but in the city meant nothing, in the city it was the reflection of a million streetlights, a million million outdoor lights scattering uncountable quadrillions of orange photons up into the night air like a seeping pale orange mist…

I could hear Fletcher breathing.

I'd been sleeping on my stomach and there was a crick in my neck and the start of a little headache—too much wine!—I could feel it, like a small warm throbbing cap of pain spreading around the muscles of my scalp and forehead…

I caterpillared through the covers and away from Fletcher, until I reached the edge of the bed.

I fumbled on the nightstand for my phone.

Four-thirty.

Mom and I would have to be at the train station by six if I was going to get to work on time…

MOM!

I'd completely forgotten about Mom. About Poetry Man. And OMG she was back at the Airbnb by now, right? She wouldn't have spent the night someplace else. Or maybe she was at the Airbnb but not alone? Maybe she was right now lying in bed next to a man listening to him breathing and checking the time and—

And I needed to get back to the Airbnb and chase that horrid Alan person out of her bed only what if she wasn't there? What if she was at that horrible Alan person's apartment? Would I have to take an Uber to that horrid Alan person's apartment and bang on the door and insist she come with me that very moment? Or what if that horrid Alan person was a serial killer and—

"Hey, beautiful," Fletcher murmured, and I felt the bed move and then he was reaching over and pulling me back toward him and OMG this was intoxicating and what about Mom and—

Oops. Closing the door again for a bit...

• • • • •

"Okay if I call you a taxi?"

"Of course." I was crouched, gathering up various bits of clothing that had somehow gotten scattered around the bedroom floor. Because I got it. Fletcher had to catch a plane back to St. Louis today, and thanks to our little linger-in-bed interlude this morning he was cutting things close. So he needed to put me in a taxi and send me on my way. And anyway, this is how couples like us roll, high-powered couples running businesses in different cities at the same time. Right?

I stood up and the throbbing in my head intensified for a moment.

I sat back on the edge of the bed.

Also, in a way, it would be a relief to be in a taxi. Because the uneasiness in my stomach about Mom was back, big time. Uneasiness and guilt because the whole point of this trip was for me to somehow rescue her, to break whatever enchantment was working on her, and sure, the other purpose of the trip was to spend time with Fletcher, but I'd had that time and I'd let Mom down. Mom and Candace and Winchell and Quill. So it was a bit of a relief to feel like I was closing out my wonderful bonding time with Fletcher and could now turn my attention entirely to this other nagging problem in my life.

I'd borrowed Fletcher's charge cord to add a little juice back to my phone.

I tapped out an innocent little text.

U up? B there in 15.

Thinking as I hit send that hopefully fifteen minutes was enough time for her to rouse Poetry Man and get him the hell out before I strode into the apartment and discovered him and mom in bed under the covers, engaged in, er, exploring each other's iambic pentameters.

Ugh. Stop it, Marion Flarey. Get dressed and think about something else. Think about Fletcher. You have a few more minutes with Fletcher. Use it wisely, girl.

I could see him through the door to the bathroom. He was shirtless and the muscles of his back and arms and shoulders flexed as he bent toward the mirror over the sink and cleaned up the edges of his beard with an electric trimmer. And you know what? That was what I wanted. More than anything. To wake up every morning with this gorgeous man, to look into the bathroom every morning to see this gorgeous man trimming his facial hair…

He turned the trimmer off and turned toward me, and it crossed my mind as I watched him walk to his dresser and open a drawer and lift out a perfectly folded black tee shirt that maybe we could postpone that taxi by a few more minutes? And here he was coming back over toward me and I bet if I smiled at him in a certain way, he'd put that shirt aside…

His phone buzzed, and he picked it up and read a text and I watched his fingers—perfectly proportioned just like the rest of him, masculine but refined—tap out a reply.

"Welp, Marion, guess what?" he said, looking up. "Looks like I'll be back in Tibbs this week."

My heart jumped happily. And had I heard that right? Fletcher? Back in Tibbs? This week? Could this really be happening? "When?" I gasped. Headache forgotten. Mom's possible horrid nighttime escapades forgotten.

He pulled the shirt over his head. "Yep. I have a couple guys who are interested in buying the brewery."

"Really?" I said again and my heart jumped even more happily because—stupidly, it turns out—I assumed he was talking about St. Louis. He was selling the St. Louis brewery, what else? Which meant he wouldn't have to travel as much, he could be in Tibbs more and we'd be able to meet in the city more and maybe start taking other trips together. Right? "Are you meeting them today?" I said happily.

He picked up a bottle of cologne from the dresser and unscrewed the top and tipped the bottle against the palm of his hand. "No. I'm in St. Louis today." He set the bottle down and swiped his palm against his neck and then muttered, more to himself than to me, "This means I have to find someone by tomorrow to run St. Louis, though, now that I think about it. Damn it."

I felt a sudden flicker of confusion. "Wait," I said. "Which brewery are we talking about? That you're selling?"

"Tibbs," he said, screwing the top back on to the cologne bottle. "Booch4U."

What? "Really?" My voice sounded funny. "Booch4U? I don't understand."

He gave me a quizzical look. "Yeah. Is that a problem, Marion?"

A problem? You mean a problem like: until that very moment, I didn't realize he was planning to sell our brewery?

"Marion?"

I didn't answer. Because I was struggling to control myself. It was the lack of sleep. It was the non-acceptable amounts of alcohol last night. And the worry about Mom and—

I heard him moving toward me.

He had my chin in his hand and was forcing me to raise my eyes and look at him.

"I'm sorry," he said. "Didn't we talk about this? I thought we'd talked about this. I thought you knew."

I blinked back a sudden wash of tears. "I—uh." I blinked again. "I knew you were thinking about selling it. Maybe. One day." Blink, blink. "But I didn't know it was—I didn't know it would be right now."

He gave a subtle little bob to his head, his eyes still on mine, as he absorbed what I was saying. "I see," he said. "But of course it's for sale, Marion. Everything is."

Everything?

"It's what I do, Marion." His head bobbed slightly again. "I get these businesses going and then I sell them. That's where the money is. You know that."

"Yes. Of course. I know," I said in a voice that I was trying to make sound reasonable but came out with a little catch in my throat.

"Hey," he said again, and he dropped my face and pulled me into his arms. "I didn't mean to upset you. It'll be okay. It won't change anything. You'll still have your job."

"My job?" I pushed myself back, jolted all over again. Like he'd zapped me with another shock before I'd even absorbed the first one.

"Marion?" His forehead puckered in a confused little frown. "You need the job. Right? That's what you told me."

Couldn't argue with that one. Student loans, owe Winchell money, bad habit of spending money I didn't really have on old fairy tale books, blah blah blah. "Yeah," I said. "It's just that..."

But I trailed off. Because it seemed so ridiculous, now, to say what was in my heart.

That the brewery wasn't a job, to me. It was so much more.

It was me and Fletcher. It was our life together.

That, to me, the brewery was a cornerstone of a story I'd been telling myself that went something along the lines of once upon a time, two people who'd been torn apart found each other again, and opened a wonderful little kombucha brewery together in Tibbs, New York, and got married and moved into a big stone house and had a family and ran their brewery and lived happily ever after.

And such is life.

The story Fletcher had been spinning in *his* head?

It was completely different.

I looked around the room. Aware, once more, of the gorgeous, expensive furniture, the chic floor lamps, the plush wool rug I was standing on with its beautiful art nouveau pattern, and of course the glass wall and beyond that, the New York skyline.

It was so beautiful. So rich.

So exotic.

And I'd known all along, of course, that Fletcher lived in a different world than I did.

This world.

I just hadn't thought, until that very moment, that maybe the story I'd been telling myself was missing some important bits. That I'd been thinking in a vague way that yeah, Fletcher and I would spend weekends in Manhattan or jet off to cool places to vacation, Europe or Japan or Thailand or Java or someplace. But that I'd thought of all this as interludes to our real life, the life that we'd spend together in Tibbs.

What a fool I'd been.

I needed to do a re-write.

Fast.

I cleared my throat. "Of course I understand, Fletcher," I said. "I'm sorry I reacted that way. I'm a little tired, is all."

"No worries," he said. He still had that concerned look on his face. "Like I said, nothing will change. I promise."

Nothing?

I let him fold me back into his arms, and then we kissed.

Me thinking, *good. Do this.*

Kiss me and make it better.

• • • • •

And then I was sitting by myself in the taxi, telling myself that I needed to calm down, that it was okay, it was going to be fine. I mean, the guy's got a business to run, and it doesn't take a Sherlock to see that he enjoys it, or to figure out that the more successful he is, the brighter our future as a couple. And just because his story turned out to be different than my story didn't mean his story was wrong.

And he'd still have the house in Tibbs. So even if he didn't have to come to Tibbs for the business, he'd come to stay. To see me. And I could always meet him in New York or fly to some other city to spend time with him. Right?

The taxi turned onto 21st Street and I checked my phone again and now there was a text from Mom.

I'm up and ready.

My stomach lurched queasily, and I couldn't help but think again about the lady enchanted by her evil lover. Which meant, what?

That even a Very Good person can become Bad if they fall into the wrong hands. If they let themselves become enchanted and the enchantment captures their minds and makes them think that what is true is false and what is false is true.

We pulled up to the curb and I told the taxi driver to wait, because if Mom and I were going to get to the train station in time we were gonna need another ride, right now.

I keyed in the passcode and climbed the stairs and keyed in the passcode to the apartment and stepped inside.

Bracing myself for what I might find. For the sight of Poetry Man standing and stretching and scratching himself and rubbing his eyes and grabbing my mother and planting a little kiss on her lips and saying, "See you again soon, I hope?"

Ugh.

28

But, phew. Poetry Man wasn't there. No Poetry Man, and even better, no evidence at all that a demonic lover had been lurking about, casting spells on my unsuspecting mother. Her bed was made, the pillows all plumped and the bedspread smooth. She was standing up as I walked in and now she gestured at our backpacks on the floor next to the door. "I packed your stuff," she said. "And I got you a coffee."

She handed me a Starbucks venti latte.

"And I bought a New York Times, too, of course." She smiled dreamily. "We can read it on the train." But then she looked at me more closely. "Marion? Do you feel okay?"

No. No, I did not. I felt wobbly and my head hurt, and my insides felt like maybe the demonic lover had set up shop there, to do whatever demonic lovers do. Gyre and gimble. "It was a bit of a late night for me," I explained wanly. "The taxi's waiting for us. Shall we get going?"

She nodded.

But there was a crease between her brows.

• • • • •

The train seemed noisier and janglier this morning than it had on the way into the city. But fortunately the coffee settled my stomach a bit, so I sipped it and peeked at my mother. She'd opened the paper and was happily scanning the columns of tight text.

"Anyway," I said, cautiously. "How'd it go for you, last night?"

"It was lovely. I had a lovely time."

Oh dear. That sounded suspicious. *Lovely?* What did she mean by that, "lovely?"

"Some of the poetry was quite good," she said.

"And how was Alan?" I asked, studying her face closely but discretely as I waited for her answer.

"Wonderful."

Oh, God. I took another sip of coffee to fortify myself. "Wonderful? How so?"

And if she'd been a girlfriend girlfriend, she'd have taken the bait. Because what girlfriend girlfriend doesn't want to share? When she'd spent at least part of the night with a man she'd just met the day before?

But instead, Mom shrugged and turned to the next page of the paper. "Just—wonderful," she said.

Because she wasn't a girlfriend girlfriend.

She was my mother.

"And how about you?" She looked up from her paper. "How was your date with Fletcher?"

"It was fun," I said, keeping my voice bright and relaxed. "It was perfect. I met some of his friends. We had drinks on the roof of their apartment. We could see the Empire State Building. And then we went out to eat, one of the best meals I've ever had."

And then I went quiet, because I felt like I was sounding more and more fake the longer I talked. Because yes, I'd had fun. But my fun had been painted over, this morning, with something not fun at all. Like a gorgeous mural, defaced by graffiti.

I looked down at the white plastic lid of my coffee cup, thinking again about how much I'd misinterpreted Fletcher's plans for our life.

For his life.

"Marion?" Mom said. "Honey. What's wrong? What happened?"

"It's nothing," I said.

Right. Try convincing your mother that nothing's wrong.

While the tears start sliding down your face...

29

So, the whole point of my planning a trip with my mother to New York City was that we would reconnect. Bond as mother and daughter.

Because I was worried about her. I could tell something was wrong and she wasn't talking about it and I wanted to create a space where she would feel safe enough to discuss it with me. Because my mother is a solitary soul in a lot of ways, and that's not always healthy, right? You need to be able to unburden yourself to another human being, once in a while.

And what better human being for a mother to confide in than her daughter?

So what happens?

The exact opposite.

I ended up being the person doing the confiding. Unburdening myself. Telling her that Fletcher was going to sell the brewery, and how it had taken me by surprise, and it seemed so very different than what I'd imagined was going to happen between us, and how was I supposed to deal with that?

"Oh, Marion," she said when I had finished. "Come here."

She held her arms open and I leaned over and she put them around me.

Like I was a little girl again.

Which only made me cry harder.

"It'll be okay," I heard her say when at long last the tears began to slow.

"I know," I whispered. But I didn't know. Not at all.

"Marion," she said, "I'm going to tell you something I've never told anyone else before."

So okay. Those were pretty intriguing words. Intriguing enough that I felt a little twitch inside me, like Curious Marion had raised her head and was now paying attention, so that Distressed Marion didn't seem quite so real anymore. Like Distressed Marion was put on hold, for now.

And I couldn't help thinking: this is it. She's going to tell me the truth about herself. About Alan, maybe. What she did last night.

About her marriage. About some other affair…

And then, sure enough, after a couple of moments when I could feel her gather her thoughts, her first words were, "It's about your stepfather."

Curious Marion now put Distressed Marion completely aside. "Oh yeah?" I said aloud, while inside I was thinking: here it is. Here it comes…

"I think, in some ways, Fletcher might be a little like him."

Huh?

So that was not what I expected. Not at all.

Fletcher? Handsome, successful, Fletcher? Was like *Winchell?*

I sat up, leaning away from my mother so I could see her face. "What do you mean?"

"Oh," she laughed her mild laugh. "I don't mean they're exactly alike. Just in one way." And she pressed her lips together for a couple seconds, like she was taking special care in how she chose her words. And then she nodded like she'd made her decision. "It has to do with money. No, not money. With the material world."

And I suppose, as she said those words, I started to get an inkling of where she was going. But only an inkling. "I'm not sure I understand," I said, feeling a bit of a pucker between my brows. And what did my mother know about Fletcher?

"Winchell is a dear, dear man," she said. "And I love him very much. But he is very, very peculiar about money."

Okay. I couldn't help but laugh a little then. Because "peculiar" was an understatement. The man was obsessed with money, really. One of these people who thinks about money constantly, constantly reminds everyone around him about money, about how much things costs. About how difficult his finances are.

But then my amusement faded, replaced again by confusion.

Because Fletcher wasn't tight with money. On the contrary. He spent freely. Because, unlike Winchell, he'd been born into wealth. So he'd never needed to stop himself from spending too much. He'd never had to worry that, no matter how fine things were today, they might fall apart tomorrow. He'd never known what it was like to think you'd damn well better hang on tight to whatever bit of money you have in your hand, because you never know. Fletcher would always be completely safe, financially. No matter how much he spent, there would always be more. When his father died, he'd come into an enormous inheritance. Money, investments, property. And in the meantime, he had all the tools and support he needed to build his own business empire, an empire that would churn out additional wealth, the sort of wealth that most people could never dream of.

How was he, in any way, like Winchell?

Mom felt my confusion. She read it in my face. "What I mean," she said, "is that maybe they both measure things in terms of their material worth."

The pucker between my eyes deepened into a frown. And yet, I suddenly started to understand.

Mom had a point.

But I'd never looked at it that way, before. That being poor and obsessing about money—money in the form of the household budget or the grocery bill or the utility bill—was as materialistic, in a way, as being rich and obsessing about money in the form of your investment portfolio.

Or the business you'd founded that you now planned to sell.

And as I sat there, beginning to understand, I realized something else.

I realized that Mom was the complete opposite.

I'd never heard her worry about money.

Not once. Not even in our family's darkest days, when Candace and I were in high school and Dad's business had gone bust, and we'd gone from comfortable middle-class people who—according to Winchell, anyway—were on our way to becoming rich, to living on a shoestring.

Memories of that time washed suddenly through my mind. Dad, pacing. Shouting at us, shouting at Mom. Cursing the guys who'd started the company and then messed it up so badly. They'd run afoul of the government. They'd gotten caught cheating.

He was a mess. He gained weight. He started drinking too much.

I remember him saying he was ruined. A ruined man. How old-fashioned the words sounded, like something from a 19th Century novel. I remember his fear. And I could almost smell our fear as well, me and Candace's, as we let his fury and panic infect us, pull us into the swirling sinking whirlpool of failure that suddenly defined our father's entire life…

But not Mom.

Mom was seemingly untouched.

I don't think I'd noticed it, at the time. But I could see her, too, in this sudden flashback that played out in my mind. How calm she'd been. How she would listen to him and remain completely calm. How she never argued, never got angry at him but also never really took his side.

It was then that she began doing art again. She'd let her art lapse for years. She'd been helping Winchell with the MLM. But suddenly she began to disappear into her workshop to do pottery. She began taking it to shows, selling it.

And all this time, I'd assumed she'd done this for purely practical reasons. Because she realized she needed to earn money—now that Winchell was a ruined man—and so she set out, quietly and practically, to do just that. And so she'd come home from one of her art shows with a few hundred dollars—cash, those days, there was no Apple Pay in those days—and leave it on the kitchen counter. She never said a word about it, which I sensed even then was because of Winchell's pride, that it would have seemed humiliating to him that he was now a complete financial failure, dependent on his wife to pay the bills, to put food on the table for his family.

And that—all of that—had seemed to me at the time as Mom, being practical. But now I saw that it was something else. I saw that it had come out of her very nature. It was in her nature to remain calm, to turn her attention to art and to what art represents, a different world, a world apart from the concerns about money and food and shelter.

It was a spiritual thing she had done. A spiritual choice.

The money she made from it was more of an after-effect than a motivation.

Her eyes were on my face, searching my face, aware that I was putting things together, thinking about things in a new way.

"When Dad's business went under," I said, "it must have been really hard on you."

"The hard part was watching the man I loved forget who he really is." She looked away for a second, then looked back. "He lost his center. He did some terrible things."

Ace.

"What things?" I whispered.

"I can't—it wouldn't be fair of me to tell you." She looked away again. "He's my husband, Marion. He's not perfect. Nobody is. But he is a good man, at heart. He just needed to find his way, again."

"And did he?"

"I think so." She sighed. "Maybe. I'm not sure."

But then her expression changed, and I saw a gleam of something else. Determination, maybe. But also humor.

Devilish humor.

"What?" I said, because now I was all-over curious again.

"Sorry?"

She didn't realize that her face had given something away.

"Mom." I touched her arm. "What else? What else happened?"

"Not sure what you mean, Marion."

"Come on. You can't fool me. You didn't just sit quietly on the sidelines during that whole thing. You—"

Hah. She gave me a bit of a guilty look. She was caught and she knew it.

But if I expected a full confession, I was sorely mistaken. "Some things in a marriage are between the wife and the husband only. But let's just say that sometimes, my husband needs a bit of a nudge."

I sank back against the train seat.

Clearly, I wasn't going to get any more out of her on that topic. Not that day.

But I was thinking, again, about Ace.

Maybe Candace was wrong. Maybe Mom knew what had happened. Maybe she knew about the stolen money and how Winchell had thrown Ace out of the house.

"Mom?"

"Yes, dear."

"What about Ace? What did—"

But before I could really formulate my question, her manner changed. Her face, which had taken on a soft, dreamy expression, became tight. "What do you mean?"

"I'm just wondering. I wasn't around. I know he and Dad had some sort of argument—"

She gave her head a vigorous shake, cutting me off. "You've been in touch with him, haven't you."

I felt my face get hot.

How had she guessed?

"Just tell me he's alive and okay, Marion. You don't need to tell me anything more."

"He's alive," I whispered. "He's okay. He's—"

She raised her hand quickly to cut me off again. "As long as he's alive, that's enough."

"I don't mind—"

"No. That's enough."

She picked the paper back up and unfolded it and opened it to the Metro section.

I'd come very, very close to breaking my promise. Because what I was going to say, before she cut me off, was that I wouldn't mind telling her. Telling her more.

But she didn't want to hear it. Any of it.

And so we stopped talking. She read her paper and I closed my eyes and dozed and thought about my little brother. And how much it must hurt my mother that she'd lost him. That one of her children who had left hadn't returned, and would maybe never return, because something awful had happened that made it impossible for him to return.

And I couldn't let that happen.

I decided all over again, there on that commuter train as we sped away from the city and toward the rest of our lives, that somehow, some way, I was going to fix this thing.

30

The first day of work after we got back to Tibbs was a bit of a blur.

A blurry nightmare.

I had to rush straight to work when we got home. And a dose of ibuprofen helped my headache, but I still didn't feel right. A bit weak and dazed like my brain couldn't keep track of things. I kept having to ask customers to repeat their orders, which made me feel stupid and OMG my tip jar had never looked so empty and forlorn.

It was the hangover, but also the shock, of course. The shock of realizing that the Happily Ever After I'd woven together in my mind was a complete fantasy with no relation to reality, because reality included a prince charming who had a completely different idea about HEAs than I did.

Which is a problem with tender, new relationships, right? You haven't had a chance to work out the HEA vision details. You haven't had those hours and hours of heart-to-heart talks that new couples need to make sure they're picturing the same castles and courtyards and carriages and heirs.

And conquests.

But I slept like a rock that night, and the next morning I felt a bit more settled.

And when I ventured cautiously into the dome that morning, it seemed like Candace was maybe feeling a bit friendlier. She said "morning" and took a mug from the cupboard and handed it to me instead of shooting me a dirty look. Which gave me hope that maybe we'd be able to have a mature and rational conversation about Quill, and maybe I'd even be able to start reading him bedtime stories again, because I missed that, and fairy tales weren't going to hurt him no matter what Candace might believe.

And so, by the time Winchell dropped me off at the brewery, I'd made my peace with my new reality.

In fact, maybe things were going to be fine. Sure, it was a little setback, because Fletcher wouldn't own the Tibbs brewery anymore. But I would still be the tasting room manager. Hopefully. And that put me in a highly advantageous position. Because Fletcher hadn't jumped on any of my ideas of how to improve the brewery, but now I'd get a second chance.

With my new boss.

And I would shine. I'd be the wunderkind of kombucha brewery tasting room managers. And one day Fletcher would come to Tibbs and stop by the brewery and my new boss would be there and remark that wow, of all the assets he'd acquired when he bought the place, the most valuable by far was Marion Flarey. Her instincts are so astute, Fletcher! Did you have any idea what you had here? And wait until you see the books! We've doubled our revenues and our restaurant business is taking off, and breaking news! Next week a crew from Saveur magazine is coming in for a photo shoot! And I still don't know how Marion found that amazing chef who isn't her brother but we actually have people flying in from all over the country just to eat here.

They're flying in from Seattle. From L.A. From Paris! They're flying in from Paris to eat at Booch4U!

And Fletcher's eyes would widen in astonishment and I'd feel him looking at me as I blushed softly before rushing over to greet another party walking in the door.

And then later that night (he'd wait for me for hours after close because we were so busy it would take a long time for the place to empty out) we'd be lying in bed in each other's arms and I'd be almost asleep when he'd touch my cheek and say, "I was thinking, Marion. As much as you love Booch4U, have you ever thought of joining me as a full-time partner and helping me with my other breweries?"

I looked up. I looked around the tasting room. And I could see it now, just like it would be. The new décor. The party of four that had flown in from Paris, sitting over there in the corner, exclaiming rapturously about the food.

All I had to do was come off as credible and professional and knowledgeable to my new boss, and I could make it happen.

I grabbed my phone and went online and right then and there ordered a bunch of books on business and marketing, because maybe I couldn't manage going back to school, but who needs a degree today when you can read books by the leading experts in their fields?

And I hit the payment button, and then stood up and got to work.

The Booch4U buyers were coming tomorrow.

My new bosses.

The ticket to my new future.

I'd have this place looking perfect by the time they got there. Scrubbed, straightened, sparkling.

Because Fletcher might think he was selling a brewery?

But I, Marion Flarey, would be selling to the same buyers.

Only I'd be selling something else entirely.

31

I arranged to borrow Winchell's truck that next morning. Because even though my probably-new-boss and Fletcher wouldn't arrive at the brewery until one o'clock, I wanted to get there early so that I could do a final check and make sure everything was perfect, and if I drove myself, I wouldn't have to worry about Winchell dawdling or deciding, en route, that he had to stop at an ATM, and making me late.

I parked around the side and let myself in the back door, a metal door that was heavy and tended to stick, so that to open it, I had to brace my shoulder against it and push.

I flicked on the light.

And I heard myself shriek.

And then I heard myself shriek again.

The entire floor, in every direction, was covered in dark water.

In every direction.

The place. Was. Flooded.

Dark water with soft little waves rippling toward me from the direction of the tasting room.

• • • • •

So.

Step one?

Give into a minute or so of pure panic.

Standing there. Saying, over and over, "Oh my God oh my God oh my God."

Step two.

Look at my phone.

It was 10:03.

Only three hours before Fletcher would be walking in with my soon-to-be-new boss.

Oh my God oh my God oh my God.

I had to calm down. I had to calm down…

Calm down, Marion Flarey.

Think.

Then I noticed something else.

A faint spraying noise.

It was coming from somewhere deep inside the building. Which is an old barn, in case I never mentioned it. So it's big. The front, the part facing the road, is where the tasting room is, but more than half the building is broken up into rooms that we use for brewing, and storage, and office space, and also a kitchen although, as I have mentioned, we don't use the kitchen for much except extra storage and a staging area for caterers when we host private parties.

The spraying water noise seemed to be coming from the bathroom area.

And I had to do something. I had to fix this, somehow, before Fletcher got there.

I started toward the sound. My feet sloshed as I walked, and a seeping wetness began climbing instantly over the soles of my flats. And I made it halfway down the passageway between the back door and the brewing area when the lights flickered and went out.

I screamed again.

Because there are no windows in the back of the barn. So for a second I was standing in pitch black, or so it seemed to me, and the idea of standing in pitch blackness in a growing pool of water and next, of course, my mind goes to: oh, my God, what if I slip and fall and hit my head and isn't it true you can drown in an inch of water, and couldn't the flood cause a short and now I'll be electrocuted?

Then I realized that my eyes were adjusting and oh. It wasn't pitch dark, actually.

There were lights. On the ceiling. Those emergency lights that come on in buildings when the power goes out.

Calm down, Marion. Calm down, and focus, and figure out how to fix this.

I opened the closet next to the storeroom where we keep the mop and bucket, because when there's water on the floor what you do is you mop it up, right?

I started wheeling the bucket toward the spraying sound.

When it suddenly it struck me that I was being a complete idiot.

Fix this yourself? With a mop?

Really, Marion? You complete idiot? Because I had no idea what I was doing, and this was a disaster and how could I possibly fix it? And wasn't this exactly like the hapless apprentice in the story—you may know the Joseph Jacobs version or the Disney one—who thought he was so smart, and started fiddling with his master's spell book, and uh oh, accidentally summoned demonic forces, and oh crap, the demonic forces were now filling the master's chamber with water…

I could mop and mop and mop but hear that spraying noise?

I'd never keep up with the rising flood.

I was doomed. I was doomed…

And then it hit me.

I may not know a sorcerer.

But I knew a plumber.

RB.

RB is a plumber.

• • • • •

Tell you what.

RB is more than a plumber.

He is a friend.

Because when I called him, he was at a job, of course. A big, important job, installing plumbing for some guy who must be rich because, I found out later, he was building a McMansion on a hilltop overlooking a golf course.

A house that was about 40 miles away, incidentally.

And what did RB do, when his ex-girlfriend called him with a barely coherent blubbering story about a flood and pitch black and gushing sounds and wet shoes and prospective buyers on the way?

Tell you what he did.

First, he talked me through how to find the water shut-off to the building.

It turned out to be near the back door, tucked into a corner.

So I twisted the knob, and that stopped the gushing noise, at least.

And then he said, "I'll be there as soon as I can."

That's RB.

I sloshed to the front of the building.

The water wasn't as deep in the tasting room. But it was still a disaster.

And then I rang Fletcher. It was time to tell Fletcher.

He didn't pick up.

I texted him.

need to talk. bit of a problem here

That got his attention. He phoned me immediately. And I told him about the flood and that I'd shut the water off and that RB was on the way.

He was real quiet at first, but then started in with that businessperson's mind of his. Questions, questions, questions. How much water, what time had I gotten there, could I see the water from the tasting room. That sort of thing.

I knew why. He wanted to know what he would be walking into, in less than three hours, when he showed up with the prospective buyers.

I could hear the stress in his voice. "What time did you say RB would be there?"

"About an hour."

"That's not soon enough. You gotta get someone there right now."

I knew why he was saying that. He knew the clock was ticking, and he wanted everything fixed and cleaned up before 1 pm.

But to be perfectly honest, it irked me a little, too. Because I was the manager, right? And it was me who was there, standing (literally!) in the middle of a major disaster, and I was fixing it the best way I could, calling a friend because I knew he was a friend and would drop everything to help, which to me seemed like a pretty good deal. And Fletcher's response was, basically, to tell me that my decisions were wrong, and I should do something completely different.

But Fletcher was also my boss.

"Okay," I said. "I'll let you know what I can do."

"And call Josh."

That's our brewer.

"I already texted him," I said, triumphantly. Because for real, Fletcher. I am the manager. Of course I knew I had to get our brewer over there, pronto.

Then we hung up, and I did as I was told. I called other plumbers. Five other plumbers. Every plumber I could find in the area who didn't have abysmal Yelp reviews.

And guess what else?

None of them could get there any sooner than RB.

Ha.

In fact, only one of them would have been able to get there that day.

I mean, this is Tibbs, New York. It's not like there are twenty plumbers in a twenty-mile radius.

So I admit it, I felt a little vindicated when I texted Fletcher back.

no good on finding other plumber. will do best to get things cleaned up by 1. Josh on the way

I sloshed back to the storage room and cut a cardboard box apart and made a "sorry, closed today, plumbing emergency" and taped it on the front door.

I updated our Facebook and Instagram pages.

And then RB was there.

He had a helper with him, a teenage kid who naturally reminded me of Ace, not only because he was built a little like Ace, but mostly because it made me wonder whether RB had hired him for the same reason he'd once hired Ace. To help out a kid who needed a mentor and a paying job.

And they lifted this big wet-vac thing off the back of RB's truck which I guess he'd stopped and picked on the way to the brewery. And then RB got to work. He replaced a pipe leading to the men's room, which had apparently cracked at the joint or something, while his helper kid vacuumed water, and I lugged soggy things out the back door and spread them out on the strip of lawn behind the barn, in the sun. And then Josh-the-Brewer showed up and was all like "oh wow, man, check it out, flood-o-geddon!" Grinning like this was an enormously funny cosmic joke instead of an enormously tragic cosmic disaster.

He got to work lugging brewery stuff out to lay it on the lawn, too.

Little brown crickets were everywhere. Jumping up out of the grass and weeds, all excited, and crawling all over the stuff as we laid it out, like we were magical beings that had suddenly appeared to erect a magical little brown cricket kingdom.

Lucky, happy crickets.

• • • • •

"Okay. It's fixed," RB said about an hour later. "We'll leave the fans. They'll help dry everything out."

I'd moved to mop duty by then. Wheeling the big yellow plastic bucket through the brewery, sopping up water, wringing out the mop. But now I straightened and pushed my bangs back from my eyes because they were slipping out of their barrette. "I don't know how we can thank you, RB," I said.

We were in the little hallway between the office and the tasting room, and now I saw a car pull in.

Fletcher.

I felt a knot in my stomach. Because of all days, why did flood-o-geddon have to strike today?

"It's not your fault," RB said.

Reading my thoughts.

We walked together to the back door and stepped out into the sun. Fletcher was walking toward the building, looking at all the stuff spread on the ground and shaking his head.

"You've had quite the morning, eh?" he said when he reached us.

He sounded distant and formal. Which was to be expected. He was thinking, at the moment, about selling a business. Not about his girlfriend.

"They'll be here in about fifteen," he said. Meaning the prospective buyers.

Then he shook RB's hand and thanked him and turned back to me and asked if Josh-the-Brewer was there, and I said he was.

"Well. Let's see the damage."

I found myself trailing him and RB as they started inside. You know how that is? When you are the least important person, almost forgotten.

By the way, in my opinion things didn't look so bad, considering. It smelled wet but not musty or muddy. The cement floor was already starting to look a bit drier, in spots. But Fletcher peered around as he went, assessing things, the office (thankfully spared), the storage room (thankfully the only things that got wet were the supplies on the bottom shelves), and the brew room (Josh-the-brewer grinning because it would take more than flood-o-geddon to harsh that boy's mellow).

Then we headed toward the front and suddenly Fletcher stopped.

His body stiffened.

He turned around and gave me strange look.

I'd never seen that expression in my sweetheart's eyes, before.

It was a hard look.

"Who's that?" he said. "Who's that, in the tasting room?"

I shook my head, confused. Not so much because of the words but because of the expression on Fletcher's face.

But fortunately RB answered. "It's my assistant. I asked him to put one of the fans up by the bar."

"Your assistant," Fletcher repeated, looking now at RB but then back at me.

And then it hit me.

Fletcher knew that Ace had worked for RB. And I'd talked to Fletcher about Ace which gave Fletcher the idea that Ace was in town, and then he'd seen RB's helper and admittedly the kid had a passing resemblance to my little brother, the same height and build. And Fletcher had jumped to a conclusion.

A wrong conclusion.

"Don't worry, Fletcher," I said, forcing a falsely cheerful little laugh. "It's not who you think it is."

But I don't know if Fletcher even heard me, because RB spoke at the exact same time. "What do you mean?" he said. "Who did you think it is?"

Ugh.

"He thinks it's Ace," I said to RB, jumping in hurriedly, my instinct being that we should wrap up this line of conversation ASAP.

Only my intervention didn't work. "Oh yeah?" RB said to Fletcher. "And why would that be a problem, if you don't mind my asking?"

Whoa.

Where did that come from?

"It's okay, RB," I said, feeling my pulse start to go up again. Because something here was ratcheting up, and I wasn't ready for it, and it's not like my stress levels were anything like normal. "Shall we check the tasting room?"

But Fletcher wasn't about to let the moment slide. "There's no issue," he said. "As long as everyone understands that Ace Weekes is not allowed on these premises."

He was stressed. Obviously. Or he wouldn't have come across like that. Hard, like that.

He was my sweet, sexy Fletcher.

"It's okay," I said again. Trying to smooth things over. I turned to RB. "Fletcher and I had a conversation about Ace. We agreed—"

But RB didn't let me finish. He was going after Fletcher. "I suppose this is about that bogus story, right? Ace breaking into your house?"

I froze.

Because of course RB knew about it, too. Tibbs is a small town. Everybody knows everything.

RB must have known there was bad blood between my boyfriend and my little brother.

So why was he getting into Fletcher's face?

I touched his arm. Still trying to defuse the situation. "It's okay—" I started for the third time.

"You're dead wrong, Fletcher," RB cut me off again.

My jaw dropped.

What was RB saying?

"RB," I said. "It's okay. Ace admitted it. He told Fletcher he did it. He returned everything he took. He gave it back to Fletcher himself."

RB snorted, looked at me, and then looked—pointedly—back at Fletcher. "Ace didn't steal anything. He took the fall for his stupid-ass buddies, is what he did."

Fletcher rolled his eyes. "Aw, come on, RB. You can't mean—"

"I can mean. Ace was with me the night of the break-in. We were in the middle a huge job. Apartment complex. We got home late. He crashed on my couch."

I stared at RB.

Could this be true?

But then I caught another look at Fletcher, and he wasn't having any of it. His eyes were hard, narrow. Suspicious. "Do you really expect me to believe that?" he said in a sharp voice.

But RB wasn't done. "They were all kids, stupid kids," he said. "And Ace isn't entirely blameless. He's the one who—Ace knew about the house because you two—" He broke off for a moment, avoiding looking at me, then started over. "You wouldn't maybe understand this, Fletcher, but your stone house? It was a local legend. Rich peoples' place, nobody living there. Kids were fascinated by it. And Ace used to take people there. They'd hang out. Pick the lock, go inside, drink and smoke dope or whatever. Take girls there. It was a local party spot."

"Oh, shit," I whispered.

But RB was still looking at Fletcher. "But they were always respectful of the place. Ace made sure they'd be respectful of it."

Fletcher was scowling, now. "You call breaking in and trespassing respectful?"

"They were kids."

"I was a kid once, too. I didn't go around breaking into peoples' homes."

"Aw, come off it," RB said. "You know damn well that things like this can get out of control. How sometimes when you're a kid, your buddies do things you're ashamed of."

"Oh, God." It slipped out, pushed out by a little upwelling of nausea. I suddenly guessed how it had played out. Ace's buddies had broken into the place. And when Ace found out what his friends had done, he would have felt responsible, deeply and utterly and devastatingly responsible. Because he'd led them there. And for Ace, breaking into the house, partying there, would have seemed like a lark. Like harmless mischief. But then it had turned into something else. Something dark. A crime.

A violation.

And he would have blamed himself.

"Nothing stays a secret for very long in this town," RB was saying. "Ace figured out what they'd done. And he told them they would have to give everything back. But they were scared. They were all over 18. They would have done time. So Ace told you that the break-in was all him. That he'd acted alone."

"Oh, Ace," I whispered.

"And nothing personal," RB said, "but you should have known better."

Fletcher's chin jutted out "What is that supposed to mean?"

"Ace is a good kid. And you and Mayf—you and Marion were—"

And for some reason, in that moment, Fletcher looked away from RB and his eyes met mine. And it was one of those funny moments when you read something in someone's eyes that they maybe would rather you didn't see. Something about how this was my fault. That by dating me, Fletcher had gotten involved with someone, with something, that he'd rather not have anything to do with.

But he couldn't contradict RB. Not there. Not to his face.

"Whatever," he said, turning back to RB. "All I know is what Ace said."

"Guys? Can we drop this, please?" I said, my voice quavering.

We three stood there for another moment. Still.

Like we were testing something. All three of us, testing each other.

And then RB spoke, broke the moment. "Yeah, sure, good idea. Let's drop it. I have to get going. I'll send my bill."

They both turned away from me. Left me standing there. RB, heading toward the door and Fletcher, without saying a word, turning and starting toward the brewing room, no doubt to talk to Josh.

I stood there for a moment, thinking that I should go with Fletcher. I should listen to what he was going to tell Josh. I was the tasting room manager. I should be a part of the conversation he had with Josh in these last few minutes before the prospective buyers arrive...

But instead I pivoted in the other direction and trotted out the back door.

I cleared my throat.

"I'll pick up the fans later this week," RB said, lifting the wet vac into the bed of his truck. He clanked the tailgate shut.

His helper kid was ready to leave, sitting in the cab, head bent down over his phone.

I cleared my throat again. "So, uh, Ace make it home okay?"

He nodded. "I guess."

"It was awfully nice of you, to put him up in your house like that," I said.

A funny look passed quickly over RB's face. "He's a friend," he said. His voice sounded sharp. Almost like he was angry at something.

Angry at me?

"Friends take care of friends."

"Yes," I whispered.

I wondered whether Ace knew what a good friend RB was. I wonder if he knew that RB was a better friend to him than his own sister, who had believed he was a thief who'd not only robbed Fletcher's family but had also robbed his own. Who had doubted his story when he told me he'd had nothing to do with the disappearance of my parents' money.

I was faithless.

I was a faithless sister.

I needed Ace's phone number. I needed to speak to him. To tell him I was sorry. To tell him I was going to do whatever it took to clear his name.

Even if he'd told RB not to give his number out, I needed to persuade him to share it.

But I didn't get a chance.

RB was climbing into the truck and starting the engine. "I've gotta get going," he said. "We left a big job half-done. It's gonna be a late one tonight."

And I watched his truck pull away.

32

The prospective buyers showed up barely ten minutes after RB left.

They were very nice about the burst pipe flood-o-geddon, joking with me and Fletcher about it as they walked through the brewery. "Cloudy with a chance of burst pipe today, Fletch?" and "Now that's what I call a mopped floor!"

Guffaw guffaw.

I sank into the background for most of the tour, although they asked me a few questions at one point, when we returned to the front of the building. What flavors were most popular, did I like my job, that sort of thing.

And I poured them samples. And the tall one even asked me if there was anything I would do to improve the place, which was the most uncomfortable moment for me because I would have liked to know what Fletcher thought first, but since I didn't, I said that it might be nice to open the kitchen and serve food. Which I immediately regretted because it meant I had invoked the whole Ace thing again. Ugh ugh ugh.

They talked longer with Josh-the-brewer. Understandably, since he was the real talent of the operation, at least for now. At least until I fully mastered the business end.

So I eavesdropped while they asked him where he got his flavor ideas and some questions about production volume. And what it would take to ramp up production. I gathered that they were thinking in terms of bottling or canning our product, expanding into retail, expanding the business beyond the tasting room into a regional brand, maybe a national brand eventually.

Big plans.

Note to self. Buy some books about ramping up business operations.

Then Fletcher led them into the office and shut the door.

About 4 pm I took the Plumbing Emergency signs off the door. And thankfully we started to get our usual afternoon crowd, so when Fletcher and the prospective buyers re-emerged, they saw that we actually had customers, which was good, right? And it was a pretty good afternoon, all things considered. Not a record day but not bad.

And then the prospective buyers left, because they had a plane to catch. And Fletcher helped Josh bring in the stuff we'd spread outside to dry, because the forecast said maybe pop-up thunderstorms, and the last thing we needed was for our mostly-dry stuff to get wet again.

• • • • •

There's a pizza joint in downtown Tibbs.

Okay. I call it downtown. But make sure you're picturing what I mean: there's a stoplight at a four corners with a handful of commercial buildings, 19th Century storefronts like you see in all the small towns in the Northeast. The pizza parlor is tiny, only about eight tables, so mostly people get pizza or subs to go. But late on a weeknight you can get a table. That's what Fletcher and I did. We ordered slices—him two, with pepperoni, me one, with mushrooms. The pizza at this place is New York style, thin crust, huge. The slices are too big for paper plates. But because they were slices, they'd been reheated, so the bottom of the crust was crispy, the tips were hanging off the side of the plate but they weren't drooping. They were sticking straight out.

It's my favorite kind of pizza.

And they have some decent beers. So we ordered Southern Tier IPAs—served in plastic cups—and stood by the counter sipping beer until our slices were ready. Then we took a seat.

Fletcher was more relaxed. More like himself. Meaning, I assumed, that the meeting with the prospective buyers had gone well.

Which meant there was an awfully good chance he'd be selling the brewery.

I pushed the thought out of my mind.

It would work out fine, right?

I had a plan in place.

All I had to do was to keep a positive attitude.

"Thanks for handling everything today," he said as we sat down.

"It all worked out okay, considering." I pulled a couple of paper napkins out of the dispenser. "What did they think?"

He knew who I meant by "they."

"They're gonna put in an offer." He took a bite of pizza, and I did too—a little one. The cheese was pretty hot. "Then it goes to the lawyers."

Ugh.

So soon? This was all going to happen that quickly?

But what I said out loud was: "That's great."

And then the conversation died. It was weird. I think I asked him what time his flight was the next morning, although I already knew it was an early one. And he probably told me a little about the deal he was working on next.

But I wasn't really thinking about Fletcher's travel plans or business deals.

Because to be honest, I was thinking about my little brother. And then I was finished with my slice and Fletcher was eating his second slice, and I took a gulp of my beer and without really thinking about what I was saying, I did it.

I went there.

"So. Guess you must have been surprised at what RB said about my brother."

Fletcher made a face. The face you make when you take a bite of something and realize, too late, that whatever it is you put in your mouth? It's nasty. "I'd rather not talk about it, Marion," he said.

"Alright. But you know, it's kind of funny how—"

"And it's moot, anyway. He's not in Tibbs, right? Isn't that what you said?"

And for some reason, I felt a sudden surge of temper.

Because it wasn't moot.

The kid was my brother. My flesh and blood.

And hey. I didn't want to fight with Fletcher. I was in love with Fletcher. I was going to spend the rest of my life with Fletcher. And if fairy tales mean anything, they mean that when you find someone who is almost certainly your prince, you should stay the course no matter what, you should fight for what you know is right.

Right?

But what if your prince has decided he hates your kid brother? So that now you have to choose between your prince and your family?

I sat there, watching Fletcher chew his pizza, and the more I sat there, the more I realized how much I hate fairy tales. Because even though they seem like they can help you understand life and get clear on what is right and wrong, they really don't. They are as complicated as life is, or maybe life is too complicated to ever figure out.

Or maybe I didn't really hate fairy tales. Maybe I was just losing my temper at my boyfriend for putting me in a position where I had to make an awful choice.

"You know," I said in a voice that was more quiet than it should have been, considering the roiling fire that was starting to rise up in my guts. "Ace is my brother." Stating the obvious, hahahahaha. But I was making a point. "So he's a part of my life. It's not like you and I will never see him."

"Really, Marion?" And now Fletcher was angry, too. His eyes sparked in a way that struck me as weirdly unpleasant, for some reason. "Maybe your brother didn't steal from me. Maybe he did. I have no way of knowing one way or the other. But I do know he's not the kind of person I want to be associated with. So if you think otherwise—"

He didn't complete the thought. He didn't need to. It was a threat.

"Fletcher Beal," I said in a low, careful voice. Because if I didn't keep my voice low and careful, I was gonna create a major scene. And I could see the pizza parlor guy behind the counter glancing over at us, because even with our voices at a low volume, pizza parlor guy could sense the tension. "On what planet is it okay to ask a woman to choose between her boyfriend and her brother?"

"On a sane planet," Fletcher said. Very smugly.

Our eyes met. And in that moment, I knew I was standing at a fork in the road. I was about to choose between two stories, and one would take me in one direction, and one would take me in another. And choosing one direction meant the other had reached The End, stick a fork in it, it's done.

And I knew it was entirely up to me. That if I wanted to keep Fletcher, all I had to do was de-escalate. Nod and say "um hmm" and tell him I understood him, even if that would have been a bit of a lie, because he was being totally unkind if not unreasonable. And it would be settled, and I'd be on the sweet road to having it all: a gorgeous, wealthy boyfriend with an amazing future and sophisticated friends. And we'd date for a bit and then get married and start a family and why would I even need to spend time in Tibbs, let alone hang around the Weekes-Flarey nuthouse? I'd be able to live in Manhattan and eventually some other gorgeous place we'd pick out together, say a beach house in Malibu or a chateau on a mountainside in Aspen. And wasn't that the future I wanted? A golden, spangled future, crowned by the undying love of an amazing man?

And maybe Ace wasn't a thief, literally. But if I chose my little brother, the price I'd pay was this enormous treasure. So choosing my little brother was the same as robbing myself of my rightful future, stealing my own precious future from myself and throwing it away. And for what?

But—he was my brother.

I stood up.

"Fine," I said. I picked up my plastic cup and chugged the last of my beer. "So guess what, Fletcher. You can have your sane planet all to yourself. Enjoy."

And I turned on my heel and headed toward the door.

I heard him call me. Once.

"Marion!"

But (a sign, folks, a sign) he didn't follow me.

He didn't follow me.

He didn't fight for me.

I got into Winchell's truck and drove back to the dome.

And I pulled into the driveway.

I parked.

And then everything inside me exploded.

I'd just wrecked the most perfect relationship.

I'd just wrecked my perfect, fairy tale relationship with my rich, handsome prince.

Oh my God, Marion Flarey. You are such an idiot.

And I sat there in the driver's seat of Winchell's truck and sobbed.

Have you ever cried until you were dizzy?

Yep. That's what I did that night.

I cried until I was dizzy.

33

So I finally wore myself out, crying, and just sat there in the truck, in the dark.

Feeling dazed.

Trying to think. To form some kind of a plan.

But my brain wouldn't work. I'd given up on Fletcher, and I needed to somehow get my family to come together, to fix what we'd done to my little brother and bring my little brother back.

But that's as far as I could go.

I turned the truck's ceiling light on and craned my neck so I could see myself in the rear-view mirror.

I looked horrible. I looked like a cry-bomb had exploded all over my face.

I switched the light back off and sat for another moment.

And then something caught my eye.

The door of the dome had opened.

Quill was standing in the doorway, backlit from the inside lights.

And a moment later he came running down the steps and across the little bit of yard between the dome and where we park the cars.

"Aunt Marion?"

He stopped next to the truck, just outside the driver's side window.

"Aunt Marion?" he said again.

Ugh.

I opened the door.

"Hi, Quill," I managed to croak.

"Mom said to check on you."

So much for escaping detection. Which is the problem with my family, in a nutshell. You have no privacy. You think you're living your life, making your own decisions, you think you're in control of what they know and don't know. But then you find out that they're paying a lot more attention than you expected. That they've noticed that you pulled into the driveway a half hour ago and are still sitting in the car.

Truck.

Whatever.

"That was nice of her," I said, the exact opposite of what I felt. "I've just been sitting here thinking. But I'm pretty tired. I'm going to go to bed."

I swiveled my legs around to get out of the car, but Quill didn't move.

"She says it's okay if you want to read me a bedtime story," he said.

"Oh." Interesting. "Are you sure?"

He nodded. "She said you're sad and it would make you feel better."

Sad?

How'd she know I was sad?

RB.

RB had told her about the plumbing disaster.

That had to be it.

Quill was still watching me.

"Well," I said, "how about you? Do you want a story?"

He nodded again, vigorously this time.

"Okay. Run tell your Mom that I'll get you ready for bed."

I hustled to the camper, to the little bathroom in the camper and splashed water on my face, hoping it would calm down the blotchy red of my cheeks, the rather brilliant red rims of my eyes. So that Quill wouldn't mention to his mother, tomorrow morning, that Aunt Marion had looked like she'd skidded her face across a rough patch of pavement.

I heard the screen door springs twang and the door bang shut.

"Brush your teeth, Quill," I called down the hall from my bedroom to the other end of the camper, and I climbed onto my bed and kicked my shoes off, and they clunked, first one and then the other, onto the floor.

I listened to Quill brush his teeth and change into his pajamas. Then he appeared in the bedroom door, holding a book.

I cleared my throat. "Whatcha got there?"

My voice sounded almost normal.

I recognized the book. Cute little collection of English fairy tales.

He didn't talk, just climbed up into the bed and snuggled next to me, like he does, and opened the book to the third story.

"This one," he said.

I winced. "Uh—I dunno, Quill."

He'd picked The Rose Tree. Which you might know by that name, or you might know the Grimm version, The Juniper Tree. "It's kind of scary. Your mother—I think your mother would like me to read you nice stories, before bed."

Quill was looking down at the illustration on the page. A black and white drawing of a boy sitting against a rose tree, looking up at a singing bird.

The drawing is framed by a quote from the story.

My eyes caught the quote.

My little brother, whom I love, sits below and I sing above.

Oh my God. I was going to lose it again…

"What's the story about?" Quill asked. "Why is it scary?"

"An evil stepmother kills her stepdaughter," I said. "And then—" I hesitated. Because next, the stepmother feeds the daughter's liver to her father. Because guess what: fairy tales aren't the sweet, childish stories that some people would like us to believe. Fairy tales are about life. And life is about pain and betrayal and death and the unspeakable things that people sometimes do to one another. "Look, let's just find a different story, okay?"

"Okay," Quill said, because he's a really, really good kid.

He flipped further into the book. Passing, I noticed, the stories without any pictures. "This one?"

Binnorie. The illustration, here, showed the harpist from the story. The harpist being a character who finds a drowned princess.

"Geez," I muttered under my breath. What're the odds that the boy would pick another story that is basically about murder and beyond-the-grave revenge. "This one is kinda scary too, Quill." I took the book from him. Because clearly it wouldn't do, to let the boy choose the story this night. "Here," I said, coming to Earl Mar's Daughter. "Let's do this one."

And Quill was fine with my choice. And it was the perfect story for a little boy's bedtime read. Well, besides the princess getting pregnant, in secret, from her enchanted lover. Which Candace would probably now decide meant that I was influencing Quill to one day run around getting girls pregnant, which would have been ironic considering how her son had come into being.

But, oh, well. It was better than a stepmother cooking a murdered girl's liver.

"Can we read another one?" Quill said. "I'm not quite tired, yet."

I didn't argue.

The very next story in the book was a skip. Mr. Miacca. I could tell Quill was intrigued because the illustration shows a little boy hiding under a chair, and the chair has a giant sitting in it, and the giant is holding an axe. But we moved on to the story after that. Whittington and his Cat. Nice story about a young man climbing socially from poverty to Lord Mayer of London.

And then I sent the boy to bed and plugged in my phone and shut off my light.

A screech owl flew by the camper, making that weird, otherworldly call they make that sounds like a cross between a horse whinny and a woman screaming.

How bizarre, really, that of all the fairy tales in my books—of all the fairy tales in the book there on my bed, where Quill had left it—the boy had picked two about murdered siblings speaking from beyond the grave.

The screech owl called again and a shiver went through me.

And then, all at once, it hit me.

It had been right there in front of my face, and I'd missed it, but now it finally hit me.

The singing bones.

My family was haunted by the singing bones.

34

I jumped out of bed.

I didn't bother putting on my shoes.

I unplugged my phone and tiptoed through the dark camper, past where Quill lay in bed already stilled with sleep, and I slipped out the door and across the dirt and around the dome.

I went to Mom's workshop, and pushed the door open and went inside.

I didn't turn the light on. I used my phone's flashlight, casting the light over the shelves against the wall—the shelves of Mom's wind chimes.

I found the one I wanted. Glazed dark blue, the same color as the wind chime Quill had wanted to give to Effie.

I picked it up, and the femur-shaped clappers clanked musically as I walked back around the dome and up the front steps.

• • • • •

Candace and Mom were on the couch, Candace staring at the television, Mom with her feet curled under her, poetry book on her lap. Winchell was tipped back in his oversized leatherette easy chair, clicker in one hand, Surprise curled up in the elbow of his other arm.

Their heads turned in unison when they heard the door close behind me.

I strode over and grabbed the clicker from Winchell and pointed it at the television and hit the Off button.

"What's going on?" Candace said. "Are you okay?"

I held up the wind chime. "Mom," I said. "You need to explain this."

She didn't answer. But I saw something flicker in her eyes.

She knew where this was going.

Candace, on the other hand, did not. "Marion," she snapped. "Turn the show back on. Are you out of your mind? What are you talking about?"

"I'll tell you what I'm talking about," I said. "I'm talking about a fairy tale. How, once upon a time, there were two brothers who went out into a forest to try to kill a wild boar that was ravaging the kingdom's farmlands."

"Oh, for crying out loud," Candace muttered.

"Shut up." I glared at her. "This is important."

I could feel my Mom's eyes on me.

She knew.

I looked at Winchell. He was pushing the lever on the side of his recliner, sitting up, looking at me like he thought I was crazy.

"I won't tell you the whole story," I said. "But the point is, one of the brothers killed the other. Which happens, in fairy tales. They can get pretty bloody, or whatever. But then, many years later, a shepherd finds one of the dead brother's bones, and he carves it into a mouthpiece for his horn."

I fixed my eyes on my mother's.

She knew.

"And the bone sings," I said.

My mother gave a barely perceptible nod.

"And the singing bone tells the secret. It tells what happened to the brother," I said.

And then I looked at Winchell.

His expression had changed.

He wasn't looking at me like I was crazy, anymore.

He was looking at me like I was scaring him.

"And now," I announced. "This family is gonna start telling our secrets about Ace."

"Oh, shit," said Candace.

"Okay Dad," I said to Winchell. "Your turn."

But Winchell didn't look at me. He looked at Mom. He couldn't help it, I suppose. Because, you see, we think that thoughts are nothing. We think that they are invisible and that as long as they stay thoughts, they don't affect things, they don't touch things.

But we're wrong.

Thoughts are things. Not things you can touch or taste or smell. But they are things. And the thought-thing that was in the room, that night, was Winchell's secret about Ace, about that day almost five years ago when he'd killed his son. Well, not killed him literally. But figuratively, he'd killed him. He'd betrayed him and rendered him dead to our family. That thought-thing was now there, in that room, hovering in the room in front of us. And part of that thought-thing was that Winchell had never come clean with Mom. And so it was like the thought-thing had these little claws, and some of the claws were hooked into Winchell and some of the claws were hooked into Mom. So he couldn't help looking at her.

Because Mom knew that the bones of her chimes were Ace's bones, his singing bones. Singing a secret about her son.

A secret that needed to be told.

And now Winchell knew that she knew.

"Dad," I said. Because he didn't want to speak. He didn't want to tell Mom. "No more secrets, Dad. Out with it."

And Mom's face was drained of color, but she was looking at Winchell too, now. "What is Marion talking about, Winchell?" she said. "What secrets?"

"Ace is bad," Winchell muttered. "That's all anyone needs to know. Bad seed."

"Marion," Candace said. "You're stirring things up. You shouldn't—" But she didn't finish her thought, because it was too late to stop this and she knew it.

Because Dad was looking at Mom, and now his face was white. And when he spoke, his voice had changed. He wasn't muttering any more. He sounded uncertain, almost pleading. "He took money from me, Lana," he said. "From us."

"Oh?" Mom's voice registered surprise. But her manner didn't fit her voice. She looked too still. Almost stiff. "What money, Winchell?" she asked.

Oh, my God. Something strange had flickered across her face.

Something almost like a smile. Only craftier.

So was this it? Did this have something to do with what was going on with Mom? Not in the literal, surface sense but in the sense of an enchantment, of Mom being enchanted in some way?

Only maybe it was Mom who was the enchantress?

I glanced back at Winchell. His expression was like the face of a little boy who'd been caught swiping cookies. He couldn't hold Mom's eye at all. He was staring down at the floor. "I'm sorry. I put it away. I never told you. I had some money left over when the business failed."

"Quite a bit of money, then?" Mom said.

But her voice? When she spoke?

She was not surprised. This wasn't a surprise to her.

She knew.

She knew about the money. She knew Winchell had squirreled away the money without telling her about it.

She was pressing him, now, not because she didn't know, but because she did. She knew everything. And this was what she'd been thinking about, on the train ride back from New York. This was what she'd kept back when she'd told me that Winchell was peculiar about money, that he placed too much importance on money.

And now Winchell was well and truly caught. Nodding yes. The strained, miserable nod of a caught little boy.

Mom closed her book and set it next to her on the couch. All very deliberately. "Go on," she said. "How much?"

Oh, my God. How funny, to watch Winchell try to form the words. To tell Mom exactly how much money he had hidden away.

Hidden from her.

"Ah," he stammered. "Ah." And then he forced it out. "A hundred—and fifty—thousand."

"I see," Mom said.

And then she stood up and looked at me and Candace, and then back at Winchell. "And when, exactly, were you going to tell me about this money?"

Winchell looked up at her. Pleading look in his face. A please-have-mercy look. "I was afraid. I was afraid."

They were staring at each other.

And suddenly Mom's shoulders slumped. And the expression on her face switched and she was no longer the enchantress. She was the middle-aged wife who had carried in her heart, her secret—her secret about her husband's secret. "You were afraid of the truth," she said in a quiet voice. "You were afraid because you'd promised me you'd make us rich, and you failed."

"But I was going to make it good, Lana," he said. "There was enough left. We would have been fine, if Ace—if Ace hadn't—"

"Don't bring our son into this," Mom interrupted, her voice sharp.

"He had the receipt," Winchell said, as if he hadn't heard her. "The withdrawal receipt. From the bank. He admitted—"

"You're missing the point." Mom turned away. "You're completely missing the point, Winchell. You think it's the money that matters. It's not. I couldn't care less about the money."

And she stood up and, without another word, crossed to the back of the dome and to the staircase to their bedroom.

And a moment later the door closed behind her.

"Good one, Marion," Candace muttered, shaking her head.

“We have to talk.” My voice was shaking but I was sure of this. I was sure I was right, that I’d done the right thing. That I was on solid ground. “Don’t you guys see we have to talk?” I said.

Neither of them answered me.

Candace stood up and took the clicker and pointed it at the television and turned it back on.

And Winchell just sat in his recliner with his head bowed.

I doubt he even noticed when I left.

35

Plumbers leave for work very early.

Which meant that if I was going to catch a plumber, I needed to be a very early bird. So the sun wasn't even up, yet, when I snuck out of the camper the next morning and borrowed Winchell's truck, and a little while later I was banging on RB's door.

I waited.

Nothing.

I banged again.

A light inside turned on and I held my breath, listening.

And then I heard the sound of someone fumbling with the door latch and then the door swung open, and RB stood there, surprised expression on his face.

He ran his hand through his hair. "Mayfly?"

He was dressed in sweatpants.

Sweatpants, only.

Not again!

I forced myself not to look at that bare chest...with those muscles...and dang. RB—I mean, Candace's boyfriend—sure kept that body of his in nice shape...

"I need Ace's address and phone number," I said, keeping my eyes focused on the man's face.

He shook his head. "Marion. We went through this already. He doesn't want—"

"Listen to me, RB," I cut him off, holding up my hand. "I've got some things to tell you."

And we went inside.

He heated some water and fixed a couple mugs of instant coffee.

And I told him everything. About Winchell's secret money and that Winchell thought Ace had stolen it, how I'd come back to RB's house and talked to Ace and he'd denied taking it but even if he had, Mom wouldn't care. Mom just wanted him home.

"Jesus," RB said.

"Exactly."

He sighed. "So what are you going to do?"

I felt myself straighten up, slightly, in my chair. "I'm going to talk to him. I'm going to tell him that it doesn't matter what happened. Mom wants him here. And if talking to him by phone doesn't work?" I sucked in my breath, then let it go. "I'll go talk to him in person."

"How do you plan to do that?" he said. "If you think I know where he lives, Marion, you're wrong. I don't. I have no idea. I don't even know what city."

Ugh. That was bad news.

"But you have his cell number, right?"

RB winced.

"You're not breaking your promise," I reminded him. "You promised you wouldn't tell us he was in town, and you didn't. I found out but that wasn't your fault, and anyway, you and Ace were close so why wouldn't I ask if you knew how to get in touch with him?"

He sighed.

He sat there another moment.

Then he got up and left the room, and a moment later he came back with his phone, and my phone buzzed.

He'd texted me Ace's number.

He sat back down and looked at his half-finished mug of coffee. "But Marion. If you talk to him and..."

RB's voice trailed off. But I knew what he was going to say.

"I'll find him," I said, my voice firm despite the odd, giddy feeling that suddenly burst up from my heart into my head. "I'll go find him."

"How can you possibly do that? You don't—"

"Yes, I do," I interrupted. "I know where he lives. He lives in Las Vegas."

RB gave me a sharp look. "Did he tell you that?"

"Uh huh. Only I'd already guessed, because of the hat," I said. "The Golden Knights cap in his backpack. Remember?"

RB nodded. And then he got a thoughtful look and stroked his beard, and I got the feeling he was going to say something more about Ace. But he didn't. All he said was, "Okay. Tell me how it goes when you call him."

• • • • •

It went…badly.

It should have been simple.

I went back home to the dome and let myself in. Nobody else was up, yet. I brewed a pot of coffee, sat at the kitchen table, flicking through some Instagram accounts, trying to distract myself with memes.

Because I needed to wait. Because Las Vegas is on west coast time, and I didn't want to wake Ace up. He worked as a cook. People who work as cooks need to sleep in, mornings.

But finally I couldn't stand it anymore.

I texted

hey. ace. it's mayfly

My phone said *delivered.*

I waited.

I waited five minutes. Fifteen minutes.

I had another cup of coffee.

Texted again.

we need 2 talk

God, I couldn't stand it.

Mom came downstairs. Looking like a ghost in her bathrobe. Smiling wanly at me.

My phone buzzed.

I grabbed it.

But it was RB.

heads up, think he's PO'd

Uh, oh.

I texted back: *bec u gave me his #?*

RB: *y*

Great.

I texted Ace again: *pls?*

Waited.

Waited.

My phone buzzed.

Ace!

But then I read the text.

sry mayfly but past is past

Oh, no!

I began to tap my phone keyboard. Something rambling, about how the fabric of our family was ripped to shreds and we needed to be together, to find forgiveness, to start over. But then I realized as I was typing that I was being stupid. Mom was at her computer now, scanning whatever secret website she checks every morning, any minute she'd turn around and see me—and I was afraid what she'd read on my face.

So I jumped up, ran out the door, sat down on the front steps, and finished composing my text.

I hit send.

I waited.

Nothing.

I went a little crazy. Sent about three more texts, telling him how sorry Dad was, how Mom was a mess, how we loved him and wanted him home.

Nothing.

Time to escalate.

So I hit voice call and called him.

He picked up.

"Look, Marion," he said. "you don't understand. You all need to leave me alone."

"But Ace, I believe you. I believe you didn't do it. We can fix this."

"Not us, Marion. Me. It's my thing, Marion. I'll come home when I'm able to pay the money back. Not a minute before. Now drop it, please."

And he hung up.

And I sat there thinking oh my God. Oh my God.

He was making it about the money, too.

Would somebody please stop making it about the money?

And my phone buzzed, and my heart leaped, thinking it was Ace and he'd had a change of heart. He was going to tell me he was sorry and ask me to please help him, help make Dad understand that he wasn't a thief, that he hadn't stolen the money.

But it wasn't Ace, it was RB.

did you talk to him?

Which tugged my heart a bit, because there's RB for you. Checking in on us because of how much he cares about my family.

But when I tried to tap out a response, I realized that I couldn't think of what to say.

I was still sitting on the dome's front steps, and the sun was up, now, the sky was bright blue, and a yellow swallowtail butterfly was dancing in the air in front of me. And a couple of crows flew out of the woods toward the dome, and one of them must have landed somewhere behind me, the dome roof. He started cawing in a loud, croaky voice.

And I didn't know what to tell RB.

That it was over? That I'd tried my best to get through to Ace and I'd failed?

No. I couldn't bring myself to do that. Because if I admitted I'd failed, it would make my failure real. And I wasn't ready to accept that my failure was real.

And I sure couldn't tell RB that as a student of fairy tales I had one more card to play, because what if he tried to talk me out of it? What if he told me to let it go, game over?

So instead of texting RB, I dialed Josh-the-brewer.

"Hey," I said. "Need a favor. Can you run the tasting room for me for a couple of days?"

And then I opened the browser on my phone and bought myself a plane ticket.

An expensive, late-minute plane ticket. To Las Vegas.

36

So. Before you tell me I was completely crazy to hop on a plane to go to Vegas, after Ace was so adamant that I should leave him alone, hear me out. In fairy tales, when siblings set out into the world and don't come back, the remaining siblings set out and try to find them. It's how it's done. Of course, the way it usually works is that the oldest goes first, then the middle child, and then the youngest. But regardless. The first two who leave get into awful trouble. They fall under a terrible enchantment, or maybe get lured into a life of vice. And then the youngest sets out last, and eventually saves the other two, even though the youngest is usually the most naïve or whatever.

So our situation wasn't exactly the same. I was the oldest—by only a couple months, but it still counted—and I'd managed to make my way back home, pretty much in one piece, although maybe overeducated and underemployed and a poor track record, relationship-wise. And Candace, the second sibling, had also made it back home, also more or less in one piece, overlooking, for now, the out-of-wedlock son and her upcoming divorce.

It was our baby brother who had failed to return.

And now my family, instead of coming together to bring him back, had acted like a bunch of stubborn idiots.

Obviously, I had to do something drastic.

I had to set out and find our little brother and bring him back.

Because the lesson for all of us was plain, as far as I was concerned.

We'd let money split us apart. Split our family apart.

I needed to go back out into the world, and find my little brother, and release him from his enchantment where it seemed like what mattered was that stupid missing money, and bring him home and put my family back together again.

Which is how I found myself, early the next morning, slipping out of the camper in the dark and walking down the driveway to meet my Uber.

It was foggy and quiet and cold. I shivered as I picked my way back and forth down the switchback driveway.

The car was waiting for me.

I climbed in, and sat quietly, grateful the driver—an older guy with a grizzled beard and a John Deere cap—wasn't a talker, and settled into the back seat and began mentally preparing myself for what was going to be a very long day. Because there are no direct flights to Vegas from anywhere around Tibbs. It's a lot more complicated. To get from Tibbs to Vegas, you first get yourself to a smallish city with a smallish airport. Then you go through security and find your gate (not too hard in a smallish airport) and wait to board and board a smallish plane and then wait to take off. Then the smallish plane, assuming nothing goes seriously awry, flies you to airport number two. This will be a city large enough to merit real airline respect. Say Chicago or Philadelphia or Minneapolis, depending on which flight you choose. There, you wait to deplane, then navigate through your second airport, where a single terminal is larger than the entire smallish airport you navigated a few hours ago. You find your new gate and wait to board your largish plane, which is the one that will deposit you, assuming nothing goes seriously awry, in Vegas.

I'd booked a flight, that day, that started in Syracuse—a two-hour drive from Tibbs—with a transfer in Chicago.

My Uber wound through the backroads for a half hour and then reached the four lane, Route 81, and I looked out the window and my mind drifted, and then my phone vibrated.

It was a text from RB.

mayfly? can you talk?

And I felt a flash of guilt, because I still hadn't answered his text from the day before. So I started tapping out a response. Something long-winded about how yeah, I'd done my best, but Ace refused to listen to me and now I was going to plan B.

But before I finished, another text came through.

need to talk about going to vegas

I frowned. What could he mean by that?

So I backspaced over my long-winded text to delete it and typed out a new one. This time, only one word long.

why?

"What airline did you say?" the Uber driver asked as I hit send, and I told him, and then felt my phone buzz again only great! Now RB was calling me?

I really didn't want to talk to RB.

I touched the red phone receiver icon thingy to decline the call, then waited, watching my phone, and sure enough a minute later he sent a new text.

can you talk?

And okay, it was nice that he cared so much and everything, but now I felt a pulse of irritation. Because the last thing I needed was for RB to interject his opinions about what I should do to deal with my little brother. And shouldn't the guy be at work by now?

I swiped my screen to wake my phone again.

thx, not a good time. tomorrow?

There. Done. Because this was my story, not RB's. This was me, setting out to find my sibling and bring him home, metaphorically if not actually. And the last thing I needed was for RB to meddle, or worse yet argue about how it would be best if I just let it go. Drop it, Marion, let Ace live his life. If it's meant to be, he'll come around eventually.

And then I turned my phone to Do Not Disturb and dropped it into the front pocket of my backpack, because it would be like RB to keep this up, and the last thing I needed was to run my battery down before I got to Vegas. I was going to need my phone in Vegas. I was going to need Uber again when I got there, for one thing.

I watched the Syracuse cityscape slide by, and then a few minutes later we reached the airport.

And if you've flown recently, you'll know how it makes you feel. You become this non-person, shuffling through lines, police-y people checking your identification, taking pictures of you, looking into your luggage. And like people do, I surrendered to it, which on the surface is for purely practical reasons, because if you fuss, you'll be dragged, kicking and screaming, out of the airport. But all day long I had this bizarre feeling, like I was two people, and on the surface I was surrendering for completely practical reasons, but the second Marion was surrendering to something else entirely.

In one of the fairy tales I'd refused to read to Quinn—Binnorie—the murdered princess is drowned. Her sister pushes her into a millstream. She doesn't die right away. She drifts for a while, crying out to her sister to save her.

And that's what I felt like that day, only instead of a millstream I was drifting in streams of people eddying through cordoned mazes and down jetways and in and out of bathrooms. I had no power over what was happening to me. It wouldn't matter what I said to anyone, nothing could be done for any of it. If my life was over, my life was over.

The dead princess was beautiful, by the way. She was dressed like a bride, a white dress with a golden girdle, and she had pearls and jewels in her hair. So as the story goes on, your heart breaks for her, and for her singing bones that later tell the secret of her death.

But there's another bit of the story that's easy to overlook, because the murder happens pretty early and it's so shocking and horrifying and entrancing that it carries you along like the current of the millstream carries the drowning princess.

But go back to the opening paragraph. The circumstances leading up to the murder were...complicated. Because there was a guy involved. And by "involved" I mean the whole thing was really his fault, too, the jerk. He plighted his troth to the elder sister. Then he changed his mind and decided he wanted the other one. So you can understand why the jilted sister might be upset. And although the story doesn't divulge any ugly details, you have to wonder. Did the younger sister encourage him? She certainly hadn't refused him. If she'd refused him—if she'd run to her sister and said, "you won't believe this, William just made a pass at me, the creep! We're both better off without that dirty two-timer!"—there would have been no murder.

And that's the thing about human relationships, right? A wrong leads to a wrong leads to a wrong. And this particular story doesn't tell us if the murderer is herself executed. It ends with the harp made of the dead sister's bones, having delivered its awful message, snapping apart.

But we can suppose that at the least, the younger sister's life was ruined, too.

And what was I doing, again? And why was I trying to use fairy tales to figure things out when obviously all they did was confuse me even more?

I had a window seat on the big plane, the one flying from Chicago to Vegas, but it wasn't much of a refuge because the middle seat was taken by an overweight boomer lady with long straggly hair and clickety fingernails whose big squishy arm kept bumping into me.

And at first there was nothing but clouds below us, but then I looked out and it was clear, and I could see the patchwork Midwest fields below us and I felt a little dizzy at being up so high, and what was it I hoped to accomplish?

What story was I in? And why, oh why, was it someone else's story and not mine? Why was I up there so high in the sky when this should have been Ace's story, because wasn't Ace the thief? Wasn't he the one who was supposed to climb the bean stalk and steal the giant's treasures, only he wasn't a thief, so did that mean I was? And hadn't it crossed my mind that by trying to fix my family I was robbing my own future and sure enough, here I was, looking down on the earth and hoping that I wasn't doomed to fail, to fall and be smashed to smithereens on the cold, hard ground?

And I tried to sleep but couldn't. And then I felt the plane start to shift and descend. I looked out of the window again, and felt a little squeeze of anxiety start to form in the pit of my gut. Because when a city is a long way away, it's like a little dot in your mind. And you're thinking, no problem. It's a little dot. I can find a person living in that little dot. But as the plane reached that last five minutes or so of the flight and the foothills gave way to the valley, I got hit in the face with how huge Vegas is.

Because from 4000 feet it wasn't a dot anymore. It was enormous.

I pulled the plastic window shade down, like blocking out the view of that enormous city would make it better, and shut my eyes, and gave myself a little talking to. And so, okay, I used fairy tales again because what else did I have? And in fairy tales, when siblings set out into the huge wide world to rescue other siblings, do they go all wobbly just because, as they set out, they have absolutely zero clue what direction to take? Do they suddenly start to think that there is no way in God's green creation that they are ever going to find this little speck of a human being but that, on the contrary, they will likely wander around in circles for fifty years until they drop dead?

No.

No, they do not.

They face the challenge bravely.

No. More than bravely.

They face the challenge with the absolutely irrational conviction that somehow, they will stumble onto that tiny speck of a human being. Against all odds.

Because it's destiny. It's an epic quest, a quest that has the backing of something sacred behind it.

It can't fail.

It just can't.

Right?

37

I started my search very logically. Ace had told me the name of his friend—the artist who'd done his tattoos—and I'd double-checked the name by looking at old Ink Master clips. And then I'd found his address, which was on Fremont Street. So I'd get an Uber and start there. Smart, eh? I'd find his tattoo artist and ask him where Ace worked.

Man, it was hot.

And it was only 1 o'clock in the afternoon.

And just as I'd expected, when I woke my phone to get the Uber, there were a bunch more texts from RB, but I didn't read them. Because what good would it do to read a bunch of texts, now, from RB?

I'd let him know what happened after I found my brother.

And I wanted to clear my head. So I asked the Uber driver to just drop me anywhere, I'd walk the rest of the way. And Fremont Street, in case you've never been, turned out to be a wide street with a big chunk that's been turned into a pedestrian walkway covered by a domed roof, which meant you were out of the sun, at least. A blessing. The street was wide, flanked on either side by restaurants and bars and casinos that looked like they were about a hundred years old. People everywhere, some couples and families, mostly touristy-looking. Gaggles of girls my age or a little younger, laughing and chattering and carrying drinks. Gaggles of men my age or a little younger clapping each other on their shoulders and pointing at the casinos. Vendors sitting or standing in what I guess were designated spots, or anyway there were these circles painted on the pavers and the venders were set up in the circles. There was a guy selling sculptures made from aluminum cans, and a woman making roses out of palm fronds. A guy was handing out sample packets of skin lotion. He pressed one into my hand. And homeless people, guys in wheelchairs with homemade signs. And then we passed a pair of women dressed like dominatrix cops who tried to flirt with passersby and get them to stop. They wanted to put handcuffs on people for photo ops.

I tried not to stare at everything. I mean, I wasn't born yesterday. I'd been to New York City, for crying out loud.

I passed a hugely obese man wearing a bikini and bunny ears. I pretended I hadn't seen him.

I reached a tower at the far end of the walkway, and after pausing to study it for a minute I realized what it was. It was a launching platform for a zipline, of all things. There were trapdoors on the front that opened, and people strapped to the cables suddenly emerged and glided overhead toward the other end of the street.

I went around the zipline tower and reached the end of the pedestrian walkway and stepped out into the blazing sun. And then I was sorry I'd decided to walk, because I was thirsty and hungry. I should have eaten breakfast in the airport before I boarded the plane or bought one of those stupid airplane meals or something.

And the guys at the tattoo parlor weren't too eager to help. The owner, Ace's friend, wasn't there and when I asked the other guys, they weren't too helpful.

"Oh yeah, Ace," one of them said. "Good guy. But no idea where he works. On the Strip, I think."

"As a cook, right?"

They looked at me suspiciously.

"I'm his sister," I told them. "I'm here to surprise him. Late birthday present."

"Yeah. All I can tell you is, he started a new gig in one of the casino restaurants."

"Any idea which one?"

"Try the Venetian."

Ugh.

I reserved another Uber. It was late afternoon, by then. Hot. Inside-an-oven hot. The air burned my throat. And the minute I stepped out of the Uber and onto the Strip, that feeling came back. The feeling that I was two people, only it was stronger now, or I should say I felt more like Unreal Marion than the real one.

I told myself it was the heat. The heat and stimulus overload. Because the sidewalks were so crowded and the buildings on the Strip are so oversized and gaudy and unreal. And the sidewalks along the Strip aren't so much sidewalks as a sidewalk system. Some pieces are at street level and some are not, you navigate by maneuvering up and down and in and out, at times you have to enter buildings, at time you are outside, there are escalators in places or stairs that you have to take. So to get to the Venetian I had to take a moving sidewalk that ramped up to this faux world that looked like Italy. Sort of. I mean, there's a canal, right? With gondolas that you can ride on. And part of the canal is outside, but then it enters the building. I found another chunk of canal when I stumbled onto this huge room that is a replica of the Piazza San Marco in Venice. Even the roof overhead is painted and lit so that it looks like real sky, with flying birds and clouds.

Technically, I knew where I was. I was in a casino in Las Vegas.

But inside, I was wondering how much I really know about anything.

I started to notice that there were restaurants all over. The entire circumference of the faux piazza was restaurants and shops. And I still hadn't eaten anything all day. But now was not the time to think about food. I needed to find Ace.

I stopped at one of the restaurants at random. Canaletto, it was called. Even though personally, I couldn't picture Ace working in an Italian place, but I was in Venice, after all. Sort of.

I caught the eye of one of the servers who asked me if I needed a table, but I said no, I was looking for Ace Weekes and did he work there?

She'd never heard of him.

There were so many restaurants and the building? It wasn't even a building, really. It was more like a complex. It had stairs and halls and rooms connected to other rooms. So maybe it would be better to be more systematic. Maybe I should try to find a map.

I wandered around for a bit, then found an escalator and hey! I'd stumbled onto a hotel lobby. But there was a line at the concierge desk, so rather than wait to ask if they had a map, I started down a big, gilded hallway that was flanked by marble columns, polished floor with trompe-l'œil tiles that made me feel a bit dizzy, they looked like 3D blocks instead of tiles, and overhead there was an arched ceiling decorated with Italianate paintings and trompe-l'œil banners and statues.

And at the end of the hallway I found myself in the casino proper.

I lost my breath for a second.

It was enormous.

I took a few steps and found myself in a sea of slot machines. Slot machines in every direction. And they were all lit up, flashing, talking, animations scrolling across the screen, animations of creatures, of people. There were animated fortune tellers, dragons, princesses, celebrities, buffaloes, wolves, cartoon characters. And I noticed that they seemed to be looking back at me. The animations were designed so their eyes seemed to be focused on the eyes of anyone who paused to look at them.

The smell of cigarette smoke pricked my nostrils.

I felt a wave of dizziness and realized that nothing around me was real, and it was pointless thinking in terms of logic. There were aisles between the slot machines but no making sense of them, they were set off from each other in crazy directions. Even the walls of the room weren't square to each other. It was a crazy, mixed up space designed to suck me in and entrance me and hold me.

I wandered around and the more I wandered the more I realized how hopeless it was. The whole thing was hopeless. I stopped for a minute to watch a woman playing one of the slot machines. A golden piggy bank on the screen suddenly exploded and rained coins. The woman watched, then took a sip of an iced drink she was holding in one hand, and when the coins stopped raining, she calmly pressed a button on the console to start the game again.

I saw her face. She looked the way people do when they watch TV. She looked like Quill had, when I'd left him on the couch to go to Effie's.

I took a few more steps. Turned. Stopped. Crossed a walkway into another pool of slot machines. And I heard some people yelling and cheering from somewhere on the other side of the casino, and then something started happening to all the lights. The lights on the slot machines, the screens, the blinking lights framing the screens, the flashing consoles. They were so colorful, faux colors because they were illuminated colors, cartoon colors. But they suddenly turned even brighter, even more colorful, while at the same time the edges of the room—the bits that were in my peripheral vision, the ceiling, the floor—darkened, deepened, darkened to the point that they disappeared, burned away by the darkness, the way the edges of the Earth disappear on the old maps. And as the edges disappeared, the kaleidoscope of lights around me grew larger, swelled up, multiplied and spread out, so that I was in this endless, endless mass of flashing talking living lights.

I hadn't eaten. I'm sure that's what it was, right? I hadn't eaten all day, and I was tired and stressed and dizzy and dehydrated, and it was sensory overload. And everywhere I looked, everywhere I turned were endless crazed lights. And people were yelling and clapping, still. They sounded like when there's party at a neighbor's, and it's late and they've been drinking, and something happens that makes them all start laughing and cheering at once.

My knees began to wobble.

And I heard someone call my name. My nickname.

"Mayfly!"

It hit me like a shockwave. I jumped, the way you jump when you are deep in thought or half asleep and someone pokes you.

I stood, listening.

I knew what direction the voice had come from.

It was calling me. No. It was reminding me of something. Something I'd forgotten. Something about why I'd entered this crazy house of lights, why I was here, what I was doing here…

I started walking in the direction of the voice, threading through the lights, ignoring the enchanted people staring at the bright cartoons because if I let myself stop, if I let myself look at them, I would forget something. Forget the voice.

And I reached a group of people. Maybe twelve or fifteen but the closer I got the more people joined them. The group was growing. They were the people I'd heard cheering and yelling, and they were still yelling, not angry yelling, excited yelling. And one of them, a man in the middle of the group, was laughing and other people were clapping him on the back and shaking his hand as he laughed.

These people… They were different, somehow.

They were familiar, somehow.

And then two of them turned toward me.

The laughing man and another man who was standing next to him.

They looked right at me, right at my face.

And then I knew. It was like I woke up. And I ran the last few steps, screaming as I ran, waking up and screaming.

"Ace!"

And I fell forward into the arms of my little brother.

38

This sounds like a cliché, I know. But I have no idea how long I was out. But that's the whole thing about passing out or fainting or whatever I did, right? You're not in a place of clocks and rulers and measures. You're someplace else. But I also knew that I was in Ace's arms, that he was holding me. And then I opened my eyes and the crazy kaleidoscope lights had faded and the dark edges of everything had brightened and I wasn't in another world, after all.

I was in a casino. In Las Vegas.

And I'd found Ace.

I'd found my little brother.

"You okay?" He was peering at my face, all worried.

"I heard you," I breathed. "I heard you call me."

He frowned. "Call you?"

"You yelled 'Mayfly.'"

He shook his head. "I didn't call you."

"I heard you," I said. "I heard you call me. I'm—I'm thirsty. I haven't eaten. I got a little dizzy."

"Here." He helped me stand up and led me to one of the seats in front of a slot machine. "You'd better sit down. You don't look so good. Hey, RB."

"I'll get her some water."

I startled again, looked up again. So many people standing around, who were all these people? They'd been yelling but now they were all staring at me…

RB?

I felt another sharp wave of dizziness.

I looked at Ace. "Was that RB?"

"Geez, Mayfly, you don't look so good. Maybe we should get you to an urgent care."

"No!" I shook my head, violently, the way a little kid does when she knows she had better be very, very emphatic or things are going to take a very, very wrong turn. "I'm fine. I'm okay. I just need—I need to eat something."

"Here."

RB's voice.

So it *was* RB.

I found his face in the cluster of people around me and stared at him a second, as my mind tried to process what was going on.

RB was here?

Not back home, in Tibbs?

He was putting a glass in my hand.

Water. Ice water.

I tilted the glass. Drank. It helped. I started to feel a little more settled. The watcher Marion began to re-enter my body, turn back again into the same person as the other Marion.

"I got dehydrated," I said apologetically after I'd drained the glass. And also craftily, because I really did not want to be dragged to an urgent care.

And I wasn't lying. The water tasted delicious. Elixir-delicious.

RB went away, then came back a minute later with more water.

The cluster of people around us had started to thin out, like whatever had caused them to group around was gone now. They were drifting away, fading back into the lights.

No. It wasn't lights. The room looked so normal, now. The floor was just a carpet. The slot machines looked like…machines. Like big toys.

I heard Ace talking to someone and turned my head. "Here," he said. "Put it in your purse."

He was handing a slip of paper to a woman. A young woman with long, dark, smooth hair and almond eyes.

"Marion, this is Yolanda," Ace said, when he saw that I had noticed them. "My girl."

Of course. Ace had a princess. Ace had found a princess. "You're beautiful," I said to Yolanda. Without really thinking. I was still, I guess, in a bit of an odd state. It was like, all I wanted to do was to say the truth, and the truth in that moment was that she was stunning.

She smiled at me. "Thank you."

And then, suddenly, I knew.

I turned back to Ace. "This is why you came back to Vegas," I said. "To fetch Yolanda."

Ace tilted his head for a split second like my words didn't make sense. And they probably didn't make much sense—I was still a bit out of it, still, so in my mind he was the last sibling to leave home. And then he'd returned, but instead of staying he'd left again, because he had to go rescue his princess.

But he seemed to understand, because he laughed, humoring me. "Sure, Mayfly. Something like that. Although—" He broke off and laughed again and suddenly grabbed Yolanda and kissed her. "Although if you'd asked me fifteen minutes ago whether I'd be bringing my girl to Tibbs any time soon—"

"I've never seen anything like this," RB said.

Which confused me.

Like what?

Two people kissing?

But I didn't ask that question, because I realized something else was bothering me.

I swiveled the chair, looking for RB. Found him, standing behind me. Alone, now. The other people had all left. It was just us four, now.

There was a worried look on RB's face. His brow was furrowed.

"Oh, cut it out, RB," I muttered. "I'm fine."

"Why didn't you answer your texts? I tried to reach you all day."

I felt my face color. "I was saving phone battery," I said sheepishly. "How was I supposed to know what you were up to? How long have you been here?"

And he rolled his eyes and shook his head. "I flew out last night."

But then his expression turned serious again, and I couldn't look at him anymore. I looked away.

Our friend. Our friend, RB.

"Guys, Marion needs food," Ace said. "Let's go get something to eat." He laughed again. A funny laugh, almost manic in a way. "My treat."

But I didn't let his laughter touch me. Not then.

I was thinking about something else.

I raised my eyes again to RB. "You came out here to talk to Ace," I said to him.

He nodded.

I considered this for a moment. Not because it was complicated, on the face of it. But because I felt like there was something else, there. Something beneath the surface, the way the enchanted kaleidoscope of lights was there, beneath or behind the silly toy slot machines of the silly toy casino.

And then I realized what it was. It was our family. RB didn't have a family of his own, anymore. And why hadn't I ever thought of him that way, before? Because although his mother had passed when he was a boy, his father had died more recently. RB was 25 when that happened. So he was a grown man, when that happened. But he was an orphan.

I realized that all of a sudden. An orphan.

No wonder he was now a part of our family's life.

We were his family now. All of us, starting with Candace and their son. Little Quill.

"You're awfully good to us, RB," I said.

He shrugged and looked away. He's not the type of person who does things for compliments.

"Guys," Ace said. "I know a place that makes great pizza. It's downtown, though, not on the Strip. Mayfly, can you make it to the lobby?"

"Yeah." I stood up to show them, and sure enough, I felt fine.

Pretty fine.

Although, when RB took my elbow to make sure I was steady on my feet, I didn't shake it off.

"But one stop, first," Ace said, laughing again.

I wasn't sure what he meant.

But then a minute later, we stopped at a row of windows with bars in front of them like in an old-fashioned bank. And Ace went up to one of the windows with Yolanda, who handed him the slip of paper she'd put in her purse.

Dumb me. I finally figured out what had happened.

"Did Ace win something? Money?" I said to RB.

He nodded. "Yeah. Right before you found us. Quite a bit of money. He hit a jackpot on one of the slots."

"Oh wow," I said. "No kidding."

Because I still didn't grasp what that meant.

39

So "downtown," it turned out, was Fremont Street. We ended up back at the place I'd started a couple hours ago.

And the pizza place was full of Evel Knievel memorabilia, which of course RB thought was the coolest thing ever.

We ordered pizza slices and beer, and sat at the bar, and I tried not to think about how I'd eaten pizza and beer with Fletcher the night we broke up. But the pizza was delicious, and as I chewed and swallowed and sipped a little beer and drank some more water, I started to feel more and more normal.

"So I guess I missed the excitement back in the Venetian," I said.

"By mere seconds," said Ace. He winked at Yolanda then smiled at me. "Mayfly," he said. "We're coming to Tibbs. Me and Yolanda."

My eyes welled and my throat felt suddenly full. "Really?"

"You know how I said I'd come home when I could pay Dad back? And you know that jackpot I won today?" He grinned.

I sucked my breath in. "But Ace. You don't owe Winchell anything."

He held his hand up, signaling me to stop. "Okay, maybe 'pay him back' is the wrong choice of words," he said. "But their money went missing, and I decided a long time ago I'd go home when I could replace it. Not because I stole anything, but because—"

"Because you're Jack," I interrupted.

He gave me a quizzical look. "Sorry?"

"Jack," I said. "The beanstalk. Jack didn't climb the beanstalk for himself. He did it for his mother. To make sure she'd be taken care of, in her old age."

Ace laughed. "Okay, we can go with that."

"But did you really win that much?" I said. "A hundred and fifty thousand?"

He glanced at Yolanda and then back at me and shook his head. "No," he said. "But it's a start."

• • • • •

After we left the pizza joint and wandered Fremont for a little while, walked in and out of some of the casinos there, and Ace and Yolanda flirted with each other and played the slots, and made jokes about jackpots striking twice in the same spot on the same day. And then Ace and RB decided they wanted to go on that zipline, and tried talking me into it, too, but I said no, even though I wasn't feeling dizzy anymore. And Yolanda said she'd wait on the ground with me, but I insisted I'd be fine.

So they bought three tickets and got in line for the ride, and I made my way to the other end of the pedestrian walkway and waited, watching people without really thinking about anything in particular, just feeling. And it was a good feeling.

It was the warm feeling of knowing that I'd found Ace. I'd found my little brother. And he was coming home.

The zipline was set up as four cables stretched the length of the street, so people would come out in groups of four. So every few minutes another group would fly overhead, and I'd look up to see if it was Ace and Yolanda and RB.

And time after time it wasn't.

And then it was. It was them, flying overhead. Big grins on their faces, whooping, arms outstretched.

RB was in the lead.

RB. Flying ahead of the other two. Flying over my head like Aladdin only without his carpet.

He didn't notice me, down there below him on the ground.

40

It was almost three weeks before Ace could get the time off work to fly back to Tibbs.

I didn't breathe a word to anyone. I told Winchell I needed to run some errands in Syracuse and no, it couldn't wait, and I borrowed his truck and drove to the Syracuse airport and waited by the curb for my brother and his beautiful, dark-haired princess.

We were pretty quiet on the drive to Tibbs. My stomach was in knots because who knows what would happen, right? They might all freak. Winchell might start yelling and Candace might start yelling and Mom might cry and fall to pieces.

The truck is a four-door, so Ace sat in the back seat and Yolanda rode shotgun, and after we'd been on the road awhile, he leaned forward and reached his hand up, and she reached back to take it. And that's how they rode most of the way, holding hands.

And then we got to the dome and got out of the truck and walked up the dirt path and inside.

And I suppose it was nerves, but I suddenly got a bit of tunnel vision again, because at first all I could see was Mom, standing by the sink, and then looking up and realizing it was her son, and then scrambling around the kitchen island and rushing toward us, and grabbing him like he was a life preserver and she was drowning.

And it was a Sunday, so Candace was home. She'd been sitting on the couch but now she was standing and staring, and her eyes were enormous, and then she looked at me and I looked away because I really couldn't deal with her at that moment, and no doubt she'd be furious at me for either bringing Ace into the house or not telling her, first, or maybe both.

And then I noticed Winchell.

He'd heard that something was going on and had emerged from the master bedroom and was standing on the balcony like he does. And then he started down the staircase and stood at the bottom of the steps, while Mom held onto Ace and said things I couldn't make out.

Winchell was watching them.

Watching Mom.

And God, Winchell looked awful. His face was pale and greenish, and he was sucking in his cheeks, and his shoulders were slumped. And what crossed my mind was: he looks like a dead man. And then I realized that he was. Because he'd driven away his son. And he'd kept not only one, but two secrets. The first about the money, and the second about driving away his son. And now the bones were singing, Mom was going to find out about the second secret. And maybe driving Ace away wasn't exactly the same as killing him, but in a way it was, and Mom had known, somehow. Mom had heard the terrible singing bones.

And what happens to a marriage when the husband drives away the child and hides it from the child's mother?

And then Ace caught sight of Winchell and turned away from Mom and in one motion began walking toward Winchell as he reached into his pocket.

He took out a folded piece of paper, which of course was a check.

He held it out.

"Here you go, Dad," he said.

Winchell's thick, old man's hands were shaking as he reached out to take the check.

But then Mom was flying across the room and stepping between them.

And she snatched the check from Ace's fingers.

“What is this?” she said in a voice that sounded too large for such a small-boned woman. “What is this about?”

“It’s the money, Lana,” Winchell said. “The money that—”

“No!” Mom cut him off and shoved the check back into Ace’s hand. “Absolutely not.” She shook her head violently. “Ace, you are absolutely not going to repay money that was never missing in the first place.”

41

Everyone stared.

Because Mom? She's built like me. Not a big woman. To put it mildly.

But in that moment, she was towering. Towering over us all. Definitely towering over Ace and Winchell.

"Ace," she said. "Put the check back in your pocket."

"It's okay," Ace said quietly. "It's okay, Mom. I'm doing this for you. For you and Dad. I want to help you. I don't care about the past."

I felt Candace's elbow jab me and realized she'd come over and was standing next to me. "What's going on, Marion?" she hissed into my ear.

"Ace is home?" I said innocently, but to be honest I really didn't care if Candace was mad at me because I couldn't take my eyes off our mother.

She was glowering, now, at Winchell.

And then I knew that Mom knew. She knew the whole thing. She knew that Winchell thought Ace had stolen money. She'd known it all along.

"Mom?" I said. "What's going on?"

"Winchell," Mom said. "Ace didn't take your money. I did. It was me."

I don't think Winchell really understood, yet, what she was saying.

Heck, I barely understood what she was saying.

"Mom?" I said again, my head tilting involuntarily because this was all so bizarre. "What are you talking about?"

But she was still addressing her husband. "The money was making you crazy, Winchell," she continued. "The money was turning you into someone who was not the man I loved."

"Oh, shit," I heard Candace breathe the words.

I watched Winchell's face as he began to understand what his wife was telling him.

And then Mom dropped her eyes to the floor. And she seemed to shrink.

And then she looked at me. "But now I see." She laughed, a short, little, unhappy laugh. "My scheme backfired, didn't it, Marion."

I nodded.

Because it had.

Mom had taken the money because she thought she would teach Winchell a lesson.

And her scheme had boomeranged.

"The money is perfectly safe," Mom said. "I put it someplace safe. But I ended up hurting you, Ace." Tears welled in her eyes and began to run down her face. "I'm so sorry, Son."

"It's okay, Mom," Ace said quietly. "It's fine. It wasn't bad. I needed the wake-up call. I had some growing up to do."

Holy crap, I was thinking to myself.

Had Ace known?

Had he known, the whole time, that it was Mom who had the money?

"Singing bones," I said beneath my breath, but Mom must have heard me because I saw her shoulders twitch as I spoke.

"Come here, Winchell," she said. "I want do show you something."

She reached out her hand. And it hovered in the air a moment, between the two of them, Mom and Dad, and then Winchell took it, and Mom led him across the room, through that big open space that is the front half of our dome to the little student desk and their crummy old computer.

And she turned the computer on, and we waited while it booted up, which seemed to take forever because that stupid computer is about a thousand years old.

Finally the computer finished waking up and Mom opened a browser.

And she typed a URL in the browser window and brought up a website.

It was an investment account.

She typed in a password.

"Here," she said.

We leaned in to look at the screen.

It was an account of some kind.

There were numbers on the screen.

One of them was a pretty big number.

"I invested it," Mom said. "The whole thing. I put it all in Family Dollar stocks during the financial downturn in 2008 and cashed it out eight years later when the stock hit 90."

"Holy shit," I whispered. "Mom. You're a stock market genius."

She shrugged. "Not really. I got lucky. But it was the recession. I thought I might as well invest in a company that caters to people who were struggling financially." She laughed, a rueful laugh. "People like us."

I looked at Winchell.

There were tears streaming down his cheeks now, too.

"Lana," he whispered. "Lana. I never meant—I didn't know."

She stood up and went to him.

"Forgive me, my love," she said.

"No, you forgive me, Lana—I can't—I can't live without you, Lana."

"Holy shit," I whispered.

"Holy shit," Candace whispered next to me in agreement.

"Should we, uh, go for a walk or something?" Yolanda asked.

Sensible girl.

So that's what we did.

We went for a walk and gave Mom and Dad a little time to themselves.

42

I wish I could tell you that this story ends with a Happily Ever After.

It doesn't.

Because I lost my prince. I didn't reconcile with Fletcher. Yeah, we talked a couple of times, and told each other that we cared about each other and that we just needed some time apart. But we both knew it was over. Something about what had happened between us, that night in the pizza parlor, was too real and too harsh. Too real and too harsh for fairy tales, and too real and too harsh for real life relationships.

And to be honest, after seeing how my parents' marriage was nearly destroyed because Winchell put money ahead of love?

It made me think, a lot, about the kind of prince I'd want to spend an Ever After with.

So, to be fair, it wasn't a Happily Ever After, but it was a pretty decent ending, because even though I lost my prince, I'd done my part to patch my family together. I'd gone out in the world and I'd found my brother and I'd brought him back home, and somehow that had managed to mend the rift between Mom and Dad.

And what can be better than that?

Of course, I still owed Effie that wind chime—courtesy of Quill.

But that's a story for another day...

Coming December 2022

The 3rd Marion Flarey title!

Fairy Tales teach the power of threes.
Now Marion's third and final Prince is suddenly back in her life ...
Has she finally found her Happily Ever After?

Sign up for my newsletter at www.KirstenMortensen.com
and I'll send you a note when *Happily Flarey...Ever?* is available!

Made in the USA
Las Vegas, NV
24 February 2023

68081243R00154